SWORD OF QUEENS

Vanessa

Batie

Salazar

SWORD OF QUEENS

JOAN MARIE VERBA

FTL Publications
Minneapolis, Minnesota

Copyright © 2012 by Joan Marie Verba

FTL Publications
P O Box 22693
Minneapolis, MN 55422-0693
www.ftlpublications.com
mail@ftlpublications.com

Cover art © Tomert | Dreamstime.com

Printed in the United States of America

ISBN 978-1-936881-11-6

Chapter 1

Early in the morning, Gill awakened to a resounding shriek. She wondered whom Tashtalon had devoured now. Whoever the victim was, it was too late to help. The great god always took what he wanted by night, after he put everyone to sleep, and no one could possibly attempt a rescue. In the morning, the family would find only an empty bed. Then the screaming would begin. Gill often thought that the suffering might be easier for the victim, devoured, and then gone, than the survivors, whose agony of grief could last for years. She sat up in bed and swung her feet around and to the floor, thinking to get dressed to find and comfort the family in their loss, when a moaning caught her ear. She tilted her head and listened.

The sound seemed to come from outside. She stood on the bed and peered through a window. She left all of them open on these warm spring nights, before the insects started flourishing. Below, she saw something thrashing on the sidewalk below. Immediately she guessed that a bola strand had fallen on an early-rising pedestrian. The shopkeepers below her rented room had hung some newly-made ones up to dry the day before.

Quickly, she put on her slippers and threw on a robe. She jerked open the door, hurried down the wooden stairs hugging the outside wall, and dashed through the alley between buildings.

At this hour, just past sunrise, the streets were empty except for the one helpless man. He lay in front of the shop, gasping for breath, hands trying to loosen the strands tangled around his neck. Cords made from the bola plant quickly wrapped around any bundle and tightened firmly if not handled with due care. Gill shouted for help. She hoped that other residents in their apartments above the shops might hear, but feared that most had rolled over and gone back to sleep after the first shriek, thinking that Tashtalon had taken another victim and nothing could be done. She rushed back to her room to get a paring knife.

Returning, she cut away at the thick strands, cursing the fact that women were not allowed to carry a sword. A sharp, heavy blade could make short work of these fibers. The man was turning blue; Gill would have gladly risked the death sentence just to put a hand on a sword to free this man. But she did her best, desperately trying to cut the cords without cutting the man's skin as well, and not being successful at either. With gestures, the man encouraged her to continue despite her clumsy efforts. Blood was oozing out over her hands, the knife, and the cord, making the task even harder.

A shadow blocked her view; a man with a white beard knelt, spoke soothingly to the man, and used his sword to cut the strand. The man rolled over, coughing and gasping. At the same time, two city guardsmen rushed up the street, accompanied by a woman pleading with them to hurry and free her husband.

Gill turned to the victim. The bearded man put a hand on the man's back. "You'll be fine," he said. "Just breathe."

Slowly, the man turned a normal color and sat up. He nodded to the rescuer. "Thank you."

"Nice work, old man," said one of the guardsmen.

Gill stood. Now that she had the leisure to look him over, she saw that the rescuer had a wrinkled face, a deep brown complexion, white hair, and a long but neat white beard. His clothes and boots were simple, sturdy, and functional. Gill thought he might be a retired guardsman.

The guardsmen helped the man up and examined the cords carefully. "These are pretty tough. Lucky cut, old man."

The rescuer arched his eyebrows at them. Stepping away from the gathering, he swung his sword at a decorative unlit candle adorning a nearby shop.

The guardsmen laughed. "Missed, old man!" said one.

The rescuer smiled. Taking the tip of the sword, he pushed at the top of the candle. It toppled to the ground.

The guardsmen stared after the old man, open-mouthed, as he strolled away, then turned to assisting the couple. No one paid Gill any attention, so she went back to her apartment. She did her best to wash the blood off her hands, robe, and gown. She hoped she would not be late at the castle.

After dressing and eating breakfast, Gill left her rented room and walked to the castle by her usual route. The streets took a gentle upward slope. The city had been built on the lower part of Mount Blade, whose snow-capped spire loomed above them. The highest points of the city were the castle, and the house of Tashtalon above that, and even they were only about a tenth of the way up the mountain.

The walk was only fifteen minutes. As she approached the castle, the buildings stopped at the sharp edge of the city, revealing a wide stone-paved courtyard. Beyond that rose a high stone wall with an iron gate, approached by steps, and then another stone courtyard into the castle itself.

The castle was huge, taller than it was wide, and the back wall stood flush with the side of the mountain. It had been fashioned of dressed cream-colored stones, fixed without mortar in a time unknown, a time before Tashtalon, it was said. A curious property of the stone caught the sun and reflected different colors depending on the angle and the brightness of the sunlight. Gill never tired of admiring it.

Higher up stood the house of Tashtalon, its door shaped like a vast mouth, a constant stream of black smoke coming from the central chimney. Its stones were rough-hewn and gray-brown, though whether that was soot or the natural color of the rock, Gill did not know.

She reached the bottom of the steps and started to ascend. At the second step, she felt a tug at her skirt, stopped, and turned. Lydia, a neighbor of her parents, stood at the bottom step, her eyes red, her face wet with tears.

"Please," she said. "Please. My son. He's gone."

So, Gill thought, Tashtalon *had* devoured someone last night. Her first, and honest, thought was that no one but his widowed mother would miss Owen. He tortured animals, vandalized shops, and was a public nuisance. But she could not say that to this grieving woman. She opened her mouth to try to speak a word of condolence when she smelled wood smoke and heard a voice.

"The great god Tashtalon has taken him."

She looked up to see Boreas, priest of Tashtalon, turn aside on his regular morning visit to the palace. In his black smoke-scented robes, he loomed over the woman as she knelt on the stairs, too upset to stand.

"Rather than weeping, you should feel proud that Tashtalon has chosen your son."

"It's not so...he ran away...we need to search."

"He did not. He was taken from his bed as are all chosen by Tashtalon. You knew he was marked for the god by his hideous deeds."

Lydia shook her head, and kept shaking it, as if she could not stop herself. Boreas motioned for one of the guards at the gate to come. "I expect you to be at Tashtalon's house at sunset, to thank him."

The guard took Lydia by the arm, set her on her feet, and hauled her away.

Boreas turned to Gill. "Take heed from this, Gill. All parents need to recognize the great honor that Tashtalon does them by devouring their sons."

Gill did not know of a single instance in which a parent felt so honored, but said nothing. Boreas put his clammy hand tenderly on her arm; Gill regretted putting on a short-sleeved dress despite the warm spring morning. The guards nodded at them as he guided her through the gate, across the pavement, and into the palace. He paused for a moment as they passed through the great hall and bowed toward Tashtalon's empty throne. Gill was glad that women had no such obligation. They continued out of the hall, up the stairs, and into the spacious room serving as the Lord Protector's office. Cyril was already there, going through the papers that Gill had neatly placed on his desk before leaving work the afternoon before.

Cyril looked up as they approached. When they reached the furnished area around the desk, he extended a greeting, first to Boreas, then to Gill. Boreas finally let go of Gill's arm, and after all exchanged pleasantries, Gill walked into the records room, which was like an enormous closet to the main room. Gill had her office there. The door was not closed except on those rare occasions in which Cyril felt the need for privacy. He did not ask Gill to close the door when she went in. Gill's perfect hearing picked up every word as she went about her daily duties.

"Tashtalon took nineteen last night," said Boreas. "Here is the list. I stopped a family member outside the gate, trying to accost Gill."

"Hmmm...that's never happened before."

"I took care of the matter."

"I see. Anything else?"

"No. I'll stay for the morning audience in case we need to instruct another such relative."

"Very well. Go ahead, and I'll meet you at the usual time." When the door clicked shut, Cyril called, "Gill."

Gill came out of her office and handed Cyril a small stack of papers. He sat behind his desk and paged through them; she sat in a chair opposite. With his head bowed, she had a clear view of his bald spot, ringed with gray hair.

With a glance to the door, he said, "Did you finish that landlord-tenant agreement?"

She gestured. "It's near the bottom."

"Ah! Found it." He looked it over and nodded. "Very good. And you deeded the land over to the woodsmen?"

"Yes, though as I said yesterday, I think we should require them to replant trees when they're done."

He shook his head. "No, we need more grassland for the shepherds and ranchers."

She shrugged. "I'm not sure why you asked my opinion when you didn't take my advice." It was an old argument.

He lifted his head and smiled. "I follow your suggestions often enough. Your opinions are always sensible, even if I don't agree." He glanced at the door again and lowered his voice slightly. "If women could rule, you could take my place."

"If greathorses could fly, we wouldn't need roads."

He laughed at the old joke and put the papers down on the desk. "Decided what you're going to do after your 23rd birthday yet? Go to the mines and make your fortune? Or go to the mountains and watch the stars through your spyglass?"

"I don't know yet," said Gill.

"May I make a recommendation?"

"Why not?"

He folded his hands on his desk. "Be sure to stay within the ring of Tashtalon. To step outside the ring is death--those are not just stories to frighten children. Many a young person has been lost that way."

"I wasn't planning to try it," she reassured him.

"And though we may confer together where Boreas and his aides don't see us, I wouldn't divulge to anyone that you have been an advisor and assistant to me these past few years. Let everyone think that you remained the mere note-taker that you were at first. Tashtalon has not killed a woman since I was a lad; I don't want it to happen to you."

"My mother and grandmother have warned me what can happen to a woman who has too much interest in affairs of state or in bladed weapons."

"Good." He relaxed in his chair with a sigh. After a moment, he took the papers and stood. "Shall we join Boreas, then?"

Two thrones stood in the back of the great hall. One was for the Lord Protector, currently Cyril, and the other for Tashtalon, forever empty. In between was a block of marble. Sometimes Cyril put papers on it; other times he put a bowl of freshly-cut flowers there. Whenever Boreas was in attendance, Tashtalon's priest stood in front of the block, next to Tashtalon's throne. Gill lingered behind the thrones, ready with pen and ink to record anything Cyril asked her to. At the moment, Cyril was listening to a report from the surveyors who had measured the boundaries for the woodsmen. They simply confirmed the information Cyril already had, so Gill was not needed. She sat, as she usually did, in a small chair in the narrow space between the backs of the thrones and the wall.

During such respites, her eyes would wander to the thrones. They were beautifully made, upholstered in rich fabric and inlaid with gold and precious stones. The Lord Protector's throne was the same size as Tashtalon's, but the patterns on the backs and arms were carved differently, as if each throne were the work of a different artist. Strangest of all, in the back of Tashtalon's throne was an odd indentation. Sometimes Gill wondered what that was, but never asked anyone about it. For a woman to touch the throne, it was said, meant death—but men never dared to go near it, either, and even Boreas never put a hand on it. Gill had learned at an early age, as did most, that it was best not to inquire into the mysteries of Tashtalon.

* * *

Boreas left after the morning audience. Gill finished her work for the day, as was her habit, in the early afternoon. When she reached the outside courtyard, she turned and took the road, sloping gently downwards, to a schoolyard. Her friend Alia sat, back to a blossoming tree, surrounded by children. Alia was taller, prettier, and stronger than Gill. She had long, straight blonde hair, whereas Gill's was short, dark, and curly. Alia had received proposals of marriage, but had accepted none. Gill had never received any. Within the ring of Tashtalon, women outnumbered men, and men were the ones with the choice. Alia claimed that she had declined marriage because she did not wish to be tied to a home and family, though Gill suspected that the real reason was that Alia did not wish to bear sons that Tashtalon might take. Many women remained celibate for that reason. Gill was willing to take the chance, but no man, so far, seemed inclined to want to take the chance with her.

Alia finished reciting the lesson and spotted Gill. The children noticed the motion, realized that the school day was almost over, and began to chant, "One more story! One more story!"

Alia smiled. "Then we shall have another story. Which one?"

Some of the boys said, "The one where Tashtalon gets all the girls!"

Gill rolled her eyes. Little boys seemed never to get enough of that story. According to the priests, before Tashtalon came there was chaos because women were evil. Tashtalon tamed women and forbade them swords and positions of power, and the world became a peaceful and settled place.

Alia smiled and replied, "No, I think I'd rather tell another story."

"Tell us the story of the sleepers!" said some of the girls.

Hearing no dissent to that, Alia recited:

Once there was a beautiful girl named Rose, who lived in a beautiful city in the forest. Every night she would leave the city to go into a clearing and look at the stars. One night, a dying star fell from the sky. But it landed in the branches of a tree, and still had some life in it. Rose saw where it landed and walked over.

"Rose," called the star. "I have seen you from heaven and how you have loved us. When I grew old, I made sure I would fall near you."

"Oh, Star," said Rose. "Is there some way I can save you?"

"No," said the star. "My time is past. But I have seen ahead, and have come to tell you that a great famine is about to descend on your land. It will last ten years, and many of your people who now live will die. The beautiful city will be beautiful no longer."

Rose was very sad hearing this.

"There is a way to save them," said the star, "but you must be very brave."

"What is it, Star?" asked Rose.

"I can use the last of my powers to put your city to sleep. They will sleep through the famine, but you must stay here, so when it is over, you can wake them. You will suffer much, and know hunger and thirst. You will be alone, with only the stars for company. Are you prepared to do this?"

"Yes, Star, I am," said Rose.

"Then watch," said the star.

As Rose watched, the grasses and vines grew and interlaced around the trees, making a living fence around the city. The branches at the top of the trees grew and tangled together, making a canopy. Rose could no longer get in.

The star sighed and died, falling from the tree into Rose's hand. In death, it was just a pebble. Rose kept it in her pocket next to her heart.

The next ten years were hard for Rose. Food was scarce, and she had to walk farther and farther to get it. But she remembered what the star had said, and when the ten years grew to a close, she went back to her beautiful city, though as she grew nearer, she was so weak she had to crawl.

Night came, and another star fell, landing in the branches of a nearby shrub.

"Oh, Star, I am so weak, I cannot wake them."

"Take me from the shrub and throw me at the hedge," said the star. "I will do the rest."

Even though the star was on a low, low branch, Rose had to struggle to reach it. But she reached it at last. Taking the star, she crawled to the city gates, now overgrown with grasses and vines, and threw the star at it. At once, the grasses and vines parted, the branches on the trees parted, and the beautiful city was beautiful once again.

The people came out of the city, saw Rose, and took care of her. When they heard her story, they found the second dead star, now a stone, and set both stars into an ornament for her head. And they all lived well in the beautiful city.

A girl raised a hand. "Is the story before or after Tashtalon?"

"No one knows," said Alia.

"It had to be after," said a boy. "We know before Tashtalon that everything was bad."

Alia and Gill exchanged looks, but said nothing.

"What was before Tashtalon?" asked another girl.

"There is no record of those times," said Alia. "We have only the stories the priests of Tashtalon tell us."

"I like the story about Tashtalon better," said one of the boys.

"Tashtalon is going to come and eat you up," said one of the girls.

"Tashtalon will shut you up," countered the boy.

Alia stood. "Now, none of that. It's time for you to go home. I'll see you tomorrow."

After a chorus of farewells and the scattering of children, Alia walked toward Gill. "I know that's your favorite story, too," she teased.

Gill smiled. "Yes, but I seem to remember that it was you who would come and tell me every time this story was performed at the puppet theater."

Alia gasped in mock surprise. "Why, that could just be."

They took the road to Alia's house. At this time of day, there was horse, cart, and pedestrian traffic, but even so, the streets and sidewalks were not crowded. City crews, under the direction of the city manager, who was in turn under the supervision of the Lord Protector, kept the roads and walkways in repair, the storm drains and underground sewer aqueducts clear. Each building had a spigot for water, flowing from a reservoir on the other side of the mountain. The houses, of stone and brick, had been sturdily built for comfortable occupation. The entire city showed signs of this deliberate and meticulous planning. Built by Tashtalon for his people, or so the priests said, but privately Gill thought it older than Tashtalon, for the records silently indicated age beyond known history.

Alia lived in a small, two-story brick house. Gill knew it as well as she knew the house of her parents, or her own rented room. This was the house Alia had grown up in, and where Tashtalon had taken her younger brother, Bruno, just over a year before. Gill remembered when Bruno was a baby, and she and Alia, only five years old themselves, would hover over his cradle, fascinated by his cooing. As time passed, however, Gill became afraid of him as he grew older and stronger, and became a tease and a bully. If Alia had not been as dear to Gill as a sister, and if Bruno had not been tame in Alia's presence, she would have avoided the house altogether. To Gill, it was almost a relief when Tashtalon took him, except that the suffering of Alia and her parents was a nightmare. Gill had been genuinely fond of Alia's parents, who had treated her as if she were a second daughter. Gill had sat with them and with Alia, night after night, after Bruno disappeared. While Alia had eventually regained her stability, the parents had sunk deeper and deeper into despair, until they had died the previous summer. Once again, Gill sat with Alia through her mourning, feeling the loss almost as keenly as Alia had. Alia had inherited the house, and now she lived there alone, becoming more of her old playful self once the cloud of her grief had lifted.

They walked up the steps to the door; Alia unlocked it with her key. Once inside, Alia turned to Gill. "What if we pack a supper and eat on the mountain?"

Gill stood speechless. Alia had always been one to stay close to home. What had changed her mind today?

Alia laughed. "I know. You're always the one to beg me to go outside the city. Let's say I've learned to see this your way."

"If I had known, I would have brought my spyglass."

"You can see the stars just as well with your own eyes."

They selected meat and breads, fruits and cheese, vegetables and sweets, and packed them all in a basket with a flask of wine and a couple of ceramic cups. Filled to the brim, the basket was too heavy for Gill, so Alia took it, as she usually did. They walked out of the city on the east side, away from Tashtalon's house, which was on the west side. Traveling up a well-worn path, they reached a flat space on the side of the mountain where city workers had carved and set stone benches.

Gill sat.

Alia set the basket down. "Do you need to rest?"

"Aren't we going to eat here?"

Alia nodded upward. "Let's go higher."

"Where?" Gill asked.

"I haven't been higher before. Wherever you go to watch the stars."

Gill stared at Alia, puzzled by her sudden interest. Gill's tales of star-watching usually bored her. When Alia simply looked back with anticipation, Gill shrugged. "All right."

There was no path, but the clover and moss grew low, and the way was easy, though unpaved. Gill reached a level area and sat in the clover. "How's this?"

Alia set down the basket, sat cross-legged, and smiled. "Just fine."

They remained quiet for a while, taking in the view. Looking down, they could see the tops of the castle and Tashtalon's house, as well as roads leading there. To the north, the mountain sloped downward to farmland, with forests on the far horizon. To the south, they could see more mountains, all progressively lower than Mount Blade, and a glimmer on the horizon could be imagined to be the sea. Westward lay more farmland; to the far west was a ribbon, the River Harrow, and more forest. The mountain itself blocked the view east, but Gill knew it was much like the view to the north.

"Mmmm," hummed Alia. "I can see why you like coming here."

"You can see almost the entire ring of Tashtalon here. Even a little outside the ring of Tashtalon, beyond the river, there."

"What do you think is beyond that?"

"I don't know. With my spyglass, sometimes I can see smoke, though it could be fog or mist, I suppose."

Alia edged closer to Gill. "Ever think of going there?"

Gill turned toward Alia. "Crossing the River Harrow is death, as is going into the forests beyond the ring."

"How do you know?"

Gill furrowed her brow. "Everyone knows. Even those few who have tried, never came back."

Alia did not reply.

"You aren't thinking of going there, are you?" asked Gill.

Alia waved a hand over the clover and the small rainbow-striped flowers growing among the grasses. "I know I can trust you to keep a secret."

"Of course." Gill shivered a little as she said that. She remembered all too well at the age of four arguing with a boy at storytelling, telling him that Tashtalon stunk. Somehow, the priest of Tashtalon, the predecessor of Boreas, had found out, came to her, and asked her if she knew what horrible things Tashtalon did to girls who defied him. Gill had rarely confided her most private thoughts to anyone again, and never betrayed a confidence.

"Have you ever thought of what the world would be like without Tashtalon?" Alia asked.

Gill considered. "You mean that the world was really better before Tashtalon came? I've thought that for a long time. We used to talk about it when we were alone in your house's attic, remember?"

Without looking up, Alia nodded. "I mean more than that. What about a future world without Tashtalon?"

"You mean a game? Like what if the sun were green instead of blue?"

Alia turned back to her, with a sober expression. "No, I'm serious. What if there were no Tashtalon?"

Gill pressed her lips together. What was Alia trying to get at? Alia loved to play games, pretend to be serious when she was only joking. Was this another joke? Or something more? "You mean what would happen if Tashtalon suddenly disappeared? I don't know how that could ever be."

"What if I were to tell you that Tashtalon could be killed?"

Did Alia have some secret knowledge? Gill could not imagine how. Gill had read all the books in the castle--how could Alia know more about Tashtalon than Gill herself? "Killed? He's a god, how can a god be killed?"

Alia looked Gill in the eye. "What if he's not a god?"

"What if he's not a god? What else could he be? No one's ever seen him...he puts everyone to sleep at night. How could he do that if he's not a god?"

"Magic."

"Doesn't that make him a god?"

"What if we could use magic against him?"

"Don't you have to be a god to use magic?"

"Do you?"

Gill was still not certain whether this was a game, a joke, a story, or real. "Can you do any?"

Alia frowned slightly. "No, but it's possible."

"How do you know?" Briefly, Gill wondered if Alia had somehow gone to the house of Tashtalon and found secrets there. But then, the house was heavily guarded and no one there would open their books for Alia--or any woman--or tell her how to kill Tashtalon, even if it could be done, which Gill doubted. And they certainly would not tell Alia that Tashtalon was not a god. No, she could not have gone there.

Alia shrugged. "I know."

"Did a star come down and tell you?" Gill asked seriously.

"Something like that," Alia replied cheerfully.

Gill sighed. She was becoming weary of this game or whatever it was. She was asking questions, but Alia was not giving her useful answers--which made Gill think this *was* a game. She turned to Alia. "Let's eat."

She smiled. "Then we shall eat."

They took supper from the basket and ate quietly. Small green furry meepers, curious about the visitors, crept toward the picnic site, chittering, but quickly dispersed when Gill and Alia smilingly shooed them away. As they finished the meal, the sun neared the western horizon. They could see a procession in the streets below.

Alia paused before finishing her dessert. "You know what they do up there, don't you?"

Gill looked down. "To the relatives of those that Tashtalon has devoured? Yes, my grandmother told me."

Alia acted as if she had not heard Gill's response. "They give them a drink--the Elixir of Forgetfulness, they call it. Remember how my parents were in a stupor for days? They could hardly feed or dress themselves. We had to help them."

"I remember," Gill said solemnly.

Alia turned to Gill. "You didn't like Bruno, did you?"

Gill shrugged and munched on an apple.

"Bruno was rough, and he liked to tease. I suppose to someone like you, someone whose brother and father are quiet, he might have seemed mean. But he was never cruel. In fact, we talked about a world without Tashtalon, too." Alia bowed her head. "I miss him."

"I'm sorry," said Gill, less because Bruno was gone and more because she did not want to see Alia sad again.

There was silence between the two. Alia finished eating, and rested her head on her upraised knees. Finally, she said, "Gill, I am going to kill Tashtalon."

Chapter 2

Inwardly, Gill was alarmed. She had heard of those who had gone mad when Tashtalon had devoured their relatives. The one comfort Gill had when Alia's parents were dying was that Alia herself had not refused food or water, and that she would not lose Alia as well. But for Alia to become insane...that idea terrified her just as much. But then, perhaps Alia was simply still playing an elaborate game? This thought calmed Gill enough to ask questions in a normal conversational tone.

"Do you know where to find him?"

Alia kept her head on her knees, not turning to Gill. "I can find him."

"Do you know how to kill him?"

"I can do that, too."

Again, Gill wondered how or where Alia could acquire any sort of information about Tashtalon's alleged vulnerabilities. This must be a joke.... "How?"

Now Alia turned to Gill. "You don't believe me."

Relieved, Gill let out a long breath. That, at least, showed Alia either was playing a game or was at least sane enough to realize the rashness of her speculations. "I'm having trouble imagining how you could do such a thing without getting killed."

Alia sat up straight. "I know. It's not without risk. But if no one tries, Tashtalon will devour us forever. That's what he does, you know. He keeps us, he feeds us, he lets us go about our business--only so he will have people to devour."

"How do you know all this?" Gill persisted.

Alia reached over and took Gill's arm firmly. "I don't want to put you in danger, Gill. You know too much already, but I couldn't keep it secret any longer, not from you. I wanted someone to know, so that if I failed...someone would remember me. Maybe try to do the same."

The thought began to creep into Gill's mind that this might not be a game, might not be madness, but a calculated plan of retribution. If she knew more, perhaps she could discourage Alia from pursuing this plan. "Shouldn't you tell me how to do this in case you fail, if I'm supposed to follow?"

Alia withdrew her hand gently. "If you choose to do this, the knowledge will come to you."

"I can't imagine how." If only Alia would tell Gill what her sources were!

Alia smiled. "You will."

Now Alia seemed to be playing games again. Gill looked around. The sun had set, and the stars were gradually coming out. "We'd better go back," she suggested. At the same time, the horn sounding the two-hour warning blared through the city. "I don't want to sleep outside tonight."

"Don't you stay here and watch the stars?"

"Once they come out, for maybe a quarter hour. Then I hurry home. But I don't want to rush tonight if I don't have to."

Alia nodded.

They picked up all their leftovers and packed the basket again. Silently, swiftly, they progressed down the mountain. The path was softly lit by glow-weed, tufts of which grew on either side. When they were young, Alia and Gill would roll in large patches of weeds, whose bits clung to their clothing and hair and made them seem to glow themselves. Once in the city, lights streaming from windows of nearby houses helped them see the way. At last, they reached Alia's door. Gill lingered just inside the entryway as Alia set the basket down.

"I'll come tomorrow," Gill announced.

Alia turned to her with a puzzled expression. "Don't you see your parents the day after you visit me?"

Gill shrugged. "It's just a social visit. They'll still see me next week."

Alia crossed her arms in front of her and grinned. "Gill...I don't need watching."

Gill turned and pushed the door shut behind her. "Alia, you just told me that you plan to kill Tashtalon, and if you fail, you want me to follow. Now if that wasn't just a game, that needs some further discussion."

Alia's smile faded. She looked down to the floor. "I wondered if I should tell you," she said softly.

Gill felt hurt. "How could you doubt that it was best to tell me?"

Alia shook her head. "Not that I thought you would betray me, but that you might be in danger."

"Then I need to know more, don't I?"

She sighed. "Perhaps I was too intense."

Gill lifted an eyebrow.

Alia chuckled softly. "All right. I was too intense." She took a breath. "I shall do nothing out of the ordinary tomorrow. I promise."

"Then I'll be back the next day."

"And miss visiting your grandmother? Gill, she has those stiff knees; she needs you to come and clean."

"I can send my brother over. It's about time he took more responsibility."

Alia tossed her head. "Oh, Gill, you know you'd miss visiting her as much as she'd miss you. Go ahead and see her. Come back on the third day, as you usually do."

Gill considered. "All right." She stepped forward and hugged Alia. "Don't do anything rash."

Alia put a reassuring hand on Gill's arm. "Then I shall do nothing rash."

The streets were nearly empty as Gill walked back to her room, and those few people she saw were hurrying to their own homes. Everyone slept from two hours after sunset until two hours before sunrise. Most slept longer, but none slept less. Those on the street at the time of Tashtalon's sleep would lie where they were until morning. The sleeping was a blessing to those with infants, or those troubled by illness; it could be a curse, even death, to those who were careless with their cooking fires, but to most it was simply a requirement that they had to meet. The horn giving the ten-minute warning sounded as Gill was unlocking her door. Glow-weed in a vase on her table lit the room softly. She managed to take care of her needs, get undressed, and get into bed before the sleep took her.

Gill woke to the sound of birds twittering. There were no screams, either from injury or from those whose loved ones had been taken by the god. Tashtalon rarely took people two nights in a row, though it was not unprecedented for him to do so. The intervals between disappearances were generally 20 days, though there had been a recorded interval as long as 102. No one could detect a pattern, and Gill had never found one, even though she had read all the records in the castle.

After work, she went to the house of her parents, which was a modest two-story building in a residential section of the city. The surrounding lawn had provided a place for her and her brother to play when they were young, with ample space left over for her parents to cultivate a garden.

As she approached the house, she saw the ice cart parked in front of it. Telford, the ice man, spoke to her mother.

"Bessie tripped on some stairs and broke her ankle. Got other neighbors bringing her meals, but I'm collecting to repair the steps."

"Of course." Her mother counted out some coins in her hand and gave them to him.

"Thanks, Mavis." Spotting Gill, he winked at her and added, "Nice to see you too, Gill."

Gill responded with a polite nod. The man took the reins of the horse and walked on.

Mavis shifted the basket of newly-bought goods in her arm and hugged Gill. "Come in."

Telford had already put the ice in the cooler. Her mother put away bread and cheese, and sat at the kitchen table. Gill sat opposite.

"Your father and brother will be late at the shop. They need to finish a table for a buyer by tonight. They said go on without them."

Gill nodded. "I'll see them next week, then. Is Clede any nearer to making a selection?"

Mavis sighed. "No. He says he still doesn't know if he wants to get married yet."

"He may. He's still 19. I'm sure he'll make a selection by the time he's 23."

"Speaking of 23, what do you want for your birthday?"

"I hadn't thought much about it."

"Not thought about being 23? Where you want to go, what you want to do? You have a whole year free to yourself, don't waste it!"

"I'm sure I'll think of something by then."

"Your father still wants you to go south and make a fortune. Then you won't have to worry about your future."

You mean, whether I marry or not, Gill thought. Aloud, she said, "Can I ask about your brother?"

Mavis seemed startled. "What do you want to know?"

"Do you ever miss him?"

"Do I miss Petri?" She snorted. "Hardly. Tashtalon taking him was the best thing that ever happened to me...and probably to him, too. He would never have amounted to anything. At least he got the honor of being eaten by a god."

"What did grandmother and grandfather think?"

"They were sad, and they still think about him, I would guess. But once he was gone, everything was quiet and peaceful. We no longer had broken plates and pots, and the neighbors no longer came over day after day complaining about what Petri had done to their property."

Gill nodded. Her maternal grandfather and grandmother currently lived by the sea with one of Mavis's sisters. She had not seen them in years.

"Why do you ask?" added Mavis.

"Lydia came to the castle yesterday," said Gill. "She was overwrought with grief."

Mavis nodded. "I heard her scream yesterday morning and rushed over. I thought I'd persuaded her to take some tea and rest, so I went back home; I didn't think she'd go to the castle. But she's snug in bed today. I checked on her again."

* * *

The next afternoon, after finishing her work for the day, Gill went to the house of her paternal grandmother. Irina lived in a small, two-room cottage surrounded by similar tidy, well-kept buildings. She was a plump, pleasant woman whose movements had slowed with age, especially when the joints in her knees had swollen and stiffened. When Gill knocked on the door, she heard an immediate greeting from within, but waited a time for the door to be unlatched.

Irina was shorter than Gill, and embraced her in a hug. They went inside; Irina sat in her old, comfortable chair, put her feet up on a footrest, and picked up her knitting. Gill started to sweep and dust, which she usually did for Irina when she was there.

Gill never had known her paternal grandfather. As a child, she had never questioned or wondered about the fact that on one side of the family, there was a grandmother and grandfather, but on the other side, only a grandmother. She had never asked about it until she had reached her teen years. Then she found that her grandfather had been taken by Tashtalon, but her parents and grandmother volunteered little additional information.

Now, though, she felt the need to know more. "Grandmother, can I ask you something personal?"

Irina smiled as the knitting needles clicked. "You can ask me anything, dear."

"Can you tell me about Grandfather?"

She stopped in her knitting and looked up. "Oh, you mean my husband."

"Yes. Can you tell me more about him?"

She shrugged. "There's not much to tell. I was only married five years when Tashtalon took him."

"Does he take men that old?"

She smiled. "He wasn't that old. He was 21. We married young. But yes, he takes young men, especially fighters, as grandfather was."

"Fighters?"

She took up her knitting again. "Yes. Brawlers, those who fight at fairs for show, guardsmen. Haven't you noticed that there are always new faces among the city and castle guards?"

Gill paused in her sweeping and thought about it. "I guess I just presumed they were transferred or promoted or moved."

Irina nodded. "Some, yes. But Tashtalon takes his share."

"So grandfather was a guardsman?"

She chuckled. "No. He was a brawler. Pick a fight with anyone. Even had a few with me."

"You?"

She nodded solemnly. "At least he had the decency to hold back while I was pregnant. But once your father was walking around, he beat him too. Your father doesn't remember him fondly, and I don't, either."

"Why did you marry him?"

"Oh, he was sweet at first. And I was pretty. He selected me, and I wanted children. He got meaner and meaner as time went on."

"So you were glad that Tashtalon took him?"

"Yes," she said bluntly. "I couldn't believe it at first. I went to bed before he did, so I thought he simply had wandered outside somewhere, picking a fight in some pub, and fallen asleep on the way home. But the priest of Tashtalon came and asked me to come and give thanks that my husband had been taken. I did. He didn't even give me that drink he gives to most of them."

Irina went back to her knitting, and Gill to her sweeping and dusting. When Gill was done, she sat in the guest chair opposite her grandmother.

"Now," said Irina, continuing her knitting, "what do you want for your 23rd birthday?"

Gill sighed.

Irina smiled. "Tired of hearing that?"

"Somewhat."

She touched the necklace she always wore: a golden chain with a key-shaped trinket at the end of it. "You know this is an heirloom."

"I couldn't take that, Grandmother."

"On your 23rd birthday, I have to give it to you."

"Have to?"

Irina put her knitting down and set it on the table next to her. "Gill, draw the curtains and check for neighbors."

"Why?"

The older woman smiled. "Tradition."

Gill shrugged and complied. When she was back in her chair, Irina said, "This is how my mother told me, and her mother told her. The tradition is supposed to go back before Tashtalon."

"Before Tashtalon?"

Irina shrugged. "That's what I was told. I don't know if it's true or not. My mother didn't know, either, and said her mother didn't know." She smiled at Gill's confused expression. "I know. It's odd. Here is what I can tell you: this is a real key that fits in a real lock. Where the lock is, I don't know, and I can't tell you when the knowledge was lost. But I was told that if I needed to use the key, I would know what lock it was."

"Were you told how you would know?"

Irina shook her head. She smiled again. "Mysterious, isn't it? My mother said she fancied that it was just a story a long ago grandmother of ours made up, to make the necklace seem important. But she was very strict with two instructions. First, that I must pass this to a daughter, or granddaughter if I had no daughter, and second, that I must do this before I die, and not on my deathbed."

"Does this mean I have a duty to have a daughter or granddaughter to pass it to?"

Irina looked at her soberly. "The line is unbroken." When Gill did not respond at once, she added, "That's why I felt I had to marry and have children."

"I want children," said Gill, "but whether I'll be selected...."

Irina got up slowly, stiffly, and put a hand on Gill's arm. "Fate will provide these things." She smiled and sat again.

Gill smiled back. "Fate apart from Tashtalon."

"If you won't tell...," Irina exchanged a meaningful look with Gill and continued, "I believe there are forces in this world which are greater than Tashtalon, and over which Tashtalon has no control."

Gill walked over, put a hand on her grandmother's arm, and looked her in the eye. "If you won't tell, I believe it too."

Gill had more than the usual paperwork at the castle the next day. By the time she reached the schoolyard, no one was there. She went directly to Alia's house, thinking, on the way, that it was strange that Alia had not waited for her. Gill quickened her pace.

She knocked on the door. Hearing no immediate response, she began to worry. Had Alia gone off to kill Tashtalon? Gill took the key to the house that Alia had given her, only to find the door already unlocked. She rushed in.

Immediately, she found herself face-to-face with an old man. Gill looked around quickly to be sure she had the right house. It was Alia's furniture, her rug, her possessions. She turned back to the man, who scrutinized her closely. She examined him in turn. Something was familiar about him.

Before she could place the man, a sound at the door made Gill turn. Alia walked in with a covered basket. "Oh, I see you've met."

"Yes," said the old man. His voice was remarkably clear for his age. "A couple of days ago, we freed a man tangled in a bola cord. But we haven't been introduced."

Alia put the basket down. "Then I shall do the honors. This is my friend, Gill. Gill, this is Eminric. He stops and visits from time to time."

Eminric continued to smile at Gill. Although it was a friendly smile, it made her uncomfortable.

Alia seemed not to notice. "I had to go out to the grocer's. I wasn't expecting both you and him on the same day. I'll put these away and be right back." She picked up the basket again.

Still facing Eminric, Gill sat. Eminric had locked his eyes on her as well; he sat opposite her.

Alia returned with a glass of wine for each of them, and put them on the narrow side tables next to the chairs before sitting herself. Gill summoned up her best diplomatic demeanor and asked politely, "And how long will you be here?"

"As long as I need to be," he answered cheerily.

"I've told Eminric so much about you," said Alia.

What had Alia told him? That she assisted the Lord Protector? That she despised Tashtalon? Gill realized she probably looked shocked, and composed herself quickly.

Eminric chuckled softly.

"Don't worry, Gill," Alia reassured her. "I haven't told him anything embarrassing. Just that you're a good friend."

Gill softly let out a relieved breath, and tried not to stare at either of them.

"Alia tells me your 23rd birthday is coming up. Any plans?" He fingered his neatly-trimmed beard.

"Not yet."

"Have you thought of exploring the world? Seeing new things, meeting new people?" He nodded to Alia over the rim of his glass as he took a sip. "Alia's turning 23 in a few more months. If you're willing to wait that long, we could all go off exploring together."

"To where?"

"Oh, here, there, and everywhere." He grinned at Alia; she grinned back.

"What about making a living? What do you do?"

"This and that."

"You're pretty good with a sword."

He inclined his head modestly. "There are those who say so."

This was all beginning to remind her of the conversation with Alia on the mountain: many words, little information. Was Eminric playing a game, too? And if so, what sort of game? Or was he the one who put the idea in Alia's mind to kill Tashtalon? But Gill did not feel secure enough about this stranger to ask these questions. Instead, she listened as Alia and Eminric talked about the weather, and sipped her wine cautiously, not wanting to become giddy or lose control. Eminric slowly drank his and asked for more. Alia refilled his glass and set the flask beside it.

At last, Alia went to start dinner and Eminric went to the lavatory. Gill drew Alia aside in the kitchen and whispered, "Alia, who is this man? Why haven't you told me about him before?"

Alia sighed. "Gill, it's just so complicated. And there's only so much I can tell you without putting you in danger."

"Complicated?" Gill blurted out, then lowered her voice. What had Alia gotten herself into? "What about you? Aren't you in danger?"

"I've taken precautions."

"Such as?" When Alia did not answer right away, Gill added, "Did he put it in your mind to kill Tashtalon?"

Alia's demeanor suddenly changed from friendly to determined. "*No one* had to put the thought in my mind that we would all be better off without Tashtalon."

Gill drew back a little, unaccustomed to Alia's vengeful tone.

"Do you like living under Tashtalon?" Alia asked.

Gill faced her squarely. She had nothing to apologize for in rec-ommending caution. "No, but I'm not about to go marching off with a sword to cut off his head when I don't even know where he is...if that's anywhere mortals can reach."

Alia's expression again softened again. She put a hand on Gill's arm. "Listen, Gill. Tashtalon may not be a god, but he is powerful, and has control over powerful magic. He can't be overcome if no one is ready to take any risks. Remember the story about the star? Rose couldn't save her people without suffering for ten years. Those stories mean something, Gill...more than you know."

"I suppose Eminric is giving you this information?"

Alia nodded. "Some, yes."

"Why doesn't *he* go after Tashtalon, then?"

Alia took a deep breath, as if pondering a difficult point. She let it out slowly. "Tashtalon can only be defeated by a woman." She paused, taking in Gill's puzzled expression, and said, "What are the greatest laws of Tashtalon?"

"That no woman can rule, and no woman can take up a sword."

"And why do you think there are laws like that?"

As Gill considered that, she heard the door to the washroom shut and footsteps cross the wooden floor of the sitting room. Eminric entered the kitchen.

"Can I help with dinner?" he asked.

"If you want to help, then you shall help," said Alia cheerfully.

That ended Gill's questioning. They put together a tasty meal; Eminric acted like an experienced cook. He dressed the small hens that Alia had brought from the market, basted them with an herb sauce, and arranged vegetables around them before placing them in the oven. Once supper was ready and on the table, Eminric and Alia engaged in a conversation about cuisine, again frustrating Gill's hopes of finding out more about Eminric's or Alia's plans.

As the warning horns sounded, Eminric showed no sign of leaving, and Gill knew she would get no further answers until he was gone. She considered staying overnight at Alia's, but concluded that, too, would not be productive. She said her goodnights and went home.

Two days later, as Gill sorted through papers in her office, Cyril came in. Gill turned to him, startled--whenever he wanted to speak to her, he normally called her into his office.

"Gill, there's someone here to see you."

"Who?" No one ever came to the castle to see *her*.

He gestured into his office. Gill rose from her chair and followed. In the office stood a black-robed assistant of Boreas. "Boreas bids you come with me," he said simply.

Gill turned to Cyril. "Take all the time you need," he said. "I won't expect you back for another two or three days."

"What's this about?" Gill asked the assistant.

"I'm not to say. Just follow."

The assistant led the way, at a great pace. Gill matched his stride but kept behind him. She was curious when he did not take the road to Tashtalon's house, but went into the city. When he turned onto the road where Alia lived, Gill's mouth went dry with a dreadful foreboding. The assistant went up the stairs to Alia's house. Two city guardsmen stood on either side of Alia's door. When Gill reached the threshold, the assistant stepped aside, and Boreas greeted her.

"I understand that the owner of the house filed a will with the city, naming you the heir," he said.

Gill nodded. Alia had done this recently, having no family to inherit. The plan was that Gill and her children would have Alia's property if Alia died unmarried and childless. But what had happened? Had Alia disappeared—maybe gone after Tashtalon with Eminric? Was that why they had looked up her heirs?

"Come in," said Boreas.

One of the guardsmen interrupted. "Do you think she should see this?"

"She's a woman," Boreas said irritably. "Do you think a woman's going to faint at the sight of blood?"

Blood? Alia could not have actually killed Tashtalon, could she? Gill did not think that Boreas would be so calm if she had.

Boreas and guardsmen moved so that Gill could enter. At first, she saw only a mound on the sitting room floor. She edged closer, and saw dried clots of black blood and shredded fabric. With closer examination, she began to make out what probably used to be limbs, some exposed internal organs, a neck, and part of a face. Alia's naked eyeball started sightlessly up at her. At the shock of recognition, Gill went numb all over.

"It is Tashtalon's doing," said Boreas. "It has been many years since he has chosen a woman. Do you know whether she broke the law of Tashtalon?"

Gill was already shaking her head when Boreas looked at her.

He scrutinized her closely. "*You* wouldn't have broken the law of Tashtalon, or encouraged her to do so?"

She turned to him with a vacant stare. Alia was dead; that was all that mattered, not some unimportant law of Tashtalon. What sort of question was that? "What?" was all she could manage to say. Her voice barely rose above a whisper.

Her listless manner seemed to convince him. He nodded. "It is good that you do not mourn for her. Anything that offends Tashtalon should be disowned. It is better that you have the house...such a nice house. I'll have the guardsmen clean the room and remove and bury the body."

Gill's head stopped shaking.

Boreas seemed to take her silence as consent. "Very well. No need for you to linger. Since she had no living relatives, there is no obligation for you to come to thank Tashtalon for his great deed in their stead. I shall do the honors."

Gill inclined her head and turned away, which Boreas appeared to take as a nod; he nodded back. In a daze, Gill left the house and walked down the stairs, but noticed nothing else until she found herself knocking on her grandmother's door.

Irina opened the door. Her eyes widened when she saw Gill. "What is it?" Irina looked up and down the street, which prompted Gill to do the same. They saw only light traffic, mostly pedestrians going about their business.

Gill walked in and sat. Irina closed and latched the door, then drew the curtains. Once seated, Gill began to weep. Her grief poured out for some time. She paced the floor, she sat, she stood, she whispered "Why? Why?" when she had voice to do so. Irina hugged Gill when Gill would let her, made tea when Gill pushed her away.

Finally, exhausted, Gill sunk into one of the chairs. Irina put tea next to her on the table and settled into her own chair. Gill picked up the cup and sipped. Feeling a little refreshed, Gill turned to Irina. "I am going to kill Tashtalon," she said softly. "I don't know how, but I'm going to kill him."

Immediately, Irina stood from her chair and hobbled to Gill with an odd expression. When Gill looked up at her, she seemed to have changed, as if her grandmother had donned a mask. Irina took the necklace from her throat and placed it around Gill's. She put Gill's hand over the key, her own warm hand holding it there as the heel of her other hand rested on Gill's forehead as if in blessing.

"You are Silmariae, daughter of Silmariae, enemy of Mace. Do not shrink from what you need to do; do not rest until your task is completed, you and your daughters or granddaughters after you." The words seemed to resonate in the tiny room.

As the echoes faded, Irina withdrew her hands and went back to her chair. She sat, put her feet up, and reached for her knitting.

Chapter 3

Gill sipped her tea and watched Irina. After a time, when she showed no sign of explaining or elaborating on what she had just done, Gill ventured, "Grandmother?"

Irina looked up with a smile. "Yes, dear?"

"Why did you give me the key just now?"

"The key? I was waiting for your 23rd birthday, dear." Her hand strayed to her throat, found nothing, and turned to Gill. Slowly, she rose from the chair and walked over to Gill. She put her hand on the key. "Yes, I did give that to you, didn't I? Or was it a dream?"

"No, Grandmother, it wasn't a dream."

"It seemed like it. I didn't know what I was doing, I didn't know what I was saying. The words just came out."

Irina padded back to her chair and sat. The expression on her face changed. "But there was a dream. I had forgotten it until now." She turned to Gill. "Do you know how some people say that they hear the hoofbeats of greathorses in their sleep on the nights that Tashtalon comes to take someone?"

"Yes."

"Last night, I heard hoofbeats in my dream...my nightmare. A murderer came to your friend Alia's house. He glowed in the dark. He opened the door without touching it. He awakened Alia from her sleep. She tried to run away; he caught her. She tried to fight him, but he murdered her...viciously." She turned to Gill again. "That's what happened, wasn't it?"

Gill had been listening to the story open-mouthed. "Yes," she whispered. "That must be...." Louder, she said, "Yes, Alia died...was murdered. By Tashtalon, so Boreas said." Then a thought occurred to her. Maybe Eminric was Tashtalon, or one of his agents. "Can you describe the murderer you saw?"

Irina looked up at the ceiling. "Let me see...yes. Youngish man, no beard, cream-colored skin, brown hair...even handsome, if one can say that of a murderer."

Eminric was handsome, but nothing else matched. Maybe it *had* been Tashtalon. No description of him existed, and if the priests knew what he looked like, they never said. They certainly were convinced that Tashtalon had killed Alia. Maybe there was some mark or sign that Gill had not noticed; her thoughts at the time had been only for Alia.

Irina continued her reminiscence. "The last time this happened, I was a girl. My mother wore the key then, and the day after Tashtalon murdered the woman, my mother told me she had a strange and frightening dream...that's all she would tell me."

Gill reached up and fingered the key around her neck. "There must be magic in the key."

Irina nodded. "That's what my grandmother thought...but women can't control magic, so says Tashtalon."

"Or they can, but Tashtalon doesn't want them to." As Irina appeared to ponder that, Gill added, "Do you know who Silmariae is? Or Mace?"

Irina shook her head. "No. I just said the names. I don't know who they are. Perhaps you can look them up in the castle?"

"I've read every chronicle written in the past 500 years, back to the time Tashtalon came. There's nothing before that, and no such name in the chronicles." This mystery was becoming deeper and deeper. Gill felt frustrated. How could she ever find the truth?

"Maybe my mother was right," Irina said. "Maybe the key came before Tashtalon."

"Maybe that's why Tashtalon doesn't want us to know what came before him."

"Maybe things were better before Tashtalon?" Irina speculated.

Gill nodded.

Irina sighed. "What are you going to do now?"

"I don't know." Gill bit her lip. "I have all these questions, and no way to get answers. Alia said something about when I need the knowledge, it would come to me, but now that I need to know, nothing's coming."

Irina smiled. "I think Alia meant what I told you: fate will provide these things."

"When?"

"Just be patient, dear. You have your whole life ahead of you."

Gill did not feel reassured.

Gill spent the next day at Alia's. The guardsmen had done excellent work cleaning up the sitting room; only freshly-sanded floorboards showed that they had been there. She searched the house, looking for papers, notes, diaries, anything that would give her a clue as to why Tashtalon would want Alia or what Alia had been planning. She had not been there long when she noticed that though the house was neat, things had been moved. Alia had been very strict about everything being in its proper place, and she was finding papers, statuettes, hairbrushes, and other items where Alia would never put them. She sat on Alia's bed, thinking. Who could have done this? Eminric, perhaps? Maybe, but from what she saw, Eminric could have probably charmed any information he needed from Alia just by asking. He would not have had to search. It was far more likely Boreas or his aides must have looked through the house. Had they found anything? If so, had they taken away what they had found? Gill sighed. She wished to know, but it was too dangerous to make inquires, to draw attention to herself.

Gill spent the night in her own rented room. She saw no need to give it up just yet. Besides, somehow just handling Alia's things had brought on waves of intense grief. In her own room, she could at least pretend that Alia was still alive.

The next day she went to work. Cyril greeted her with, "Are you well?"

"Yes, thank you," Gill answered, and Cyril never mentioned the incident again.

In the days that followed, she watched Boreas for any signs that he was suspicious of her. When, day after day, he acted normally around her, she became less tense, but remained vigilant. She became more aware of people behind her on the street, or curious about those who made eye contact with her in the markets. Most of all, she tried to spot Eminric. Would he be looking for her now? Try to take her away? At night, alone in her room, she wondered if she would ever feel safe again.

One day, as she sat in her accustomed place in the throne room, staring at the back of Tashtalon's throne as Cyril heard petitions, the thought came to her in a flash: Tashtalon's throne was where the key fit. There was no doubt in her mind.

When her work was done for the day, she walked through the great hall, as usual. The hall was empty, and her footsteps echoed on the tile floor. Hearing no approach, she quickly slipped behind the thrones. Taking the key from her neck, she held it in front of the keyhole. It appeared to be the right size. She looked up and down the back. To touch Tashtalon's throne was supposed to be death. But then, magic was not supposed to work for women. Tashtalon's words were not all true, but Gill suspected that they weren't all lies, either.

She heard footsteps and crouched behind the throne. Someone walked past the door of the great hall, but did not pause. When the sound faded away, she rose slowly. She could not stand there, indecisive, the rest of the afternoon. Eventually someone would spot her and ask awkward, perhaps dangerous, questions. She did not want to die, but the only tool she had to get the answers to the questions nagging her was this key, and somehow she knew, with a cold certainty, that it fit that lock.

Taking a breath, she lifted the key with a shaking hand, thrust the key into the hole, and gave it a twist. She did not die, but nothing else happened, either. She turned the key harder, afraid, for an instant, that it would never work. Suddenly, a panel hinged at the bottom flew open. Startled, she took a step back. There was now a square hole in the throne. A paper lay inside. Gingerly, she took out the paper. Unfolding it, she saw what appeared to be a map. Peering around the throne to be sure no one was there, she stuffed it into her bodice, patting it so that it was smooth. Carefully, she closed the panel, relocked it, and scurried out of the still-empty great hall.

On the walk home, she could hardly believe that she had done it, that it had been that easy, and that she was still alive. Was Tashtalon blind? No, he was not blind, if he killed Alia. But he was not all-seeing. Or perhaps he did have his eye on her and was toying with her? Was the key an instrument of his to lure his enemies to him? She sighed deeply. Would she ever have answers to her questions?

After supper, she settled in a rocking chair, resting. Since Alia's death, she found she needed this quiet time alone. Someone in the neighborhood was a musician, and this evening he or she was practicing a tune on an instrument with a bow and string. She rocked gently back and forth with the rhythm until dusk, when the musician stopped. She closed the windows, drew the curtains, lit a lamp, and sat at her desk, a shallow box with a hinged top set on wooden legs. Fresh glow-weed in the vase lit the room adequately for reading.

She took the page from her bodice and spread it out. It appeared to be a map, and showed the mountain range behind Mount Blade. A particular site was marked. Gill knew the place was uninhabited, away even from the paths where shepherds pastured their flocks. Insets on the map showed a stream, rocks, and other natural markers near the site. Her grandmother said that the key came from a time before Tashtalon; presumably the map did, too. If the site was marked before Tashtalon, she wondered if the area looked anywhere near the same—except, the inset showed marble columns, outlining, perhaps, a door. She turned the paper over, wondering how the paper and writing itself had been so well preserved for so long. More magic at work, perhaps? She held the paper up to the light, but there was no watermark. Who had written it and what message was she supposed to take from it? She wished she could discuss it with Alia, especially since Alia had hinted she knew secrets about Tashtalon. Would she have known about this?

Thinking about Alia caused a wave of grief to seize her. She turned from the page and put her head in her hands until the warning trumpets roused her from her oblivion.

On the day of her twenty-third birthday, she put all of her possessions at the castle into a wooden box. Much she had taken home, a little every day, for the past month, so only these few items remained. When the day was done, Cyril ducked into her office.

"Ready to go?"

"Yes."

Cyril smiled. "I shall miss you. After your year of freedom is over, if you want to come back, I can probably find work for you."

She felt warmed by his offer. "Thank you."

He took the box from her and set it down. "I'll have one of the guards bring it out. I want to show you what I got for you." He took her arm and guided her out of his office.

"You didn't have to get me anything," she protested feebly.

"Oh, but I wanted to. You have been of great value to me and I wanted to give you something of equal value."

Once out the gate, at the top of the steps, he stopped. At the bottom of the gate, one of the guardsmen held the reins of a greathorse.

He grinned. "Your present."

Gill realized her mouth was hanging open, and shut it. With Cyril at her side, she walked down the stairs. The greathorses were no ordinary horses. They were taller, stronger, and sturdier. Though they could not run as fast over a short distance, they had greater endurance over a long distance. They were more even-tempered and biddable than an ordinary horse, and less vulnerable to heat and cold. It was said that Tashtalon had fashioned them from ordinary horses with his magic.

She reached the horse's side and stroked the golden coat. The horse nuzzled her shoulder affectionately.

She turned to Cyril. "He's wonderful."

"What are you going to call him?" he asked.

"He doesn't have a name?"

Cyril smiled and shook his head. "Just out of colthood."

She stroked the offered muzzle. "I always dreamed of having a horse, and I've always planned a name if I ever got one: Kiri."

He nodded and stepped back. "I hope you like the saddle, too."

She walked over and examined it. It was a good traveling saddle, with pockets as well as hooks and rings for packs. She looked up at Cyril. Merely saying "thank you" seemed so inadequate to the occasion, but what else could she say? "It's a generous gift. I'm grateful beyond words."

"If you're happy, I'm happy. I presume you can ride a horse?"

Gill took the reins. "Yes. One of my aunts has a ranch in the foothills. I just haven't been able to afford one for myself." She pulled herself up. The guardsman come out with her box.

Cyril took the box from the guardsman. "Here, let me attach that." He secured it in a place in back of the saddle.

"Thank you again," Gill said.

"A good journey to you!" Cyril waved her off.

She rode Kiri back to her home and put the box away. Then she went to her parents' house for their celebration. Kiri drew a lot of attention, not only from her family, but from the neighbors as well. Even Lydia showed up for a while, though she said little and quickly went home.

Inside, her brother Clede gave her the traditional gift for a woman's 23rd birthday: a set of kitchen knives. Her parents gave her a new spyglass. Her grandmother gave her a tent.

"For your travels," she said.

"Going south?" asked her father, Loris, hopefully.

"At first, to look at the stars," Gill said. "Then I'll come back and think about what to do next."

"With a horse like that, it makes even more sense to go south to the mines," Loris advised. "It's about time you learned a craft or trade instead of all that book work. You can't make a decent living at that."

"Maybe so," Gill replied, knowing he would take the vague answer as agreement.

Gill traced out the length of the route she would take, and estimated that the journey to the place on the map would take two days. Kiri did not complain once as Gill loaded all the provisions she bought, using every bag and attachment the saddle had. Once Gill was out sight of the city, she never saw anyone, even when she reined in Kiri at the top of a hill to check for signs of pursuit. Kiri climbed the mountain foothills sure-footedly and without complaint. After checking a couple of sites that seemed likely, but lacked some essential markers, they arrived at what Gill hoped was the correct spot. Boulders stood in the indicated places, though not shaped exactly as in the drawings. Some trees stood where they had been drawn, though dead or stunted, and many other trees had grown up. Part of the hill itself seemed straighter than was natural, but overgrown with moss and vines. Using one of her new knives as a machete, she cleared them until she struck rock. She took off her thick riding gloves and put in a hand among the vines. The stone was unnaturally smooth. This was the place.

She cut enough of the brush away so that the stone door could be exposed. The rest of the vines she tied back like a curtain. She set up the tent and drew a flap next to the door so that that the entrance would not be visible from outside.

She examined the door. She made out hinges on one side and a metal ring above a keyhole on the other. There was no key to try except the one around her neck; to her astonishment, the lock clicked. She pulled the metal ring. At first, nothing happened, so she gripped it with two hands and leaned back with all her might. Slowly, the door ground open. Stale, but not foul, air came from inside.

Gill lit a lamp and went in. Her first impression was that she had found a treasurehouse. Objects—neatly placed on tables and shelves—glittered in the light. Looking more closely, she saw books, a rack of swords, and a glass globe that seemed to have its own light inside, among dozens of other items. Turning, she gasped. A body lay on a slab.

Quickly, she walked around the room—not much larger than her rented room—to be sure there were no other human remains, and then turned back to the slab. At the base was carved "Silmariae." Gill let out a sigh of relief. At last, some answers. Her grandmother said she was a daughter of Silmariae. Would this be an ancestor?

She walked close to the head and looked down. The skin was waxy; Gill presumed some sort of preservative had been spread over it. The face did not seem much like hers or her grandmother's, though with many generations she knew the resemblance would fade. She saw some wrinkles around the eyes; she guessed the woman had been in her forties, maybe early fifties, at death.

She brought the lamp down to examine the body closer. The corpse was dressed in armor. A sword with a plain hilt and sheath lay on the body's breast and stomach, the haft under the folded hands. She remembered the conversation between her and Alia: "What are the greatest laws of Tashtalon?" "That no woman should rule, and no woman should carry a sword." This woman had! *Which was probably why she is dead*, Gill thought.

She turned to the books, which were lined up next to an empty marble bookstand. Lifting the covers, and paging quickly through them, she found a history; what seemed to be an inventory of the artifacts and a description of their characteristics; a bound set of maps; and a book curiously addressed: "To the one who discovers this tomb." She hugged the book triumphantly. Answers, at last!

Gill had always been a quick reader. The book addressed to the discoverer of the tomb was thin, but the central message was clear: she was, the book presumed, a descendant of Silmariae and it was her task to challenge Mace. That sounded close to what her grandmother had said when she gave Gill the key. The rest of the book's entries puzzled her. She made out what seemed to be a set of instructions, but those instructions referred to names and places she did not know. The flowery archaic language, such as she had found in the older books at the castle, did not help, either. Apparently the author anticipated her confusion and recommended she read the other books, and come back to this one. She took a history next and put it on the bookstand. After a brief time, she found she needed the map at her elbow and the artifact book for reference, so she moved other tables next to the bookstand. They were heavy, but she was determined, and managed to shove enough furniture together to form a makeshift study area, though the effort winded her.

About a third of the way through the thick history, she began to tremble with anger. As she had always suspected, the legend of Tashtalon had been a lie. The world had not been in chaos before Tashtalon. It had been much larger, more populated, more prosperous. The area within the ring of Tashtalon had been called Somerlie, but another area to the north had been populated, too. That was called Asquith. Asquith and Somerlie together had been ruled by a man in authority, called a king, and a woman in authority, called a queen. The book went on to say that people from the stars, called the Wye, had come to join them, making a settlement just east of Asquith, called Eldswold. Gill rocked back and forth in delight as she read that passage. People from the stars! But Gill sobered quickly as she read that Mace, a Wye himself, had also come from the stars and made war on the humans and other Wye, nearly destroying them all.

Silmariae then came into the story. She had been one of those women in authority called a queen. Courageous and headstrong, she had undertaken a journey, hoping to kill Mace, using the sword she had been named after. Here Gill had to read carefully, and occasionally had to re-read parts, because sometimes "Silmariae" referred to her ancestor and other times "Silmariae" referred to the sword. She even moved her chair over to the slab for a time, alternately touching the armor on the body and the sheath of the sword as they were mentioned in the book, to keep track.

Even though Silmariae's body lay within reach, Gill found herself hoping, as she read the tale, that Silmariae would succeed in her mission. She found she could not help but feel saddened and dismayed when the history reported that Mace had killed Silmariae. Silmariae's adult daughter, Estes, a warrior herself who had traveled with her mother, had recovered the body and put their mother in the secret tomb pre-built especially for her. In victory, Mace declared that he was a god. "Tashtalon," the history said, meant "powerful one" in the Wye language, and his appointed acolytes began to refer to him as Tashtalon rather than by his name.

Gill paused after reading this. If Tashtalon were Mace, and she were the enemy of Mace, then what her grandmother said—and the introductory book proclaimed—was that she was expected to challenge Tashtalon. Gill remembered saying to her grandmother right after Alia's death that she would kill Tashtalon, and at the time, she meant it. Now, after her grief had lessened, and after reading about the incredible powers Tashtalon/Mace possessed, Gill wondered whether *anyone* could successfully challenge him.

She turned back to the book. The writer, whose style changed from third to first person and identified herself as Estes, did not believe that she could overcome Mace after the defeat. Mace had created the ring of Tashtalon around Somerlie, and Estes did not know whether Asquith or Eldswold existed anymore. Still, Estes wrote that she hoped a day would come when Tashtalon would be less vigilant, and one of her descendants could take the sword Silmariae and make the attempt. So she hid the body and the books and the maps, retaining only the key, and wrote that she would settle into a quiet domestic life, along with two younger sisters, who had also set down their swords after Mace's victory.

Gill put down the history, walked over to the body, and looked at the sword. She had never held a sword before. Wondering what it felt like, she reached down to lift the sword from the body. The moment her fingers went around the hilt, a shock went up her arm. Gill cried out in pain, pulled her hand back, and shook her arm. The feeling had gone out of it. Panicked, she continued to shake it, wondering if she had been permanently injured. But within minutes, the feeling started to come back. She examined her arm closely in the lamplight and saw no burn or mark. Relieved, she sank back in the chair.

Looking around, she wondered if there were other dangers in the tomb. She had already handled the books, and the furniture, without harm; those must be safe. One was an artifact registry, and one book...ah! Reaching for it, remembering when she had glanced through it earlier, she found it was indeed a history of the sword. She soon became engaged in the narrative.

In a similar manner, she poured through the other volumes of history, of geography, of artifact descriptions. She was so absorbed in reading she forgot to eat or drink until her throat was dry with thirst and her stomach grumbling with hunger. Eventually, she found herself nodding off, and not even her intense craving for more knowledge could keep her awake. She tore herself away from the books and walked to her tent to lie down. Taking a look outside, she was startled. According to the position of the sun, it was earlier than when she had gone into the tomb. But how could that be? Had time somehow magically reversed?

Then the thought came to her: she had stayed up all night. This was the next morning. Inside, she had been shielded from sleep, which she had thought impossible within the ring of Tashtalon. *His magic could be overcome, after all,* was her weary and hopeful thought as she lay down and drifted into slumber.

The next two days she took at a slower pace. At least once a day, she left the tomb, stretched her legs, and exercised Kiri, whom she tethered in reach of a spring while she was inside. She considered and digested what she had read during these brief rides. But, at last, she had read the last book, examined the last map, identified the last artifact.

She set the chair so that she was looking at Silmariae, and considered what to do next. The easiest option, of course, would be to close the tomb, take Kiri, and go out to seek her fortune, the same as every other 23-year-old did. Certainly that plan had its attractions. Mace would be a formidable enemy, and Gill's chances of defeating him would be uncertain at the very best. Silmariae, with all her training, with all her courage, with all her knowledge, had failed to defeat him. Silmariae's daughters, who had never been queens, but otherwise had been as skilled as their mother, had concluded that Mace was too strong for them. One could take the point of view that if Gill had a duty to her ancestors, that is, if she had any obligation to them at all, that duty would best be served if she married, had daughters, and passed on the key to someone better qualified than she.

Gill found, however, that she could not take that view. Her vow to kill Tashtalon, even though rashly made, still echoed in her memory. She realized she would not have used the key, not come here, if that vow meant nothing to her. Something about the day Alia died had fixed the idea of a world without Tashtalon as an attainable goal, not just a hopeful fantasy of a possible future.

Moreover, after reading the books, Gill keenly felt the sacrifices of Silmariae and her daughters. They were real to her, not simply characters on a page. Silmariae had felt that defeating Mace was worth risking her life for. Silmariae's daughters had risked their lives to hide their mother, and though they had not confronted Mace, they had been in fearful danger because Mace and his agents had been diligently searching for the sword and any descendant of Silmariae who might be able to use it, to destroy them. In all of that, somehow they had survived and passed on the key in the hope that one day Mace might be less on guard, enough for a descendant of theirs to take up the task. Even her grandmother and her grandmother's mother had been faithful in carrying on that hope, even if they were not aware what that hope was. Most of all, Gill knew that no daughter she would bear would be any more qualified than she.

Finally, there was Alia. Even though Alia had only a vague notion of the task she was contemplating, she had been well aware of the danger, and faced it until her final breath. To be less brave than her friend, in Gill's mind, was a slander to her friend's memory.

Even though the corpse's eyes were closed, Gill felt the presence of her ancestor strongly. She nodded to the waxen face. "I'll do as your daughters asked," she promised, "and let fate decide if I succeed."

She half-expected the body to rise up in blessing, but nothing about it changed. She stood, sighed, and looked around the tomb, spotting the glowing globe. She did not touch it, though she now knew it would do her no harm. Indeed, she had found through her reading that none of the artifacts in the room would cause her any permanent harm. The sword had acted as it did simply to warn her the time was not yet right for her to take it. Some magic in the sword, the books said, would be able to tell when she was skilled and courageous enough to use it properly. The book of instructions amplified the information, advising her to use the globe first. But even before that, she needed to go back to the city one last time and settle her affairs.

* * *

She stopped on the road leading to Mount Blade and took in the full view of the city and the mountain—whose original name had been Mount Monarch. Gill had seen the city from this vantage point before, but knew it only as the city of Tashtalon, nameless, faceless. Now overlaid on it was the image, the drawings, of the city of Arcacia, the southern capital in the region of Somerlie. Except for the obscene house of Tashtalon, added after the fall, it was remarkably similar in shape. But this city was barren, lifeless, Arcacia no more.

Gill rode to her grandmother's, tied Kiri at a nearby post, and walked to the door.

Irina answered, and looked up in surprise. "Gill, is that you?"

"Yes, I said I'd be back soon." She stepped inside as Irina closed the door.

"You look different."

Gill walked over to the mirror in the sitting room. She turned her head from side to side. "I look the same to me."

Irina walked behind her and put a hand on her shoulder. "It's not the shape of your face. You look more...composed, confident, mature," she said approvingly.

Gill faced her grandmother. "Do I?" she said, lifting an eyebrow.

Irina smiled.

Gill put a hand on Irina's arm. "Grandmother, I have to go away, for a long time."

Irina nodded. "I know."

"Can you have my family move my things out of my room and into Alia's, and check on the house from time to time?"

"Certainly. They'd be glad to, especially if your father thinks you went south to make a fortune."

Gill grinned. "Why don't you tell them that?"

"I will." Irina walked to her chair and sat. "By the way, Eminric was here, looking for you. He was very concerned for your safety."

"Who?" Gill was astonished. How did her grandmother know Eminric?

"The way he spoke," Irina said, "I thought you knew him."

Gill walked to another chair and sat. "I did. I saw him at Alia's. How did you know him?"

"He visited me from time to time when I was younger, before I married. I never saw him after that." She paused, then added, "If he weren't so old, I would have thought he was a suitor."

"What did he talk to you about?"

Irina shrugged. "Nothing of importance. He wanted to know about my interests, my family, my ambitions."

"And nothing ever came of it?"

"No."

"Did he look different now from when you were younger?"

Irina considered. "A little older, yes. But after you reach a certain age, you don't look that much different from year to year."

"I suppose so." Gill walked over, bent and kissed her on the cheek. "Someday, I hope to come back."

Irina kissed her, in return. "May luck go with you."

Behind the stairs leading to Gill's rented room was a horse stall for her use, unoccupied until she had Kiri. Gill had filled the feeding and water troughs before they left; these were still amply filled when she tied Kiri there, unsaddled him, and brushed his coat. She put the tent in the corner, slung her pack over her shoulder, and walked up the stairs. Turning the key, she opened the door.

Stepping inside, she found Eminric sitting placidly at her dining table.

"Don't be alarmed," he said.

"I'm not." She shut the door behind her and put the pack down.

"I was sorry to hear about Alia," he said softly, eyes downcast. "I had no idea she was so near to danger. I would have saved her if I could."

While he spoke, she walked over to the rocking chair and settled in it. "I believe you."

He turned to her. "I see you have your grandmother's necklace."

"Yes, it's my 23rd birthday, a time for passing on of heirlooms."

"What are your plans?"

Gill threw him a wry smile and shook her head.

Eminric furrowed his brow. He had never looked puzzled before.

"I'm not going to play any more games," Gill said. "Either answer my questions directly, or get out."

Eminric straightened up in the chair. "Very well." There was an air of respect in his tones that had not been there before.

Gill looked him in the eye. "Alia hinted to me that there was a weapon to kill Tashtalon. Do you know where that weapon is?"

Eminric sighed and swallowed, avoiding her gaze. "No."

Gill nodded. She had thought as much, because the moss growing around the entrance showed that the tomb had not been disturbed for years. Eminric could not have gone there, at least not recently. "Don't you think it would have been a good idea to get it *before* enlisting someone to use it?"

"How much did Alia tell you?"

"No games. Answer my question, or leave." After she had read the books, she had guessed what Eminric was up to, but she was tired of guessing.

He licked his lips. "The problem is, locating it would take a powerful finding spell that could draw Tashtalon's attention. To find the weapon first without having someone to take it would risk having the weapon found and destroyed before *anyone* could use it."

That sounded fair enough. In addition, the mention of the finding spell confirmed that Eminric was one of the people of the stars who could generate magic. Gill nodded, but wanted to fill in every last detail. "And just anyone...any woman, that is...could use this weapon?"

"No. But a willing person could be trained to. A person with strength and courage. Such as Alia...," he made eye contact with her, "...or you."

Gill chuckled at the irony of his statement.

"This is not a joke."

She composed herself. "No, it isn't. Alia's dead."

Again, Eminric looked stricken.

"Now that you've answered my questions," Gill said, "I'm curious as to what you came here for."

He turned to her with a hopeful expression. "I was going to ask you to come with me."

"No."

He shifted position in his chair. "Alia would have come with me after her 23rd birthday. I only wish I had asked her to come earlier," he added in a whisper.

"Why didn't you?" She said it as a question, not an accusation.

He sighed. "I had to make preparations. I thought there was time." His face assumed a distant, sad expression. He again turned to Gill. "I need your help."

"No."

"If you don't, Tashtalon may never be stopped. Do you want that?"

As he spoke, Gill got out of her chair and went to the door. "Alia's dead. She's dead because somehow Tashtalon found out what she planned to do."

He gasped. "You don't think I...."

"No, but Tashtalon seems to have eyes and ears everywhere. Since my plans depend on me staying alive, at least for a time, I don't think it's wise for me either to discuss Tashtalon or to be seen with you." She opened the door.

"I understand." Putting his hands on the table, he slowly rose to his feet, looking frail and worn. She closed the door after he walked through.

She went back to the rocking chair and sat back. Although on the whole she believed Eminric's story, there was always a chance, a glimmer of a chance, that he could be one of Mace's agents trying to find descendants of Silmariae to destroy, or that he was being followed by Mace's agents for the same purpose. It was a chance she dared not take.

Chapter 4

Early the next day, Gill took all she needed from her rented room, saddled Kiri, and rode to Silmariae's tomb. On the two-day journey, her feelings varied from apprehension to excitement to determination. At times, she thought of going back; other times, she hurried on the journey, eager to start an adventure, or equally eager to get it over with. By the time she reached the tomb, she had settled on the idea that at the moment, she was only making a first step. She would not be taking up the sword Silmariae—which would not allow her to use it anyway unless it magically sensed she was ready—to kill Mace; she was simply going to follow the instructions which advised her to use one of the other artifacts to gather information. Once she had reopened the tomb, she put almost everything she brought from the city inside, then lifted the glowing globe. One of the books had explained what was in the globe:

It is merely an animated force and will do you no harm. It is not a personality. It is void of feeling, and you will be void of emotion while it resides within you. It retains the memories of those who have used it before; you may experience some of those memories, even after the force departs from you. Some of your memories will be copied and retained by the force when it departs from you, to be passed on to the next user. You will find yourself taking the shape of its maker; your own shape will return to you when the force departs. The force is best used when you allow it to guide your words and actions. You may let it speak and act for you, or you may speak and act for yourself. Open up the globe and let the force rest within you; it is an excellent spy and will allow you to gather knowledge about your adversary.

Not knowing whether taking on the spy would make her feel faint, she lay on a mat within the tomb before opening the globe. When she removed the top, the light gathered itself like a large insect and flew into her face.

When she came to herself, she was looking in a mirror. Her face appeared curiously different. The general shape was more square, the nose narrower, the chin jutting out more. As she watched the image of herself, her hands took a chain with a crystal hanging from it and placed it around her neck. The key was nowhere in sight.

Gill tried to move her hands, and found she could not. She tried to take a step back, and found she could not. She wondered why she was unable to move her hands and legs, when the book had said she would be able to act for herself, but she remained calm. Meanwhile, something else moved her hands and straightened her shirt and vest. The spy had changed her clothes, probably because her shoulders were wider and her chest was flat; she felt as if she had no breasts at all. Her genitals felt swollen, enlarged, heavy. Serenely, without panic, she guessed her body had assumed the shape of a male. Despite the changes, her face still bore some resemblance to her former face, though her hair had been cut nearly to the scalp. A hand reached up and smoothed it.

Her body turned. It went to an open box of clothes at a corner of the tomb and replaced the lid. It put away a clipper, swept up the excess hair, and threw it out the door of the tomb into the moss. It took an ordinary sword from the weapons rack in back of the tomb and belted it around her waist. Finally, it took the lamp and left the tomb.

Gill watched placidly as her body fished the key out of a pocket, locked the tomb door, replaced the moss and vines, took down and folded the tent, packed the supplies, saddled Kiri, loaded him with the packs, and swung up to the saddle. She had no success in so much as moving a finger or twitching an eyebrow. Still, there were no rival thoughts in her head; no one else was there. Nor did she have a sense of possessing memories not her own. She had not anticipated that this was what the instructions meant when they said to let the spy take the lead, but she was not in the least tempted to resist this arrangement. The spy had done nothing harmful to her so far, and she was genuinely curious as to what it *would* do.

As the day wore on, she found that the spy knew how to cook and knew when to rest. When the spy emptied her bladder, she confirmed her body was now male. She also found that the spy was a better horse handler than she was; the spy had Kiri responding to subtle commands of the leg and the bridle.

Gill slept when the spy slept; woke when the spy woke. He took a westward direction, staying in roadhouses in the villages along the way or sleeping outside as they traveled through the farmlands and forest. In time, they came to the River Harrow, which had been called the River Silver before Tashtalon. The river was wide and swift, and a thick forest grew on the other side.

She had not expected to see a dock there, but the spy took it in stride. He guided Kiri to the end and dismounted. A rope-and-pulley assembly brought a wooden platform across the river. He led Kiri onto it, then pulled the rope. Slowly, they reached the dock on the other side. He secured the platform and climbed back into Kiri's saddle.

She felt a tingle as Kiri stepped off the dock and into the forest. Kiri shivered, as if shaking off water, but the spy gently urged Kiri on. In her peripheral vision, she saw bones on either side of the track, and wished the spy would stop and look, or at least turn his head. But he continued to stare straight ahead and rode on. She wondered how they had survived leaving the ring of Tashtalon when these others had died. For the first time, the spy passed thoughts into Gill's mind: the necklace the spy had put on in the tomb had a magical charm that allowed them to pass the ring unharmed. Only humans needed such a charm; animals did not.

Not long afterward, they rode out of the forest into an enormous clearing ringed with trees. She saw a vast garden with row upon row of vegetables, herbs, and vines. Men were scattered among the plants, tending them. Some had their shirts off in the warm spring sunshine; those who wore shirts had circles of sweat under their arms. A few stole glances at the greathorse and rider, but turned quickly back to their work and did not call out a greeting or a challenge.

The spy turned a corner in the road. Now they faced a vast gray stone wall with tall spires at the corners. By its length, she guessed it enclosed a town or city, though she saw no roofs rising above the wall. The wall had no windows but was crenellated at the top. In the very center was a huge formidable iron gate, open. The wall was so thick that the gateway marked the entrance to a tunnel connecting the outside and inside yards.

The spy did not slacken Kiri's pace; he guided Kiri past the iron doors and through the tunnel archway. At the end of the tunnel, he stopped and dismounted. A groom came to take the horse. She thought the groom must have been in a fight—he seemed to have a broken nose and two black eyes. But he took Kiri's reins without a word, and Kiri followed him.

The spy entered a courtyard larger than the clearing they had just left. The far horizon was blocked by hills of ash. A huge chimney and furnace stood at the northeast corner of the courtyard. Within the courtyard, men milled about. Gill saw no women, no older people, no children.

He turned to a magnificent mansion built next to the wall. The edifice was fashioned of white marble, veined with pink and blue. A walled portico indicated the entrance. He walked right to it and went inside.

The rooms and halls were spotless. Ornate rugs covered the tiled floors. Fine artwork and tapestries lined the walls. The ceilings were vaulted and painted with frescoes. He walked up a wide, open stairway to the second floor, and down a long hallway. A man with a scarred face approached and said, "Lord Mace is waiting for you."

The spy nodded. He paused at a door and knocked. A pleasant voice said, "Enter." He stepped inside and closed the door behind him.

The only occupant of the room sat in a richly ornamented, cushioned chair at an ornately-carved desk. He rose to greet the spy. His age was hard to guess, but he was perfectly formed, without spot or wrinkle on the cream-colored skin. He had no beard or stubble, and straight brown hair on his head. He examined the spy closely.

"I like this body better than the other one."

Gill's mouth said, "I find them much the same." The tone was lower than her natural voice.

The host gestured to a long, wide, rich sofa. He sat on one end; the spy at on the other. "I was wondering when you would come back. It has been centuries."

"I've been occupied."

"Have you seen Nils?"

"Not a sign."

"It has been centuries since I have seen him, too. He disappeared without a trace." He paused a moment, then added, "What is your report?"

"The world is yours, Lord Mace. What else is there to say?"

"I wish it were so. I had to go into the city, not long ago, to punish a traitor myself."

"But you always deal with such traitors, Lord Mace. And afterwards, no one dares to challenge you."

"They forget too quickly, these humans." He stood and paced. "I give them food, water, sleep, rain in season.... I even bring some here to live with me, and what do they do? Do you know how I found out about this traitor? Her brother, whom I brought here under my protection, tried to escape. We captured him before he reached the ring, or he would have been dead before I could examine him. And what did he do? He defied me." Here Mace's tone and appearance changed, like a thundercloud overwhelming and menacing a clear sky. He made a fist and clutched it close to his chest. "He said that I would not last forever, and that there were those in the city who said it. When I asked him who, he confessed it was his sister. So I made an example of her."

The spy passed an image into Gill's mind: that of the body of Bruno, naked and broken on a rack, the strongest tools torturing his body, the strongest magic invading his mind and wrenching a secret he would have rather died than tell, destroying his mind and dooming Alia.

Mace's anger was fierce. Had Gill been in her usual mind, she knew she would have fled in terror when he turned to her again. But she felt not a trace of fear, and the spy looked up placidly.

"But surely, Lord Mace, it was only those two of a city of thousands."

Mace relaxed a little, his appearance was now less threatening. "I wish I could examine all as they are brought in, but they would be useless to me."

"These traitors always betray themselves. Have any escaped your notice?"

Mace nodded and sat. "True."

"Think of the thousands, nay, millions, who would never dare oppose you. Who have lived with you for years under your countenance without a thought of rebellion."

Mace nodded again. "You are a good counselor, Sloan. I miss my counselors. All I have around me are these humans, who do not understand me." Almost to himself, he added, "If only they had not made me angry."

A soft knock interrupted them. Mace looked up. "Yes?"

The door opened, and a man with a scarred face—but not the same one that she had seen in the hall earlier—stuck his head in. "You called, my lord?"

Mace stood, and so did Sloan. Mace waved the newcomer in. "Yes. Sloan, this is Rand, my current overseer."

Rand folded his hands in front of him and bowed slightly. Sloan nodded. Gill wondered if she had seen Rand somewhere before, maybe passed him on the street in the city? She was sure she knew no one by the name, but the face seemed vaguely familiar.

"I want you to give Sloan a fine room. He is to go anywhere he wishes, and he is not to be harmed."

"Anything you say, Lord Mace."

"Stay as long as you can," Mace said to Sloan.

"I will, my lord."

Mace turned away, a definite dismissal. Sloan and Rand left quickly; Rand shut the door behind them. Rand gestured Sloan to follow; as he did, Gill noticed a limp that Rand had not shown in the presence of Mace. They walked almost to the end of the hall, when Rand stopped at a door and opened it. Sloan walked in ahead of him.

The room had a large bed with richly dyed coverings. The furnishings had carved knobs, scallops, and diamond patterns; a rug with flower patterns woven into it adorned the floor. An open door in the corner of the room showed a spotless washroom. Opposite the entrance, two large glass doors opened onto a balcony.

"Fine with you?" asked Rand.

"It is."

Rand nodded. "If you want anything, my room is at the top of the stairs."

Sloan nodded in turn. When Rand was gone, Sloan went to the glass doors and opened them. Standing on the balcony, he could see the entire courtyard. To the left were the stables. A little beyond was a staging area, where men sparred with swords while others watched. Because the onlookers were neither cheering nor shouting encouragement, Gill supposed this was just practice. Sloan fed a thought to her that sometimes Mace amused himself by watching fights. Further on were the furnace and chimney she had noticed before. On the far side she saw the hills of ash, and at a distance in front of them, a large, two-story building she presumed to be a barracks. In the middle of the courtyard stood a sort of carousel, turning, but in place of wooden horses were men, chained and naked, with the sun beating down on their backs and chests. To her right were covered booths resembling open-air markets, where she saw food preparation, metalworking, and other crafts. To the far right were pens, some with poultry, some with sheep or goats, and one with cows. Each area was occupied with men working; none were crowded.

Sloan went back into the room, closed the glass doors, and strolled into the hall. The corridor was empty; he walked to a door near the opposite end of the mansion and opened it. This room, like the others, was huge. There was no rug on the floor; only tile. Against one wall was a metal table with restraints and a drain. A hose with a spigot was neatly coiled nearby. On the walls she saw racks and shelves of tools and instruments: needles, screws, tongs, knives of every length and shape, shining and spotless. Other devices she did not recognize at all. Sloan walked over and picked one of these up. Sloan's finger pressed a metal button; an arc, like a small lightning, came out of the end. He pressed the button again and the device ceased its action. He replaced the device and took another. As he examined it, the door opened.

Mace walked in. Seeing Sloan, he smiled. "Shall I get a body for you?"

"No," Sloan said tonelessly, and put back the instrument. He walked over to Mace; Mace put a hand on his back and they both left the room.

"I think you could do better than I," Mace remarked.

"No one could match your artistry, my lord," Sloan answered.

Mace gave Sloan's back a few friendly pats and walked away.

Sloan walked down the stairs and out the door. The first place he went was the stable. He found Kiri easily; the young groom was brushing the greathorse fondly.

"Does it meet with your approval, sir?" the youth asked, trying, but not succeeding, to hide his nervousness.

"Yes," said Sloan. He gave Kiri a few gentle strokes and walked on. There were both greathorses and ordinary horses in the stable. All were healthy, glossy, and well-cared for.

He crossed the sand-and-gravel floor of the courtyard to the booths, passing the carousel without a sideward glance. As she had seen from the balcony, some booths were concerned with food preparation, some with various crafts. She noticed that of the men working there, none was without a bruise or scar. Some had more, some had less, but all had them. In an enclosure set off by itself, she saw a youth lying on a table and paused. Three men surrounded the table, going back and forth with tongs and other instruments, coolly applying them to the restrained youth, who made no sound, though his eyes were tightly shut and his mouth moved wordlessly. Edging closer, she saw the youth was Owen, Lydia's missing son. The torturers looked up as Sloan entered, but went back to work when Sloan backed out of the booth.

As Sloan walked to the pens, Gill wondered if the experience of being tortured himself had given Owen any insight into or sympathy for the animals he had tortured. But then, as Sloan leaned on the pens, looking inside, she saw poultry limping around with bent wings, or broken beaks. No, she thought, neither Owen or the others seemed to have learned anything. Comparing the condition of these animals to the horses, she guessed the difference in treatment was due to Mace's attitude toward food animals in contrast to his feelings about horses.

Sloan returned to the mansion and found the kitchen. As he entered, he felt a tingling and looked up and around. He smiled. Again, Gill was given information: that there was an enchantment at work to prevent poisoning. Indeed, the faces and eyes of the workers here were vacant. Sloan took dishes and bowls and glasses and helped himself to a hearty meal, which he ate at one of the kitchen tables, ignored by the kitchen workers.

As he ate, Sloan had a view of almost the entire kitchen. Gill saw no cooking fires. A ceramic box had pots on its top, which the kitchen folk stirred, and which were emitting steam. Other workers opened doors, putting unbaked goods in, and opened them again, taking baked goods out. Again, Gill saw no fires. Other cabinets emitted a cold breeze when opened, but Gill saw no ice. She wondered if this were all done by magic.

When Sloan returned to his room, the packs he had placed on Kiri's saddle were there. Mace, or one of his servants, had also provided elegant clothes. Sloan went into the washroom and filled the tub there. Gill watched with interest as Sloan adjusted levers, putting his hand under the water as it came out to test the temperature, and making further adjustments until the water was just right. As the water ran, he put his travel-stained clothes in a basket and took a long soak. When finished, he dried off, dressed, and lay on top of the bed to rest.

By the time Sloan awakened, the sun had set. He slid out of bed and walked to the wall. He touched a panel and the ceiling lit, illuminating the room bright as day. When he went out into the hallway, light also came down from the hallway ceiling, apparently from the beams between the ceiling frescoes of the flowers, birds, and animals, which, now that Gill thought of it, did not look like any flowers, birds, or animals she had ever seen.

Sloan continued outside to the tunnel in the wall where he had entered the fortress and found a door. Opening it, she saw a staircase.

The staircase moved upward when he stepped on it, and brought him to the top of the outer wall. There he leaned on the crenellations and looked up at the stars. Gill spotted the Tether right away: the brightest star in the sky had another star circling around it. Gill had found, using her spyglass, that the brightest stars looked like tiny disks, and some had other fainter stars circling them. Two had colored rings around them. Most stars, even with the spyglass, were mere points of light, but some of those, too, had a fainter star circling them.

"Looking for home?" said a voice behind her.

Sloan noticed a glimmer in his peripheral vision and turned to see Mace approaching. Gill knew from reading the histories that all Wye glowed in the dark; Mace's radiance was anything but subtle. Mace stepped forward, put a hand on Sloan's shoulder, and pointed upward with his other hand. "Home," he repeated, and put his arm down. "I think about it all the time."

Sloan's eyes fixed on a particular red star and turned back to Mace.

"Still," Mace said jovially, "it is better to be here, where we are in charge, and the world is at our command." He inhaled loudly, as if savoring the air. "The air is good here, too." He walked away, disappearing into the night.

Sloan returned to his room. He used the panel to turn off the lights, though Gill could still see dim lights outlining the door and the entrance to the washroom. He changed into a nightshirt and went to bed.

The next day, Sloan occupied himself with examining the wall more closely. Gill discovered it was actually a building, though the windows and openings were all on the courtyard side, or in the tunnel. Sloan went from chamber to chamber, looking, examining, feeling. She had no idea what he was looking for, and he did not communicate his purpose to her. Perhaps, she thought, since Sloan's function was to gather information, he was simply making sure that Gill saw everything there was to see. He searched a wide array of rooms—some for storage with shelves and cabinets, some empty except for a piece of furniture or a panel, and some with gadgetry whose purpose she could not even guess at. Sloan paused in his search only to go back to the mansion to eat. On one such foray, walking through the mansion to the kitchen, he passed the door to a room. She heard voices inside; he stopped.

"What? Do you mean Mace isn't going to torture him? Isn't *he* the favorite," an unfamiliar voice complained.

"No use to torture *him*," Rand answered. "He's not human."

"Not human? I thought Mace's people were all dead."

"Dead as dust."

"Then what is he, a badger?"

"He's a copy."

"A copy? Copy of what?"

She heard Rand sigh. "He's a copy of one of Mace's old friends inside a human body. That's what Mace told me, anyway."

"What happened to the human?"

"I don't know; Mace didn't tell me that. Devoured, maybe. He can't feel anything, that's for sure."

"You mean if I cut him, he wouldn't feel it?"

"He'd know it, but it wouldn't bother him. Slice his arms off—he'd only lie there and stare at you. Strip him naked and put him on the carousel—he wouldn't care. He can't feel love, hate, or anything. He's just an empty shell that can talk."

"Then what good is he?"

"Like a pet, I suppose. Comes when you call, keeps you company."

"I still don't think it's fair, that all of us are tortured and he isn't."

Rand sighed again. "Haven't you learned yet? It's not what's fair, it's what Mace wants. And Mace doesn't want him harmed. You know what happens when Mace gets mad."

Sloan walked away to the kitchen; Gill heard nothing more. Again, Sloan helped himself, but when he saw the workers putting food on a tray, he put his own plates and bowls on a separate tray and followed the worker. The man went to Rand's door and knocked with a foot. Rand opened the door and the worker went inside, setting the tray on a table. Sloan followed. The worker left and shut the door behind him; only the two of them remained in the room.

"May I join you?" Sloan asked.

Rand extended a hand to a table. "Go ahead."

Sloan picked up a fork and began to eat as Rand put a spoon in his soup.

Rand looked over at Sloan's tray. "Solid food," he said nostalgically.

"You can't eat it anymore?"

Rand shook his head. "Hurts too much."

Sloan looked over Rand as he continued to eat. Rand was the oldest human at the site—maybe in his late fifties or early sixties, though Gill suspected that torture could make a person look much older than he actually was. But now that she had a closer view, she noticed broken teeth, gouges in the tongue, scars on the lips....

"Staying long?" Rand continued between sips. He had been stealing glances at Sloan just as Sloan had been examining him; Gill guessed he was intensely curious about this newcomer.

"As long as I need to." Sloan answered evenly.

Rand accepted that as an answer. "He's calmer since you've come. I think you remind him of the time when his friends were here."

"The other near-immortals."

"Yes." Rand swallowed, a hard swallow. "How many were there?"

"Of his friends, four," Sloan responded between bites. "Von, his closest friend, then Isalene, Galeron, and Kelric."

"Only four?"

Sloan nodded. "Originally, maybe 50 came with him from his home in the stars."

"Why did he leave? He never said."

"He destroyed his homeworld."

Rand lifted an eyebrow. "He did?"

"Some sort of experimentation. Poisoned the land, water, and plants. Everyone had to leave. Most scattered to other worlds. One large group pursued Mace and his followers here, to prevent him from ruining yet another world."

"More than the 50 that went with Mace?"

Sloan nodded again as he munched on bread. "Two of the sky ships came to this world. Mace on one; Mace's opponents on the other."

"How many opponents?"

"Oh, some hundreds."

"That many? What happened to them?"

"Presumably killed when Mace defeated them in the war."

"And Mace won with only 50?"

"Less than that. On both skyships, some went mad on the way here. Then, many on Mace's side died in the war, too. At the end, only his four friends remained."

"How did he win, then?"

Sloan wiped his mouth with a napkin. "He had the greater magic. The opposition, it is said, created an artifact of magic to oppose it, but it was lost."

Gill knew Sloan was referring to the sword Silmariae, which had been created by Wye magic especially to defeat Mace, and which had been given to humans to use.

"So that's why he's afraid of traitors. He's afraid someone will find it."

"And use it," Sloan confirmed.

"How did the four get killed?"

"A mistake. Mace's friends, knowing that a strong artifact of magic was out there in an unknown place, tried to form a counter-spell. Mace, however, thought they were conspiring to oppose him, and destroyed them while they were working. When he realized his error, I understand his anger shattered the hills nearby."

"Can he make the counter-spell again?"

Sloan shook his head. "Each of Mace's people had a unique magical talent. He killed the one who could make the counter-spell."

"Hm. And all his people dead now."

Sloan resumed eating and did not reply. Gill received an impression that Sloan had no information about whether other Wye were still alive or not. Gill deduced that if Rand assumed that all Wye except

Mace were dead, it was because Mace thought so. Mace, therefore, did not know Eminric was alive. Gill wondered if there were other Wye alive besides Mace and Eminric.

"Any more of you?" Rand asked Sloan.

"Most of my kind were lost. We have to be carefully preserved. Because our maker is dead, there will be no more of us."

Gill recalled from reading the artifact registry that the animated force named Sloan had been created by Von, Mace's friend, who had tried to restrain Mace's violence, only to be killed by him. Von had left the globes in the custody of humans to keep track of Mace in the event of his death, hoping the humans could use the information gleaned from the animated force to keep Mace contained. Von told Mace only that he had made copies of his memories that could inhabit a body and keep Mace company if Von died before Mace did.

While Gill was thinking, Rand finished his soup and set the bowl aside.

"What are your origins?" Sloan asked, continuing the conversation. Apparently Sloan sensed he might be able gather more facts from Rand if he kept him talking.

Rand coughed a laugh. "Don't think about the past. Too busy surviving."

Sloan nodded and concentrated on finishing his meal. Gill received the impression that Sloan had determined he had learned all he could here and it was time to move to somewhere else.

Rand assumed a thoughtful expression. "I had a wife and child in the city. The child should be grown up now. He never came here, anyway."

"Would you go back if you could?" Sloan appeared ready to talk some more if Rand seemed willing to say more.

Rand's face hardened. "No. All they are back there are a bunch of weaklings. Fools. Here, someone gets out of line, you thrash him. Over there, they call that mean. I tried to whip my son into line and all I got was grief for it. I tried to whip my wife into line and the neighbors called me names. Here, I can thrash someone anytime I want and everyone looks up to me."

"It's different here," Sloan confirmed.

Rand picked up a glass of ale and drank. "Back in the city, if you come across a woman named Irina with a grown-up son named Loris, you'll see. I bet their lives are a mess. They're sorry I'm gone, that's for sure."

Chapter 5

Sloan left his tray in Rand's office for the workers to pick up. Gill considered the information she had just been given. Although she now realized that Rand was her grandfather, she felt nothing toward him—neither love nor hate nor pity nor anger. She was an empty shell, as Rand had said, thought without emotion.

Sloan returned to the chambers within the wall, searching again for a long time, but seeming not to find what he was after.

The next day, Sloan crossed the yard to inspect the other restraining walls, passing by an area where a few men practiced swordplay. Suddenly, one turned and swung his weapon toward Sloan. Immediately, Sloan drew his own sword to parry the attack. Gill had forgotten that Sloan wore a sword. He had the moves of an expert fighter, visibly frustrating his opponent. In her peripheral vision, she could see others gather round, standing quietly at a safe distance, observing, but not cheering or interfering.

In response to a particularly sloppy move by his opponent, Sloan delivered a kick to the man's midsection which sent him sprawling. He disarmed the man and threw the sword out of reach. Immediately, another opponent engaged him, an opponent more skilled than the last, and yet Sloan was scarcely breathing hard. This time Sloan disarmed the opponent with a savage thrust of the sword. The man yelped in pain and held his arm limply. Still another man stepped forward, murder in his eyes, but Sloan parried the strokes expertly.

"What is this?" thundered a voice.

Gill saw most of the spectators drop to the ground, kneeling or bowing. Sloan did not react to the voice until the latest opponent dropped his sword. Only then did Sloan turn to see Mace. Rand stood a couple of paces behind. Mace looked flushed, stimulated, hungry, and the air crackled as if a thunderstorm might be approaching, though the day was as hot and clear as the previous ones.

Mace thrust his finger at each of Sloan's opponents in turn. "Into the furnace!" he ordered.

As others came to take the designated men in hand, the man still standing in front of Sloan pleaded, "No!"

Mace strode forward and struck the man in the face. A tooth came loose and something cracked; Gill guessed the jaw or cheekbone. "When I punish you, you do not question me, you understand? You do not talk back, you do not protest, and you thank me for giving you what you deserve! I am your god!" He turned savagely to the other men. "Do you hear?"

The kneeling men murmured, "Yes, my lord."

Mace turned back and the man nodded as best he could, with the blood running out of his mouth, dripping on the sand and gravel. Mace put a hand on Sloan's back. "This man is not to be touched. That is my order, and that is all." He turned and started toward the mansion. Passing a kneeling man, he paused and pointed. "Prepare yourself," he said. Without waiting for a response, he stalked back to the mansion. Rand met Sloan's eye. His expression showed he thoroughly approved of the demonstration. Then he, too, turned and followed Mace, again carefully concealing his limp. The kneeling man Mace had pointed to rose and followed more slowly.

Meanwhile, Mace's executioners were hauling the designated men away. Gill detected the strong smell of ammonia; several men had lost control of their bladders. Sloan sheathed his sword at last and continued toward the walls. Presently, screams reached his ears from the direction of the furnace, then died away.

As Sloan walked back from the walls, he saw the man Mace had told to prepare himself come out of the mansion. He moved slowly, looking pale. Sloan saw fresh bruises and cuts, but passed the man without stopping. Gill saw no one else move to help him, either.

Inside, at the top of the stairs, stood Mace, wiping his hands with a towel and conferring with Rand, who held a book in front of him. Mace spotted Sloan and gestured for him to come. Sloan walked up to them.

"Inventory is lower than I thought," Mace said to Sloan. "Such weak creatures; they do not last long. A couple died last night, no reason." He turned to Rand. "This time gather several more. Enough to last for a while. Tell them to get stronger specimens." He waved at Sloan again. "Can you go?"

"Yes," said Sloan.

A caravan of five greathorses and carts assembled in the yard that evening. Sloan saw the drivers put on a necklace similar to his, so they could cross the ring safely and remain awake at night. Rand gave one of the drivers a box with more charms, apparently so they could bring the victims across the ring as well. A yard supervisor threw a large net of thick cords—standard rope, not bola cords—into each cart. When they were ready, Rand signaled them to leave the fortress, but remained in the courtyard, watching them leave. They took the road eastward, crossing the river and swiftly traveling through Somerlie. Sloan, on Kiri, matched their pace. Toward sunrise, they turned toward a barn and everything went in. Sloan slept when the other men did. As the sun set, they woke, ate, saddled and hitched the horses. Two hours after sunset, they opened the doors of the barn and went out on the road.

On the second night, a rider on a greathorse met the caravan. Sloan was not close enough to hear the conversation, but a cart left the caravan and went north. None of the other men spoke of the encounter.

Early on the third night, they came to the city. The carts split up. Sloan followed one cart, which stopped at Telford's house. Gill wondered why they stopped there. Telford was not a particularly sturdy man, strong enough to haul ice blocks, yes, but not a prize. Sloan dismounted and followed them; they had a key which opened the door. Inside, she saw the men slide a hidden panel in the kitchen wall. They took out a book and spread it out under the light of a lamp. Sloan stood behind them and looked over their shoulders.

She read a list of names. Owen's caught her eye. So Telford was an agent of Mace. On his rounds in the neighborhoods, he could keep an eye out for likely victims. Mace's agents must be all over the city, she thought, with more agents along the roadways, for the use and secrecy of their barns.

One of the men copied the names and addresses and put the book back. That done, the gathering began. A magic charm opened the houses. Strong men removed sturdy men from their beds and placed them in the carts. They spread a net over them and placed a necklace over each of their heads. When the cart was full, they went toward the city gate, meeting other laden carts. By the second hour before sunrise, they were back in a barn.

The victims did not wake. Sloan passed Gill the information that the net had a spell which kept them asleep until it was removed. Had the families only known how near their relatives were, Gill thought, it would have been possible to rescue them. Perhaps that was why they were given an elixir to keep them docile in the days following the abductions. She also noted that none of the men from the fortress tried to run away and rejoin their families. Considering that Mace had spies in the city, and that they knew that Mace himself could come into the city after them, to do so would have meant death. Would their families even recognize them after years of torture and brutality?

The next days they took the straight road back to Mace's fortress. The night the river came into view, Sloan guided Kiri off the road. A light to the north had caught his eye. He took out Gill's spyglass—Gill had forgotten he had brought it—and saw the cart which had left them earlier. Sloan put the spyglass away and rode through a field of rising grain toward it. If the other carts noticed Sloan's absence, they gave no sign.

Sloan approached the cart cautiously, urging Kiri only close enough to discern the barest details. The lantern swinging on a hook near the front of the cart showed two men in the driver's seat, and one figure in the back, presumably netted. She saw no escort.

Sloan guided Kiri away from the cart's path, giving them a wide berth and circling ahead of them into a small orchard. There he dismounted Kiri and hid behind a bush. After they passed, he ran out and climbed into the back of the cart, keeping his head down. He slid next to the sleeping figure and looked up. The drivers did not even glance back. Gill presumed they were probably tired and worn out from their night's journey, as all the drivers were towards sunrise.

Once Sloan's eyes adjusted to the darkness, Gill could identify the victim. It was Eminric. A faint light shone about him. Slowly gathering the net, he took it into his hands and spread it over the drivers, who nodded off immediately. As they slumped, he grabbed the reins and stopped the greathorses.

Sloan sat back in the cart, watching as Eminric stirred, groaned, and sat up. Eminric's glow brightened as he regained his wits and quickly took in the situation. He looked across the cart to Sloan. "Have we met?"

"Have we?"

"You're Sloan, aren't you?"

"Yes."

He retrieved a travel pack from elsewhere on the cart, and slid off. He turned and said, "Thank you...and thanks to the one whose body you're occupying."

"Go," Sloan said simply.

Eminric disappeared into the night. Sloan left the cart, went into the orchard, and gathered brush. He piled it in the cart and put a tarp over it. As he worked, Kiri ambled up to the light. Sloan took Kiri's reins in one hand and gathered the net in the other. He threw the net back over the tarp, leapt on Kiri's back, and slipped into the orchard. At a safe distance, he saw the drivers recover their senses.

The taller one spoke first. "You fall asleep?"

"Seems so," said the shorter one.

Abruptly, the taller one reached back; he wrenched away the net and the tarp. The shorter one climbed back and tossed out the brush. He shook his head over and over.

"How could he be gone?" said the taller one.

"Tashtalon will devour us!" sobbed the shorter one.

The taller one reached over and touched his shoulder. "Wait a minute. No one knows why the agent summoned us, but us. And the agent never speaks to Tashtalon directly. He won't know that we ever had a prisoner, much less that the prisoner escaped."

"But he's a god, how can he not know?" the shorter one whined.

"Even a god doesn't know everything."

"But what do we say? The others know we left the caravan."

"Just say the agent told us he found people to bring back, but we found they weren't suitable. He'll be mad at the agent, not us."

The shorter one silently climbed back into the driver's seat and they started the cart again.

After taking Kiri well south of the path, Sloan galloped ahead and reached the river before either caravan. The main party reached the docks first.

"Where did you go?" one of the men asked.

"I wanted to stretch my horse's legs and race here ahead of you."

No one questioned the explanation. Gill suspected this was partly because they were tired, and partly because they thought it was too dangerous to question Mace's favorite.

They started taking the carts across. Sloan and Kiri went with the first. He watched as the last cart caught up and came across.

The fortress was well-lit. When they came through the tunnel and into the courtyard, Sloan dismounted and handed Kiri's reins to a groom. A glimmering figure walked out of the mansion; Mace had come to inspect the cargo. Rand followed and began collecting the necklaces. Mace looked at the first four carts and seemed satisfied; those drivers went to the barracks. At the last one, he frowned, threw off the net, and took off the tarp.

"You dare you bring back an empty cart!" he demanded of the drivers.

The taller driver looked down humbly. "Our agent told us he had some people for us, but we found them unsuitable for my lord."

Mace turned to Rand, who stood nearby. "The next time a caravan goes out, tell that worthless priest of mine to have that agent killed."

Rand bowed.

Somehow, Sloan knew that the agent would not be given a chance to tell his story before he died.

Mace took each of the drivers in hand, and threw them about three meters away. "Worthless indeed if they were less suitable than you!"

Apparently relieved that their punishment would be no worse, the drivers scrambled to their feet, bowed, and stumbled back to the barracks.

The next day, when Sloan went into the courtyard, he found that a tall cage had been set up in the yard, and when the nets came off, the still-sleepy men were hauled out and thrown in. When they all looked awake, beginning to talk to each other and shout questions, a man that Gill had seen often in the yard came and paced in front of the cage.

"Silence! Listen to me!" he shouted, and the men quieted. "I am only going to say this once, because all of us have had the same questions as you and we're all sick of hearing them.

"You are now in the fortress of Tashtalon. Here we call him by his real name, the Lord Mace. His word here is law, and never to be questioned. You cannot leave, and it is death to try."

At this, some of the men started to mumble.

"Quiet! It is your duty to be silent when your betters are speaking to you; one more word and you will become like them." He pointed to the carousel and the men chained there. Many heads turned; Gill heard gasps.

One of the younger men in the cage raised a timid hand.

"This is not a school! You do not ask questions! You do what you are told, or you die. You belong to Lord Mace now, and your only thought should be to do his will." The men remained silent, and the speaker continued. "If you do as you're told, you will live; if not, you will die. It is that simple." He paused again, but no one spoke. "Now we will let you out, and someone will ask you what you can do so we know what work we will assign you to. You will only answer questions; you will not ask any. Is that understood?" When he received no answer, he motioned to have the door opened. Other men came and each took a newcomer in hand.

Gill looked at all of the faces, but there was no one whose name she knew or who she was acquainted with. She noted that many of the men looked relieved. After being told from childhood that all those who had disappeared were devoured by Tashtalon, they probably had expected instant death. She wondered if, once they found out what life was really like under Mace, whether they would have wished that they had died upon arrival instead.

Once he had looked over the newcomers, Sloan went back to the mansion and carefully started exploring rooms. Most were empty sitting rooms or bedrooms. One room contained a large library, with hundreds of books on shelves. Sloan went over and paged through one. With Sloan's help, she could read the letters and understand the language. It seemed to be a novel, about life on another world. Sloan replaced the book.

Once out of the library, Sloan resumed his tour, but nothing else drew his attention. At three of the doors, Sloan began to reach for the door latch, only to have his hand pushed back by an unseen force. He drew his hand away and moved on. Sloan gave information to her: these were Mace's private rooms, protected from entry by his spells. As he walked further down the hall, he passed the torture chamber, heard noises, and paused. Very slowly, very quietly, he cracked the door open.

Mace was not inside. A newcomer, blindfolded but otherwise naked, lay spread and restrained on the table. The same man who had given the men their initial instructions stood over him. Two other guards lingered nearby, backs to the door.

"Be silent and listen to me, and you will survive," said the man to the victim. "Mace tortures all who come here; it is his pleasure." The victim winced but did not say anything. The man continued, "It offends Mace for you to cry out, protest, or plead. Do not do so. Mace may stay with you for a long time or a short time, whatever pleases him. I have come with you this first time to tell you what to do. From now on, when Mace tells you to prepare yourself, you are to come here, undress, and lie upon the table until Mace releases you. Do you understand?"

The victim nodded.

Sloan eased the door shut and went on his way.

After he had eaten a midday meal in the kitchen, Sloan heard a sound like distant thunder and felt a crackle in the air. He walked to the mansion's entrance. Rand stood there looking out into the court-yard. Following his gaze, Sloan saw a man writhing at Mace's feet.

"Mace went out in the yard," Rand explained. "He startled a new man holding a tool. The tool flipped up. Would have put Mace's eye out except for his magic."

As Sloan stared at the spectacle, he sent Gill a thought—that this was how Mace's associates died, when Mace flew into a rage. The very air was stifling. The ground trembled. Mace's victim dissolved in silent agony, little by little, until he was dust.

The ground continued to vibrate. Sloan looked around. Gill saw that the remaining men had either fallen prostrate, or had run and hid. Debris started flying. Rand eased himself down as quickly as he could, covering his head with his hands. Sloan hastily lay next to a post, but something fell on his leg. He heard a crack and looked down to see a stone block slide off his ankle. Gill felt no pain—or, rather, there was a knowledge of pain but no sensation of it. Sloan did not flinch either, but continued to look down at his leg.

A shadow fell across it. Sloan looked up to see Mace looming over him. "Your leg is hurt?" he asked curiously.

"Yes."

Mace turned to Rand. "Get something to immobilize it." He turned back to Sloan. Rand, unseen by Mace, had the luxury of getting pain-fully to his feet and quickly limping away.

It occurred to Gill that if Sloan had not been controlling her at that moment, she would have been screaming in terror. Instead, Sloan lay quietly as Mace gingerly touched Sloan's boot and eased up the pant leg to determine the extent of the injury. There was some bruising, but Gill suspected the ankle, hidden by the boot, had been hit hard-est. She was aware of the swelling within the boot, pushing against it, despite the lack of pain.

A man quickly came out of the mansion and handed over a brace. When Sloan's leg was immobilized, Mace gently lifted Sloan in his arms. "Leave me," he said to the man, and to Rand, who stood just behind the worker. The two quickly disappeared.

As Mace went into the house, Gill again reflected that without Sloan, she might have fainted from panic. Sloan, however, inspected the ceiling frescoes calmly as Mace carried him through the house, and into the chambers within the fortress walls.

Now Gill wondered where Mace was taking her. Sloan had searched all the rooms and had found nothing that could be of use in this situation. Mace turned and it seemed as if he would walk directly into a wall. Sloan did not even blink, which meant that Gill saw the wall—or the illusion of a wall—give way into a room.

A long marble table stood in the center of the room. Mace carefully laid Sloan there. He went to a wall lined with shelves. On the shelves she saw innumerable items and artifacts: small lamps, jewelry of various designs, other objects she could not easily identify. Mace opened the doors of a cabinet on the wall and took out what appeared to be two metal vambraces, adorned with gold and silver filigree and encrusted with rubies and emeralds. Mace locked them on his wrists and put a hand on Sloan's chest. "Do not be afraid," he said softly. "You will sleep, and waken to health."

Sloan closed his eyes. Gill, however, could still hear Mace moving around in the room, and wondered why this time she had not slept when Sloan had. Her finger twitched, and Gill realized that she had done it. Had Sloan left her now? What was she to do if he had?

Still, she felt no apprehension. She listened to Mace talk to himself, and realized as he did that he was speaking another language, and that she could understand him.

"How I have missed you, Von," he said. "When they are here, it is almost as if you were still here with me."

A long silence followed. Her curiosity nagging at her, Gill ventured to open her eyes slightly. Mace stood above her feet, looking down, hands over her ankle. A strong light shone between his hands and her skin. She closed her eyes again.

Not long afterwards, she felt a hand on her chest again, and in the same strange language, Mace said, "Awake, my friend."

Sloan woke. Mace slid an arm under his back and eased him into a sitting position. In Gill's own language, Mace said, "You are well again."

Sloan slid off the table and tested the leg. It was sturdy. He nodded his thanks.

"You must go," Mace said sadly.

"Yes," Sloan answered. Gill noticed that Mace's arms were free of the vambraces once more.

"Come back." It was half a request, half a question.

Gill said with Sloan's voice, "I will come here again."

Mace smiled, took her arm, and led her out. The room actually had a door, which opened without Mace touching it, but disappeared into the illusion of a wall once they stood in the outer corridor.

Mace guided her to the mansion, and let her go. "Return soon," he said softly, and walked down the corridor. One of the men whom Gill was accustomed to seeing in the house walked toward Mace, and bowed as he was about to pass. Mace silently took him by the arm and led him, unprotesting, into the torture chamber.

Gill returned to her room and packed her things. She felt Sloan lingering in her mind, but he did not assert control. Gill moved her own legs and arms now. Traveling pack over her shoulder, she left the mansion and went to saddle Kiri. As she did, Rand walked in.

"You're leaving?" he asked.

"Yes," Sloan said simply.

Rand sat on a bale of hay. "Will you be back?"

"No," Sloan replied.

Rand nodded. "Just as well. Some of the men are mad at you because you're Mace's favorite. They want to kill you even if Mace kills them."

"I know," Sloan said calmly.

"I'll be going, then," Rand said, and limped away.

Sloan left soon afterwards. The sky, which had been fair all the days he had been there, gradually became covered by clouds. As he pulled the platform across the river, the first raindrops fell, and as he rode eastward, a steady rain began. No lightning, thunder, or wind accompanied the clouds. Sloan ignored the wetness, and Gill was neither chilled nor miserable.

The rain continued the next day, but started to ease the third. The only respite they had from the weather was when they stopped for the night at a roadhouse, where Sloan slept in a bed and Kiri slept in a stable stall. By the time they reached the city, the rain had stopped. Sloan dismounted just outside the city gates and bought food at the markets. After he loaded the supplies onto Kiri, he continued toward Silmariae's tomb.

As Sloan made camp, Gill found that Sloan had kept the key all this time in a fold of the tent, which, at Mace's, had remained rolled up. Inside, Sloan returned the necklace he had worn all that time, picked up his globe, and opened it. Gill flinched as light surged out of her, formed itself into a ball, and deposited itself into the globe. Exhausted, she replaced the lid and slumped to the floor.

Chapter 6

She had no sense of falling asleep until she woke, screaming, in darkness. At first, she did not know where she was. But as her eyes adjusted, she noticed the soft light shed by Sloan, now back in his globe. She realized that she was in the tomb, and deduced the lamp Sloan had brought in had gone out. As she dragged herself to her feet, she realized the clothes she wore did not fit well. She put a hand to her chest and felt breasts again. Her genitals had returned to their accustomed female form.

She went to the pack that she had left in the tomb before Sloan had entered her body. She refueled the lamp and struck a light. Rummaging through the pack, she took out a fresh shirt, pants, socks, and underthings. But those did not quite fit, either. Looking at her arms and legs, she found they were thicker, stronger. She remembered the trunk that Sloan had taken his clothes from, and tried items on until she found several that suited her.

Once clothed, she walked outside. The sun was out, and judging from the amount of droppings Kiri had left, she had slept at least a day. Sloan had left a bag of oats for Kiri and tied him in reach of the spring. Kiri came and nuzzled her shoulder; she patted his head affectionately. She went back to the tent, making a good meal from the food Sloan had bought. As she cleaned the crumbs, she began to tremble.

A madness gripped her. All of the outrage, terror, and grief that Sloan had set aside while she was with Mace welled up all at once. Gill stalked into the tomb, paced, pounded the walls, screamed and wailed, until she slumped, exhausted, into a sitting position. In a daze, she hauled herself to her feet, stumbled outside, and was caught in the spell of sleep.

In the morning she found herself lying on the tent's canvas floor. She rose and made breakfast. When she was done, she rode Kiri bareback for a short distance, but turned back soon when she began to tremble again.

This time, however, she only sat, knees up, arms on knees, on the floor of the tomb with her back against one wall, at the bottom of a well of oblivion. Slowly, she came back to her senses, and began to consider what to do next.

A quiet life as far away from Tashtalon as possible was her foremost thought. She could go south as if nothing had happened, make her fortune, and build a remote cottage somewhere to live out her life. If she did nothing to reveal her feelings for Tashtalon, and did not go back to the city where she would be under the eye of Boreas, maybe she could live out her life in complete safety. Others Mace would take, of course, but what were they to her? Her grandfather, certainly, was one she would not want to be brought back, and was better gone. Weren't they all? Weren't they all getting what they deserved?

But then she remembered Alia, and that unhappy groom that tended Kiri, tended Kiri very well, while she was there. Sloan had never asked his name. Nor did he ask the names of dozens of others he passed while he was there, men who did not look mean or menacing, but just wanted to stay alive one more day.

What could she do, anyway? A power that could put an entire region to sleep nightly, a power that prevented any unwanted touch, a power that could turn someone to dust at will—how could she overcome that? She turned to the body on the slab. Silmariae, the queen of the northern realm of Asquith and the southern realm of Somerlie; Silmariae, the greatest swordfighter who had ever been; Silmariae, keeper of the most powerful sword ever forged—had failed to overcome Mace. Who was Gill, in comparison? How could she succeed where Silmariae had not?

She rubbed her face with a hand. Slowly, she rose to her feet and walked to the globe. She picked it up. She wanted Sloan to possess her again, so she would not have to feel all these things, not have to think all these things. Sloan always knew what to do. Then a thought came to her: could she take Sloan into her and defeat Mace?

But the thought left her as soon as it came. According to the histories, Silmariae had taken Sloan into her for a time, but found she could not use the sword with him inside her, and she needed the sword to defeat Mace. Sloan never challenged Mace; in fact, he quite often humored him. She put the globe down.

Taking the chair, she straddled it, resting her chin on the back, and faced Silmariae. She felt weary. She knew there was no going back. Once again, she felt the weight of the sacrifices of Silmariae, Estes, Alia, Eminric, her grandmother, and the countless others who had dedicated their lives to keep the hope alive that one day, Mace would be gone. She could not dishonor them by refusing to try to defeat him.

She slid the chair aside and approached the slab. The book of instructions had advised that after she had gained all the knowledge she could from Sloan, she was to take the sword and go north. There the instructions ended. All that was left was for her was to try to take the sword. If the magic in the sword judged her competent and worthy, she would be the one committed to defeating Mace. If not, she would have to go on without the sword, and try to find another woman to take Silmariae. She thought of Eminric and his centuries-old quest, for surely the reason he had tried to enlist Irina, Alia, and her was to find someone willing to use the sword.

She stood next to the slab and hovered over the hilt. It was placed lightly in Silmariae's folded hands; she ought to be able to extract it easily. Carefully, she grabbed the scabbard and drew it away. Silmariae's hands fell to her breast. With one hand holding the scabbard, Gill placed her fingers around the hilt, and felt a warm surge of power move up her hand and wrist, all the way to her shoulder. This time there was no pain, no shock. Gill pulled the sword free. Almost of itself, it made an arc in the air and landed, point touching the floor. Gill put both hands on the hilts and announced, "I am Silmariae, daughter of Silmariae, enemy of Mace. I will not rest until he is defeated."

After the vow had gone out of her, she gasped, feeling as if something had caught her in a grip and now released her. At the same time, she heard what she thought was a distant shout. She looked around, and even ducked out of the tomb, but saw nothing, heard no echo. She stepped back into the tomb and held the sword up to her face. It glowed fiercely, but she could look into the carved runes on the blade comfortably.

The book of instructions said that it was very important to assert control over the sword at all times. She would have to start now. "Look, you," she said, addressing the artifact. "I'm getting weary of words being put into my mouth, so keep quiet."

Not even a tingle answered her, though the sword dimmed slightly. With her mouth set in an attitude of grim determination, she started to prepare to leave. She put the sword back in its sheath and set it on a table. She turned to the wall, where protective armor hung on pegs. This was battle armor made by the Wye, the people from the stars, not the ceremonial armor that Silmariae's body wore—how did she know that? She turned to the corpse, then to the globe. Silmariae had taken Sloan into her. Sloan had some of Silmariae's memories. Now Gill had them, too. Furthermore, Gill thought, Sloan now had some of Gill's memories. She smiled and thought *that* would be interesting for the next person to try.

She went through the tomb, knowing precisely what to take and what to leave behind. She was at once an experienced campaigner and a rank novice. Unexpectedly, everything seemed lighter and easier to move than before Sloan possessed her. She paused for a moment and felt her arms again. They did seem thicker. All of Sloan's activity must have built muscles.

At last, she had gathered all she would need. By the time she left and locked the tomb, the sun had set. She decided to stay the night. Looking up and determining the position of the stars, she reckoned it had been a little less than a month since her 23rd birthday. It seemed forever ago.

Gill set out the next morning, wearing the magical charm that Sloan had worn in order to cross the ring of Tashtalon. The key she placed in a special pocket in the scabbard, and she had to fight off the impression that the key and the sword were whispering to one another. Kiri's mood seemed to have lightened with hers; he pranced and pulled at the bit as if eager to be on the road.

A minor river, the River Stone, flowed southward from the forest that lay north of the ring of Tashtalon. Gill saw no other name for it in the maps, and presumed that the name had not changed at the coming of Tashtalon. It was easy to see how the river had gotten its name: the sand bank was narrow on each side, and rocks were plentiful on both banks and in the riverbed itself. The water was clear, except for the deep central channel, which was a muddy at the bottom, though the water remained still largely translucent. According to the maps, the headwaters were inside the great city of Maclin, capital of the northern realm. All Gill had to do was to follow its winding ways northward.

This area within the ring of Tashtalon was largely farmstead or pasture. Gill saw no one on her first day's journey, and expected to see none as she traveled farther. With clear skies and warm weather, she did not set up the tent at night, but simply unfolded the bedroll and slept in it. That was cozy enough, even wearing the armor, which was comfortably light and flexible. The necklace, however, prevented her from being taken by the sleep of Tashtalon, and sometimes it was difficult to sleep on the hard bumpy ground.

Five days north of Silmariae's tomb, she was nearly at the northern edge of the ring of Tashtalon. She stopped for the evening meal, built a campfire, ate, banked the flame, and settled to sleep.

She was awakened by Kiri nuzzling her shoulder and Silmariae nudging her leg. Quickly, she got out of the bag and turned her back to the river just in time to see three figures emerge from the brush. They charged at her, swords raised, screaming at the top of their lungs. Gill ran to Kiri. Knowing from her experiences at her aunt's ranch how greathorses reacted to a perceived attack, she evaded the sword of the lead man and pushed him into Kiri. Kiri neighed loudly and lashed out with his hooves. That reduced her opponents to two.

The survivors gave Kiri a wide berth. Gill was hard pressed to keep them both at bay. Silmariae almost moved on its own to defend Gill and strike her adversaries. Some lingering memory of swordfighting skills told Gill of every weakness, every opening; Silmariae landed blows and then mortal wounds. Two men lay on the ground, unmoving. Quickly, she twisted around only to see Kiri with his hoof on the third man. She scanned from horizon to horizon to see if there were any other threats. But the sword was quiet, telling her there were none.

Gill sat on the ground, breathless. Silmariae grumbled. She cleaned the blood off the blade, then sheathed it. She looked at the bodies, wondering what to do next. She did not have a shovel to bury them. A bonfire, larger than her small camping fire, might draw the attention of any unknown associates that might still be lurking out there. She could lay stones over them, but that would take time. When she got her breath back, she stood and looked over the bodies. The signs of torture definitely identified them as coming from Mace. The faces were vaguely familiar, but she did not know their names.

She built up the campfire again and checked Kiri. The horse was uninjured, but blood-spattered. She cleaned and brushed his coat, then, bareback, rode him a little way out of the clearing. Three unattended greathorses grazed there. She saw no carts, and no signs of any others. She remembered the distant shout when she had drawn the sword in Silmariae's tomb. Somehow, Mace must have been aware of her drawing the sword, and had sent assassins to kill her.

She gathered the reins of the greathorses, brought them close to the campsite, and tied them to a small tree. With luck, she would be in Maclin in two more days and could pasture the horses there. As she rode Kiri through the brush again, she stopped. A tall, thin, glowing figure stooped over the bodies, examining them curiously. At Gill's approach, he looked up and smiled.

"You woke me up!" he said brightly.

Although he did not sound as if he expected an apology, Gill said "sorry" as she dismounted Kiri and tied his reins to a nearby tree.

Gill turned to find the figure walking toward her, arms outstretched. He was clothed from neck to thigh in a dark material which fitted him like skin. He carried no weapon, bag, or pack. His hair was silky and brown. In the back of her mind—perhaps some memory of Silmariae's—something said "friend." She did not resist as he embraced her in a long hug. "Silmariae," he said happily.

"Yes," Gill said when released, presuming that he had recognized the sword.

He stepped back and indicated the men. "They tried to kill you?"
"Yes."

He shook his head. "That was not nice."

"I thought so, too."

He examined the bodies more closely and looked up. "From Mace. I can tell."

Gill nodded. Although he did not look young, he impressed her as being childish. Her fragmentary memories from Silmariae provided no further hints about him, however.

He continued to ramble. "I will help you. I'll take care of their horses, too. You go back to sleep."

"Help me?"

"Hide the bodies decently. Don't worry."

"Are you going to the city?"

"Oh, no. Just came from there. I'm going home." He gestured eastward. "It's been asleep too, but it's still there."

Gill realized he was referring to Eldswold, which was the settlement of the Wye. "What's your name?"

"Leni. Go to sleep now."

Gill felt she still needed to be on her guard; other agents of Mace could be around. On the other hand, after the day's journey and the battle, she was tired. She knelt and lay on the bedroll, facing a smiling Leni. She intended simply to rest, and keep at least one wary eye open in case of trouble, but she blinked, and suddenly it was morning.

Startled, she scrambled to her feet. Leni was gone, and so were the extra greathorses and the bodies. She checked Kiri and the saddlebags; nothing had been taken, nothing had been damaged. An echo of memory deduced that Leni had magically put her to sleep. She sighed, and set about making breakfast.

Ready to travel again, she turned Kiri northward. About midmorning, a tingling on her skin and a brief protest from Kiri told her that she had crossed the northern border of the ring of Tashtalon. The river had narrowed to a stream, and, as she traveled on, to a brook. She camped by it that night, and, starting out early next morning, she began looking for the outlines of a city. But instead of the clearings and farmsteads she might expect close to a city, she found the trees and brush becoming thicker and taller. The stream disappeared in the undergrowth. She could not see very far ahead of her, and Kiri was nearly swimming through the grasses. Gill was about to urge Kiri into what appeared to be a thicket when he stopped, refusing to go on. Silmariae murmured.

Gill put a hand on the hilt. "I heard; now be quiet," she said sternly, and dismounted. She walked up to what was almost a wall of grasses and vines and put her hand forward, meeting something solid. She drew Silmariae to clear the brush and get a better look. Before she could put the blade to the greenery, it moved aside, and what appeared to be a huge iron-clad door opened.

Quickly, Gill waded back to Kiri and urged him forward.

They emerged into a wide street paved with cream-colored stones. Old leaves from last autumn were scattered on the streets and walks. Gill heard a click and turned to see that the doors had closed behind her. Now that she was away from the thick forest growth, she saw a stone wall around the city, breached only by the gate.

Turning again, she looked up the street. Something inside her said "home." Indeed, the buildings to either side of her were very home-like—attractive, well-constructed. She looked up the street and saw similar handsome buildings. At the end of the road, she saw a large fountain, opening on one side and flowing eastward—the headwaters of the River Stone, as the map said. Beyond the fountain, wide marble steps led up to a majestic palace that made the one Gill had worked in seem ordinary by comparison. Towers and battlements of ivory-colored marble soared to the treetops, trees which were thrice the height of the tallest tree Gill had ever seen.

She rode directly to the palace steps. As she passed the fountain, she saw an alcove next to the stairway which appeared to be for horses. She tied Kiri there and went up the stairs. She looked for guards or watchers, but saw none.

Once inside, she found herself looking down a corridor which branched right and left. It was at once completely strange and completely familiar. She let the part of her that recognized the castle be her guide; she padded down the carpeted corridors, unwilling to disturb the profound silence.

After treading up a flight of stairs, she reached an open door and peered inside. A woman in her late teens, fully dressed, slept on a bed. Something in her mind said, "baby." She felt an upwelling of affection as she stepped to the bedside, and found herself bending to kiss the woman tenderly on the forehead.

The whisper of fabric in motion made her straighten and turn to the doorway. She saw a tall, thin man, whose skin was sepia-toned and whose hair was black. He had big brown eyes deeply set in an oval face. He wore pants, soft shoes, and a shirt that wrapped around his torso. He regarded her as one might regard someone who had lost their mind, then turned and gestured down the hall. "Eminric," he said in a low voice.

Within seconds, Eminric appeared and stood beside him. The tall man waved at Gill. "There's Silmariae."

After a moment of astonishment, Eminric's face broke out in a smile. "Gill...." He took a breath. "When I saw Sloan, I wondered if it was you."

The tall man turned to Eminric. "You're using a different language."

Gill realized that he was speaking a language similar to the one Mace had used in his magical laboratory.

Eminric turned to him. "The language of Somerlie is somewhat different now than it was 500 years ago." He extended an arm to Gill. "Come. Let's find somewhere to talk." As Gill crossed the room to him, he added, "If you had Sloan inside you, you must recognize Collin from Silmariae's memories?"

Before she could think about it, she found herself saying in an unfamiliar language, "Oh, yes, Collin and I are old friends."

Collin moaned. "I'd consider throttling Von if he weren't dead already."

"Oh?" Gill blurted out.

Collin turned to her. "Von didn't think through the implications of his creations imprinting memories of one or more individuals in one mind. Silmariae used Sloan herself, and after that, she sometimes acted like Von, Sloan's creator." He gestured back into the room. "Do you know who that is?"

She swiveled around and looked at the woman again. After a few seconds' thought, she said, "Saris. My youngest."

Collin groaned again.

"No," Eminric said gently. "That's your great-aunt, many times over. Her oldest sister, Estes, was your many times great-grandmother."

Collin touched Gill's shoulder and said sympathetically, "I know it's good for you to have the memories, but you can't let them take over, or you'll lose yourself."

Eminric put a hand on Collin's back. "There's time for that. Let's sit and talk first."

As they walked down the hallways, Eminric in the lead, Gill said, "Isn't this a city? Where's everyone else?"

Eminric drew breath to answer, but Collin spoke first. "Everyone in the city except you and me and Eminric are asleep. I asked Eminric to wait before wakening the humans."

"Is it something like the sleep of Tashtalon?"

"Tashtalon?" Collin asked.

"Yes and no," Eminric answered. "Here's the pantry. Let's sit."

The room Eminric entered was a small kitchen, though it resembled the kitchen at Mace's more than it did the kitchens in Somerlie. Eminric opened various cupboards and brought out breads, cheeses, butter, jams, and juices. Collin helped set the table while Gill sat in a wooden chair and watched.

"You did a stellar job of preserving things," Collin remarked. "There's not even an accumulation of dust after all these years."

Eminric smiled. "Yes." He sat when Collin did and pushed some of the food over to Gill. "Have you ever tasted 500-year-old bread before?"

She began to reach for it, then drew her hand back. "Five hundred years?"

"Don't worry," said Collin. "It's still fresh." He took a loaf and a knife, sliced three pieces, took one for himself, and set down the knife.

"Did you know there had been a war with Mace?" Eminric asked her.

"Yes, Estes wrote it down in the history I read."

Eminric hastily swallowed his bread. "Where did you find that?"

"In Silmariae's tomb, where I got the sword."

Eminric exchanged an astonished glance with Collin. "How did you find all these things?"

"The key my grandmother wore...there was some magic in it. After Alia died, the magic came out somehow. I recognized that the key fit a lock in the back of Tashtalon's throne. When I opened it, I found a map to the tomb. I had been there and back when you last saw me in Arcacia."

Eminric shook his head, open-mouthed.

"Who's this Tashtalon fellow?" Collin asked.

"Mace," said Eminric and Gill at the same time.

"And he lives in Somerlie now?"

"No, he lives where he always has," said Eminric. "It is interesting and ironic that when he took over Somerlie, he told his agents a story that the Queen's throne in Arcacia was his, and it stands there as a symbol of his power."

"That's the *Queen's throne*?" Gill said.

Eminric smiled kindly. "I see that Sloan was only able to give you bits and pieces of Silmariae's memory. Otherwise, you would have known from her that that was her throne."

To cover her embarrassment at her lack of knowledge, she reached for one of the slices Collin had left on the plate. "This is 500 years old?"

"Yes, that's how long it has been since the final battle with Mace," said Eminric.

"I thought we were doomed," Collin said. "Just five days ago...well, you know what I mean...Silmariae, the sword, communicated Silmariae's death scream. Then the entire Wye army was wiped out."

"I survived, but they didn't know that," Eminric amended.

Collin waved a hand above his head. "A dark cloud came in from the southwest, with the image of Mace reflected in it. I thought it would be the last thing I would ever see. We all did. The next thing I knew, I woke up, here and now."

Eminric bowed his head solemnly and sighed. He raised his head again and began speaking in a low voice. "I barely was able to gather my wits and strength. With the armies gone, Mace had the leisure to create a spell that would seek out and destroy all intelligent life. He left Somerlie alone—that part of the realm had fallen to its knees—and went to the only places that had power left to oppose him: Asquith and Eldswold. I did the only thing I could; I stretched out my power. I sent out a spell of oblivion, and then commanded all to find a safe place to lie down. Once that spell was in place, I brought everyone into a state where there was no body activity, and then I preserved them."

"Suspended life, we call it," Collin interrupted.

"Once Mace's spell had dissipated, Mace's magic told him no one was alive, and he assumed his spell had killed everyone."

"He couldn't tell you 'suspended' everyone?" Gill asked.

"No," said Collin. "We were dead, by medical definition, but revivable. Our magical specialists have always said it is only possible to suspend an individual—certainly not an entire city at once—and even then not for more than a few years. I didn't think it could be done, and my magical specialty is in the healing arts." He turned to Eminric. "In fact, I still wouldn't have believed it if it hadn't happened to me. No one knew you were that powerful."

"Especially me. But I had nothing to lose." He took a breath. "Later, I added touches to discourage any further searching, such as additional forest overgrowth and a spell to keep animals from entering the city."

Gill paused between bites. "The star story. You lived the star story."

"Story?" Collin asked.

Eminric smiled faintly. "My story, though I didn't *exactly* live it." He took a breath. "After Mace thought he defeated Asquith and Eldswold, he put an impenetrable barrier around Somerlie. I couldn't get in for 100 years until he relaxed the spell so that the barrier was only deadly to humans. Once I did get in, I found the descendants of Estes, but they had no knowledge of Asquith or their ancestry, and no idea where Silmariae was. So, for a time, I wandered from place to place as a storyteller, hoping that my little parables would one day inspire someone."

"They did," Gill affirmed.

Eminric spread soft cheese and jam on a slice of bread—an unusual combination, Gill thought—and said, "We knew when you drew the sword, just as the sword told us when Silmariae died. You woke up all the Wye that I had suspended, there was such power."

Collin swallowed his bite of bread. "All the humans were still suspended, though."

"Then it was you I heard when I drew the sword?"

"What?"

"Who?"

"When I drew the sword...I heard a distant shout. I looked around, but I didn't see anyone. Was that you?"

"It wasn't us," Eminric said. "It must have been..."

"...Mace," Collin finished.

Gill sighed. "I suspected as much, when those assassins came on me."

"Assassins?" Eminric asked.

"A day or so ago, I was sleeping, and three agents of Mace attacked me. Kiri and I killed them, and then someone calling himself Leni showed up. I think he must have put me to sleep, and taken the bodies and the greathorses."

Eminric nodded. "Leni and Collin were the only Wye here in Maclin when I put everyone in Asquith and Eldswold to sleep. Of course, Leni woke when Collin did—when you drew the sword. A couple of days ago Leni told us he was going back to Eldswold. He's probably there by now. You awakened all the Wye in Eldswold, too, so he won't be alone there."

Collin turned to Eminric. "If Mace knows the sword has been found, he's going to come here after it. I want you to awaken Saris so she can continue her research. There are a lot of things I want to know, not the least of which is where you got the power to do all this. If your power can increase, maybe ours can, too, and the Wye can oppose him more strongly."

"I'm interested, too, but I should awaken Allard first; he's king of Asquith," Eminric insisted.

"Is he a relative of mine, too?" Gill asked.

Eminric turned to her. "No. We understand that it used to be human tradition that a king and queen were married to each other, but the humans changed the tradition some time ago. Now the king is chosen by the men in the community, and the women choose the queen. They're very rarely spouses."

Collin drained his glass of fruit juice and dabbed his lips with a napkin. "We'd best get started, then...or," he paused, as if thinking, "maybe we'd better only waken a handful and keep the others asleep, so they'll remain alive if Mace comes?"

Eminric shook his head. "There's no point in waiting. Mace overlooked the population of Asquith and Eldswold once; he won't do it again. This time he'll create a spell which will kill everyone, suspended or not. I've only given us a respite. This time, we either defeat Mace or the world will become his to rule exclusively, all the remaining centuries of his life."

Chapter 7

When Eminric and Collin had finished eating, they left to revive the king. With nothing else to do, Gill went outside and brought Kiri to the fountain for a drink. After tying him in the alcove again, and leaving some oats from the saddlebags, she returned to the castle. On the way back to the pantry, she ran into Eminric and Collin. They were flanking a man with silvery hair and brown skin tones. All of them stopped.

Eminric turned to the man. "Your majesty, this is Gill, the one I told you about."

"With Silmariae, I see."

"Yes. Gill, this is Allard, king of Asquith and Somerlie for 18 years...or at least, the 18 years before the 500," Eminric added with a smile.

Gill executed a small bow. Allard took her by the hand. "While Eminric is reviving my people, we have much to discuss. I am 500 years out of date, and I must understand the current situation before I can make any decisions." He nodded to Eminric, then Collin, in dismissal. The two bowed and walked away. Allard led Gill down the hall.

"Are the Wye under your authority as well?" she asked.

"Only when they are in Asquith or Somerlie," he answered. "Since Ciernan is now dead, Eldswold has no leader. I suppose the Wye will select another once the current crisis is over." After some moments, he added, "Are there any Wye in the city right now besides Eminric and Collin and Leni? I was a bit muddled after the long sleep and forgot to ask."

"Leni went back to Eldswold. Eminric and Collin are the only Wye here."

He nodded.

They walked into a parlor that Silmariae's memory recognized as the king's audience chamber. It had many windows extending almost from floor to ceiling, and was circular in shape. Bookcases lined any unwindowed space. Many wooden tables, large and small, had been placed in neat assembly, as had the upholstered chairs. Allard guided her to one and sat in another with a small table between them.

Allard questioned her about the political situation in Somerlie. He was impressed that Gill had assisted the Lord Protector, but astonished that she had to do so secretly. As he talked, Gill realized that he had a shrewd and perceptive mind, a deep understanding and experience in human nature, and a vast treasurehouse of knowledge. Cyril seemed merely adequate as a ruler compared to Allard, and Boreas was a bumpkin in comparison. She also discovered that he was skilled in drawing out information; she found herself telling him much more about herself, and Somerlie, than she had intended.

Once she had explained all she could about Somerlie, he sighed and sat back in the chair. She thought that was the end of the questioning and shifted her weight, preparing to stand, but he turned to her and said, "And what about your experience with Mace? How did you feel about that?"

Gill froze. Her tongue rested against the back of her clenched teeth. She began to shake.

"Here, let me get you some water." He went to another table with a pitcher and glasses; he brought back a glass for Gill and put it in a trembling hand.

He looked down at her kindly. "I'm sorry. I'm still regaining my senses after the long sleep. Now I remember that after Silmariae put Sloan back, she could not talk about it for some time. She was chilled and shaking for three days."

Gill sipped slowly as Allard again took his seat. He waited patiently until Gill had downed half a glass and set it back on the table.

He rubbed his chin thoughtfully. "Perhaps that part can wait for another time. You've given me a lot to ponder already."

A man appeared at the door. He was in his late thirties, skin creamy like Gill's, blond hair, powerfully built. He bowed. "Majesty."

Allard waved him in. "Come in, Bryce." As the man stepped in, Allard continued, "Gill, this is Bryce. He's one of the crown's senior advisors."

Bryce noticed the sword immediately. "Silmariae." He looked at Gill with wonder.

"Yes, we thought Mace had captured it when Silmariae died, didn't we? Bryce, here's the situation: we have been asleep for 500 years. Gill, here, is a descendant of Silmariae. There is peace at the moment, but Somerlie is in the grip of Mace, and now that he knows that we're here, we can count on a confrontation. I want you to gather messengers to go through the city. Tell the people they've been asleep for 500 years, but not to leave the city until I give permission. Other than that, they should go about their normal activities. I will give out the entire story in due time."

"And I should not say anything about Mace?"

"Not at the moment. If they ask, say Mace has left Asquith alone for these past 500 years and we believe he will do so for a while longer."

"I understand, majesty."

"Thank you. Come back when you've instructed the messengers."

"Yes, majesty." He bowed and backed out of the room.

Moments later, a woman appeared in the door. She wore a sleeveless shirt, showing well-muscled arms. She had the complexion of someone who spent a lot of time outdoors. Bowing, she said, "Majesty," and stepped in.

Allard turned to Gill. "Gill, this is Rowan, one of our military leaders. Rowan, this is Gill, our new keeper of the sword of queens."

"Eminric told me." She stepped close to Gill and looked at her closely. Gill felt an echo of affection coming from Silmariae. "You're younger than I expected, but you have that same haunted look Silmariae had when she came back from spying out Mace with Sloan."

Gill put a hand to her face and wondered if there were a mirror in the room.

Rowan leaned over and held out a hand. "I am—used to be—Silmariae's bodyguard, poor as I was."

Allard sighed. "Shall I make it a royal command for you not to blame yourself for that?"

Rowan looked over to Allard. "A royal command won't change the fact that I was wounded in battle and was recovering here when Silmariae died." Meanwhile, Gill took the outstretched hand and shook it. Rowan continued, "I hope we can be friends. Might as well be, since I consider myself your bodyguard while you wear the sword." She released Gill's hand. "Looks like the sword has accepted you. You can use it, I hope?"

"I have already."

She looked relieved. "Good. We can go from there."

"You have a plan?" asked Allard.

Rowan settled into a chair. "Do we need one?"

Eminric came to the door and bowed as the others had before stepping in. "Your subjects have all been revived, majesty."

"Excellent."

Eminric sat. "If you're finished with Gill, I'd like to have a word with her."

Allard extended a hand toward Gill. "Be my guest."

Eminric turned to Gill. "It may be instructive for Allard and Rowan to listen in. Do you mind?" When Gill waved a hand in consent, he asked, "How is it with you and the sword?"

"All right. I wish it wouldn't put words in my mouth, though. Sometimes it acts as if it has a mind of its own."

"Many magical artifacts will suggest to your mind what to do and how to use them," Eminric said. "You can choose to act on those suggestions or not."

"Not with Sloan. I couldn't even move a finger."

"For the first few hours, yes."

"Longer than that. He was still controlling me when I rescued you."

"You mean you allowed him to lead you."

"No, I didn't."

He sat up straight. "Did Sloan ever do anything you didn't want?" When she did not answer right away, he added, "Did you ever torture anyone?"

"No!" she insisted.

"Could you, if you wanted to?"

She remembered Mace's invitation. "I could have, yes."

"Did you want to rescue me?"

"Yes."

"Then you were in control. Sloan couldn't do anything against your will. We call him that for the sake of convenience, but he was void of any personality. You could have asserted control anytime after the first few hours."

She thought about that, then asked, "Why did Sloan turn me into a man?"

"Von invented Sloan, and several others like him, and Von was male."

"Mace's friend."

He nodded. "Von lived here for a time. Or, rather," he gestured eastward, "he lived at Eldswold, our settlement. He went back and forth between us and Mace until Mace set himself against us. Then he stayed with Mace, until he died."

"I thought Mace had always been the enemy."

"Silmariae's memories didn't give you the full story, I take it?" When she shook her head, he added, "Don't worry. No one expects you to know everything. When he was younger, Mace was little different from anyone else—his friends say he was quite pleasant. As the years went by, his ambition grew—he wanted to possess the most powerful magic on our world. Somehow his experiments got out of control; he poisoned the planet. We all had to find homes elsewhere. Ciernan, the leader of my group, feared that Mace would try his experiment again on whatever world he landed on, thinking that the second time nothing would go wrong, so we followed him here. At first, everything was fine. When we landed, we assumed the shape of the residents here...."

"You can change shape?"

He smiled. "To a certain extent; just as Sloan changed you. There's a basic form, and by what you call magic, we can make certain alterations. We do that at whatever world we're on. It's easier than finding a world nearly identical to the one we evolved on, which is what most other space travelers do. Since the residents have already evolved an optimum form for breathing the air and otherwise coping with the environment, we simply take their shape. We don't feel that outward appearance matters; it's character that's important."

"What was your shape before?"

"Roughly what it is now. You would recognize a picture of me before I last changed shape; it's the same with the rest of us."

Another question occurred to her. "How did Silmariae get Sloan, if it was Von's creation?"

He smiled again. "Ah. You see, each of us has a unique magical ability, and our artifacts can outlast us. Our magic is more powerful when we can connect it to an artifact." He pulled out a wand from his sleeve. "This is mine." He leaned over and whispered conspiratorially, "I didn't have much imagination as a young man." He glanced to Allard and Rowan, who chuckled. He put away the wand and continued. "Von, assuming he would return, left his creations here. When he died, the council of the Wye distributed the globes, and they awarded Sloan to Silmariae's family. Other families received other globes, but they were lost." He pointed to the sword. "Varantia, the Wye who created the sword, willed it to Silmariae's ancestors in the event of her death. She fashioned the sword especially to counter Mace's magic."

"Why not give the artifacts to others of your own people?"

"It is difficult, with our own unique abilities, to handle another's magic. We found it safer, especially with our small numbers here, to award them to those of your people who could use them responsibly."

"Did Mace kill Varantia, then?"

He shook his head. "Varantia was Mace's spouse...."

"His wife!?" she interrupted, shocked.

"Yes," he answered calmly. "The season came upon them when they were relatively young, long before Mace became ambitious."

"Season?"

"It comes to some early, others late. We don't mate out of season, and since we are virtually immortal, there isn't a great need for us to mate more than once or twice in a lifetime."

She persisted. "If Varantia was his mate, why would she design a sword especially to counter his magic?"

"The mating was without issue, and they separated. She grew disenchanted with him...almost literally. When Mace destroyed our world, she came here with us, not with him. And since she knew him intimately—more intimately than a human would know a human spouse—she knew better than anyone what would affect him."

"If Mace didn't kill her, how did she die?"

"We are not certain. She was found dead with her artifact completed and by her side. Some speculated that she committed suicide; I and others tend to think that the creating of the sword took such great strength that it drained her."

She considered that a moment, then added, "Then how did Silmariae die?"

Rowan winced; Allard looked grieved.

"Sorry," Gill said.

Eminric nodded solemnly. "No apology is necessary. For you, it was centuries ago." He took a breath. "Lamentably, we aren't sure. When war came, no one doubted that Silmariae would defeat Mace. She had been in Mace's fortress, she was fierce and courageous, no one could match her in swordplay. She had the sword. And then, she was dead. Estes was with her; I presume she escaped with the body."

"No one saw her die?"

"Estes might have. Mace undoubtedly did. No one else."

In the silence that followed, Bryce appeared at the door. "I've sent out the messengers, majesty."

"Good." He turned to the others. "Shall Bryce join us?"

They all looked to Gill. "Why not?" she said.

Bryce found an empty chair and sat. "I've asked the cooks to prepare a lunch. It's after midday."

"Good thinking." Allard gestured to Eminric. "Eminric is explaining things to Gill. We're just listening."

"Ah."

"One thing I've been wondering," Gill continued. "How did Mace's agents capture you?"

"They did *what*?" Rowan said.

For the first time since she had known him, Eminric looked sheepish. "I was traveling north from Somerlie to my shelter in the forest beyond the ring of Tashtalon...."

"The what?" Bryce asked.

Allard put up a finger, catching Bryce's and Rowan's eye. "I'll explain later."

"I hope so," Rowan said.

Eminric continued. "Normally I keep traveling until I am beyond it, but I was weary, and grieved for the death of Gill's friend, whom Mace murdered, and whom I hoped would come with me to search for Silmariae. I was also saddened by Gill's refusal to come with me."

"I'm sorry," Gill said. "After what happened, I felt it was not safe to tell you. I thought there was a chance you might be an agent of Mace, or that agents of Mace were shadowing you, to find descendants of Silmariae."

He laughed. "And my first thought, when I was captured, is that you might have reported me to Boreas...until I saw Sloan."

"You were saying how you were captured....," Allard prompted. He looked eager to know more.

Eminric nodded. "I was exhausted, so I slept in a pasture, within the borders of Somerlie. An agent of Mace's must have seen me glowing and alerted Mace's men. I woke to find them throwing a net of sleep over me." He shook his head. "It was a combination of ill luck and carelessness."

Allard leaned forward a little. "We've all made our share of mistakes."

At that moment, young men and women came in with food trays. Quickly and efficiently, they moved tables and set dishes, and then, just as swiftly, were gone.

All were silent for a time as they set about to eat. Bryce spoke first, "What next?"

Allard took a deep breath. "Let's see...we don't have a queen...."

"Mmmm," Rowan said, munching a vegetable, and pointing to Gill with her fork.

Gill almost choked on her food.

Allard turned to her. "Traditionally, the women of the kingdom select the keeper of the sword of queens as queen."

Gill took a drink of water to clear her throat. "I can't be queen. I'm going out to kill Mace. I might never come back."

Allard nodded. "Commendable goal; but what if you succeed?"

"I'll think about it when I succeed."

"Perhaps you should consider it," Eminric said. "I remember Alia telling me how frustrated you were that you weren't able to make decisions in Somerlie."

Gill blushed. She had no idea Alia had told Eminric things that she thought were only between her and Alia.

Eminric smiled at her. "By the way, did you know that you and Alia were distantly related?"

Gill's eyebrows went up.

"You share an ancestor who was a descendant of Silmariae. She had two daughters. You are a many-times offspring of the older sister; Alia of the younger one."

Gill nodded. "That must be why my grandmother had the key; it was passed to her from the older sister's descendants."

"Apparently it was so secret that the younger sister didn't know," Eminric mused.

Gill let out a breath. "In any event, my instructions were to take the sword and go north. Now that I'm here, I was hoping for some advice. Before going, I would like to have some sort of plan." She looked around hopefully, anticipating some useful counsel.

Rowan snorted. "Plan," she said derisively.

Gill's brows furrowed, puzzled at Rowan's attitude.

Rowan turned to Gill. "You don't need a plan if you believe in yourself."

What sort of weakling did Rowan think she was? "If I didn't believe in myself," Gill protested, "I wouldn't have picked up the sword in the first place."

Rowan lifted a finger. "Precisely! Then you don't need a plan...just use what you've learned. You have Silmariae's memories and who knows how many others...."

"Yes, and Silmariae did, too, and she died."

"She planned too much," Rowan complained. "She didn't follow her feelings enough."

"If you don't know how she died, you don't know whether her feelings had anything to do with her death." Gill saw the men's faces contorting as she talked; when she finished, they burst out laughing.

"What's the joke?" Gill asked.

Allard took a breath and waved a hand. "Not you. It's just that you and Rowan arguing sound exactly like Silmariae and Rowan arguing."

"That's what scares me," said Rowan. "She's thinking just like Silmariae. She could make the same mistakes Silmariae did...whatever those were. If she does, she's dead."

"You may be going too far into the realm of conjecture," said Eminric. When Rowan opened her mouth, he waved a hand. "You're still adjusting from your long sleep. We can discuss these matters again at a later time."

Rowan shrugged and returned to her meal.

"What happened to Collin?" Allard asked.

"He and Saris went to her library to see if they could find anything useful," Eminric said.

Allard nodded.

Eminric turned to Gill. "You might find this interesting, Gill. On our homeworld of Wik, there was once a master of magic knowledge. This master accumulated a set of volumes called forbidden books. When he died, none of us could use them. It was said, however, that they contained everything possible to know about magic...probably some exaggeration, but he left a large number of volumes. When we left the planet, Ciernan took them with us, to prevent another species from finding and using them, if nothing else. Once we found humans could use our magic, Ciernan kept watch for a human who might be able to crack them. When Saris showed an interest and aptitude for magical history, he gave them to her."

"I'm not sure I understand," Gill said. "If they're books, can't anyone just open them and read them?"

"To open the books and see printing on the pages required a magical key that the master of knowledge made with his unique abilities... none of the rest of us could use it, or duplicate it."

"We had Wye coming in and out of here all the time, having her look up something for them," Bryce volunteered. "They said she was quite useful."

"So she was," Eminric said.

"Kept her out of trouble," Rowan mumbled.

"Meaning?" Gill asked.

Rowan turned to Gill. "Saris grew up in a family of warriors. Mother, father, sisters...she didn't have the ability to use a sword, and it was heartbreaking to see her try and fail. It was such a relief when we found something she could do."

Gill caught the word "father" and realized she had never read anything about Silmariae's husband. "Could I ask what happened to her father?" she said timidly.

"Killed early in the war," Allard said softly.

Gill nodded.

When they were finished eating, Eminric rose. "I think Gill and I could use a respite until dinnertime."

"By all means," Allard said.

Eminric added, "I'll give Gill the empty room on the advisor's floor, where she can be near Bryce and Rowan and Collin and me, since she knows us."

"Please do."

Eminric extended a hand. "Gill?"

Gill stood; Rowan stood too.

Eminric held up a hand. "Gill won't need your services right away. Let me have a moment." He nodded at Allard. "Why not ask Allard about the ring of Tashtalon?"

"Who or what the hell is Tashtalon?" Bryce said.

When they were out of earshot of the room, Eminric said, "You realize, of course, that this is a different society from the one you grew up in."

"Yes, of course."

"I'm not sure that you—or they, for that matter—realize the extent of the difference. I've been in contact with both of these human societies for centuries. You're both human, yes; you have some concepts in common, yes, but you're very different."

"I'm not sure what you're trying to say," she said.

"What I'm trying to lead into gently is that you come from a society which is much less sophisticated than this one is. Let me quickly add this is not your fault. Mace has suppressed much of your human potential for a variety of opinions and outlooks. You and your immediate ancestors have, for all intents and purposes, grown up in a prison, and your perspective has been limited to that prison."

Gill nodded. "When I was explaining life in Somerlie to Allard, he was horrified at some of the things that happen all the time, that I never even thought much about before."

Eminric nodded.

"I must say, though," Gill continued, "I don't see how Silmariae and Rowan could be friends if they argued all the time."

He smiled. "Well, not all the time. It simply seemed that way sometimes." He took a breath. "Rowan and Silmariae did not have the same sort of friendship that you had with Alia. You and Alia became friends because you and she were so much the same. Silmariae and

Rowan were almost at opposite ends of a thought sometimes, and each of them found their differences stimulating, exciting, refreshing."

Gill thought about what he was saying. "It wasn't unpleasant for them to argue?"

Eminric blew out a breath. "It probably was, on occasion. But friction between individuals or groups with strong and differing opinions is inevitable. It doesn't have to create a breach, however. Individuals can learn from it. Others find arguing exciting, competitive, even amusing." He turned to her with another smile. "You'll learn."

Gill sighed.

"When we first came to this world, there was some friction, too. But we had centuries of experience in dealing with diverse opinions, even from other species. Immortality has this advantage. And the humans here were excited to meet another species, especially since we were relatively small in number, and they were lacking in technology that we were willing to share."

"Technology?"

"The ability to do construct sophisticated items. For instance, a society with a high technology can build a city which can last for centuries in a matter of weeks."

She inhaled sharply. "The Wye built Arcacia."

He nodded. "And Maclin. Both Wye and humans lost technology after coming here. Each of us came with only one ship, and without the factories that are needed to sustain a high technological level. We lost less, because we were at a higher level, but we both live more simply than our ancestors did on the worlds from which we came."

She gasped. "You mean...," she put a hand to herself, "*we're* from the stars?"

"Why, yes, Gill, you are."

Chapter 8

Eminric eventually stopped at a room and opened the door. Inside, Gill saw carved furniture, a bed with richly woven linens, and a fine rug on the floor. It reminded her of her room at Mace's.

He pointed inside. "Your bags have been placed on the table. I've instructed the grooms to tend to Kiri."

Gill nodded her thanks; Eminric smiled and left, closing the door behind him.

She found the washroom, took a bath, dressed again, and lay on the bed for a short nap. She was awakened by knock at the door. When she called, Rowan entered with an armful of garments.

"I thought you'd like more clothes," she explained, setting them neatly on the bed. "Some of these ought to fit."

"Thanks."

Rowan sighed. "Too many people not coming back from the war."

"It must be hard," Gill replied. "For you, it was only days ago."

She nodded. "Allard told me about your friend. I'm sorry."

Gill sat on her bed. "Thanks." She paused a moment, and added thoughtfully, "Sometimes I think she would have been better suited for this task than I was."

Rowan found a chair and sat. "You don't know that."

"She was stronger than me; more suited for swordplay. I'm probably a lot like you described Saris to be—more suited for book work."

Rowan shook her head. "You don't seem that way to me."

Gill smiled weakly. "You don't know me that well yet."

She shrugged. "Well enough. And I've known Saris long enough to know you're not like her." Standing, she added, "When you're dressed, Allard wants us to have dinner together in his audience chamber. Something about *plans*." She rolled her eyes.

Gill crossed her arms in front of her. "I don't believe you never plan anything."

"Not when I can avoid it, no. Life's too changeable. I've seen too many people break from not being flexible enough."

"And I've seen too many people fall on their faces from lack of planning."

"It's a large planet; enough room for each of us," she said amicably, and left the room.

Gill was last to arrive. Allard, Eminric, Bryce, and Rowan were already there. After greeting them, Gill took a seat and listened to them discuss city matters while she ate. She was relieved to hear that the public had received the news of their long sleep calmly. The most frequent topic of conversation among the citizens was who might be the next queen. The prominent women were discussing candidates somewhere in the city.

Just as she was taking the last sip of milk, she heard a pounding, as if someone were running down the hall toward them. Moments later, Saris and Collin appeared. Saris held a book in her arms; she walked in, set it on a low table, and knelt on the floor. Collin stood behind her.

"We found it," she announced ominously.

Curious, Gill stood and took a step toward them. Saris spotted the sword immediately and stared at Gill. "My mother's sword."

"Yes," Allard said. "This is Gill, a descendant of your older sister, Estes."

Saris stood and squared her shoulders. She was tall and sturdy, but lacked Rowan's—or even Gill's—muscles. Her blond hair was cut close to her face. She wore a suit with the shirt and leggings in one piece; it buttoned in the front.

She held out her hand. "I would like to take the sword, please."

"Don't be ridiculous, Saris," Rowan said.

"Rowan," Allard warned. "This is a family matter between Gill and Saris."

Gill lifted an eyebrow. She knew that she could not have fought with the sword, as she had on the way to Maclin, if the sword had not deemed her worthy to use it. Something in her memories, however, told her that Saris would not accept this unless it was demonstrated to her, and the easiest way to do that was to allow her to try to draw the sword. "All right," Gill said, unbuckling the sword and tossing it to Saris. She caught it by the sheath. The instant she gripped the hilt, she cried out in pain and shook her arm. Gill stepped forward and took back the sword. Grasping it by the hilt, she drew it and showed the blade, which glowed fiercely, even in the brightly sunlit room. "Satisfied?" She made eye contact with Saris before sheathing and buckling the sword again.

Saris bowed her head sadly.

Eminric put her hand on her shoulder. "I know how you feel."

"Do you?" She kept her head bowed.

"It was your mother's legacy; of course I know how you feel."

She sighed.

"You were about to show us something?" Allard prompted.

"Yes, majesty." She knelt next to her book again. Looking up at Eminric, she added, "I need you to tell me exactly what happened in the last moments of your battle group."

Eminric looked pained. He covered his face with his hands and let out a sob.

Collin put a hand on his back. "Do you need some time? Do you need my help?"

He took a deep breath and shook his head. "I've tried not to think about it, for so long." He leaned back, shakily grabbed the arm of a chair, and eased himself into it. He put his hands in his lap. "Let's see. There was this maelstrom, surrounding us, battering us, sucking the life out of us. We could barely breathe. We were holding it off, but we knew any minute it would break through our barriers and reduce us to dust. Ciernan called to the others. I could barely hear—the noise was incredible. He said it was time for sacrificial measures. I didn't know what he meant...I-I thought maybe my attention had wandered during a briefing. Then they threw themselves on me. The tempest surged in. They were all reduced to dust." He bowed his head. Collin put a hand on his back. He nodded and inhaled deeply. "Then it stopped. As if it were never there. I thought Mace would surely sense me and kill me too, but he didn't. I made my way north, and saw this cloud pass overhead. I knew Maclin was in danger." He took another breath. "The rest you know."

Saris nodded. "That confirms it."

"It?" Allard asked.

She turned to him. "Eminric's battle group committed suicide."

Eminric's head jerked up. "What? But the maelstrom reduced them to dust. I was there."

"It did, but they were dead when they fell on you."

"How could you possibly know?"

She put a finger on the page of the open book. "I know. It's in here."

Rowan turned to her. "You didn't find this before?" she said, startled.

Saris glared at her. "No, Rowan, I didn't find it before. The library of forbidden knowledge has tens of thousands of entries, and every time I have a moment to trace them, someone comes into my office and pleads with me to look up something for them immediately. And it's *all* of the utmost importance, of course."

"During the war, it was," Collin said evenly.

Saris rubbed her forehead. "I'm sorry. Yes, it was important. But it kept me from getting at the knowledge I *knew* must be in there—what we really needed."

"I'm not following," Eminric said.

Collin bent close to him. "Remember back on our homeworld, the old jokes when someone would try a magic spell and failed...what would we say?"

"Uh, we said, 'You could always kill yourself.'" He turned to Collin. "But that was just an expression."

Saris shook her head. "Forbidden knowledge always happens to get out somehow...in legend, humor, old stories passed from generation to generation."

Everyone turned to her, absorbing the information.

"The point is," Saris continued, and Gill could see the flush of excitement on her face, "there is a way to increase magical power, by absorbing or transferring life energy." She waved a hand over the pages. "It's right here in this book. That's why the master made it his artifact, to ensure that he was the only Wye who could use it. He was obsessed with gathering knowledge, but he knew the knowledge could be used unethically. On your world, where murder or suicide were virtually unknown for thousands of years, releasing such knowledge would be unthinkable."

Collin sat on the arm of Eminric's chair. "We believe that there were some Wye who suspected the truth, but kept it to themselves. But it explains so much...Varantia dying making Silmariae...your magical power increasing dramatically after your battle group dies around you...."

"...Mace," Eminric finished.

"Mace," Saris said, as if she were nailing him to the wall. "He not only guessed the truth, he tried to kill all of his own people to increase his power."

"But that was an accident," Eminric said.

"That's what he told Von, his friend," Saris said, "because he knew that Von wouldn't be his friend anymore if he told him the truth...if Von knew he'd tried to kill him and everyone else on your world."

"But he didn't," Eminric said. "Very few died in the evacuation of Wik. Less than a hundred out of billions."

"The accident," Saris insisted, "was that he was so inexperienced that he killed so few when he meant to kill so many. Even taking the life force from them increased his power far above that of any Wye in your known history. He knew he could dominate any world. He knew if he could refine his technique, learn from his mistakes, he could defeat anyone."

"How could we have missed it?" Eminric said.

"Because we theorize according to what we know. War you understand from your distant past and association with other species. Ambition you understand. But killing someone—or yourself—to increase magical power? It had never been done before, unthinkable when your society had virtually eliminated murder."

Collin turned to Eminric. "Do you see now how your power increased? Remember you told Saris that you sensed that the maelstrom was sucking your life out of you?"

"At the moment I said it, I meant it as a metaphor."

"You *sub*consciously knew what Mace was trying to do," Saris said. "Ciernan *con*sciously registered it...he must have guessed before, discussed it with others outside your presence, and this was the final confirmation. So he robbed Mace of getting even more power by having the battle group transfer it to you."

Collin crossed his arms in front of him. "Then the cloud that attacked us wasn't simply Mace wanting to defeat us...since Ciernan robbed him, he was going to get the life energy from any Wye left on the world, whether in Maclin or Eldswold."

"And I robbed him of that."

"Exactly," Saris said. "So he just settles down, master of the world, and his only worry these past 500 years is if someone finds Silmariae, and he believes he has Somerlie in too tight a grip for that to happen."

"Until now," Gill said.

Saris nodded. "Until now."

"But," Gill said, "how can Silmariae defeat him? If Varantia transferred her life force to it, that's only the energy of one person, and he must have absorbed at least the energy of 50."

"Magic doesn't work on a mathematical scale," Saris said. "Yes, absorbing the energy of 50 makes him more powerful than if he absorbed one, but not necessarily 50 times stronger. Also, magical strength can weaken...for example, if one is physically injured, or if the magic is overextended. Besides, in a contest of magic, it isn't always the most powerful who wins...it can be who has the more innovative spell, and from all my studies, I can say that Varantia was nothing if not innovative."

"She knew all of Mace's weaknesses, better than anyone else could," Eminric explained.

"So you think I can defeat Mace?" Gill asked Saris.

"Silmariae can. Varantia wouldn't have made it if she wasn't certain it could. I don't know what Mother did wrong. I've been trying to find clues, with no luck yet."

"Would you be willing to help me with this?" Gill asked.

Saris sighed and licked her lips. "The sword won't take me, that much is certain."

"That's nothing to feel bad about; I doubt that it would take me, either," Rowan said.

A smile played on Saris's lips. "I'll help."

Gill happened to glance out the window and saw that it was dark outside. She looked up to the ceiling and saw light coming from the panels, just as it had in Mace's mansion. It must have kept the brightness level constant as the sun set.

Allard seemed to notice the hour also. "I think we've accomplished enough for one day. We can meet again tomorrow."

Eminric nodded. "I've set a warning spell around the city to alert me in case Mace tries to attack it. I think that unlikely, however—he would have to spend more energy to come to us than if we came to him, as he expects and fears."

"I've always wanted to be Mace's worst nightmare," Rowan said. She stood and bowed to Allard. "Goodnight."

In turn, Gill rose, bowed, and left the room. Hearing a noise behind her, she turned to see Collin following. "Do you mind?" he asked.

"Not at all."

They walked outside. The air was fresh and warm. The sky was clear and the stars were out. She walked out on the wide landing and looked up.

"Looking for Earth?" Collin asked.

She turned. "Yes. Which is the star we came from?"

Collin pointed. "See that bright blue star?"

"Yes."

"It's the faint one under it and to the right."

"I see it."

"Your world had a moon, too."

"Moon?"

Collin made a circle with his thumb and forefinger. "A disk appearing about this size, bright enough to cast a faint shadow, but dim enough to look at directly. Our world had three, of various sizes." He pointed again. "Ours is the big red star over there."

She nodded.

"Are you planning to go back to Mace's fortress?" he asked suddenly.

"I have to," Gill said, determined.

Collin turned to look her in the face. "Oh, I'm not objecting. I wanted to ask if I could come too."

"Why?" she asked, genuinely puzzled.

"I'm tired of sitting on my hands."

"Aren't you a healer?"

"That's true, but that doesn't mean I don't know any other magic. It just means that my strongest magic is in the healing arts."

As she considered his offer, she looked over his shoulder to the southern sky. She saw a glow there; not the one she usually saw among the stars, but as if lightning were passing between clouds of a very distant thunderstorm. The sky above remained clear.

When she did not answer right away, he continued. "Look. I was left behind the last time because I wasn't a warrior, and I'm not going to be left again. If I wanted to just sit and do nothing, I would have gone to some other world when I left Wik." He indicated the stars. "Out there various colony ships have made identical copies of our homeworld. Tall spires. Anything you want at the touch of a button." He turned back to Gill. "Boring. I came here because this promised to be exciting. A new world. Another intelligent species. Stopping Mace from destroying another world. I was a part of all of it—until Mace decided to go to war against us. Then, all of a sudden, I was just here to treat the casualties." He turned to her again. "Don't mistake me—that was important and I was glad to do it. But I wanted to be part of the plan, too."

"You survived because you weren't," she pointed out.

"Very true. But if you win, the world will settle down again and I'll have missed my chance once more. If you lose, it won't matter anyway."

A rumble of thunder caught her attention. High in the sky, approaching the gates of the city, she saw a cloud bank. Lightning flashed from cloud to cloud. As she watched, the clouds began to thin, change shape. A form in outline became clear.

Collin turned and looked up. "Great Stellar Nebula! Not again!"

They heard a shout from the castle doors. "Get inside!" It was Eminric.

Gill took a step back, but made no other move as an image of Mace, tall as the clouds, loomed over the city. Eminric aimed his wand at the figure. A larger image of Eminric grew around his body and shot up to the clouds. Lightning flashed between the two ghostly figures. Mace's figure seemed to flinch, but held steady. The form of Mace hurled itself against the form of Eminric. Eminric screamed.

Gill did not remember that Silmariae was still strapped to her hip until that moment. Before she could think to use it, control it, do anything with it, her hand drew the sword without her conscious direction. It seemed to vanish as she extended it.

In the sword's place, another figure, glowing, but almost transparent, grew at Gill's feet. The form was a woman, but not Gill. It grew to the height of Mace's image, extending an arm to keep the adversary at length. Gently, she pulled the form of Eminric away from Mace. Once released, Eminric's giant image vanished. Eminric himself slumped to the pavement, his dropped wand clattering on the stones.

The woman's image remained strong. Gill felt something slam into that image, though her body did not sense an impact. The next blow landed harder; she felt the womanly image faltering; she braced her feet and leaned forward, putting her leg, back, and shoulder muscles into the effort. The force slammed into her again, and again, and yet again. The womanly image held fast. Gill felt no strain, no weariness, but still wondered how long she could hold out against this barrage, which caused the very stones under her feet to shudder.

Chapter 9

Once Gill felt the castle steps vibrate, she knew the city could be destroyed at any moment. She must act. She looked for the sword, but it was nowhere to be seen. Turning her face upward, she saw a star moving across the sky. She reached up, took it, and threw it toward Mace's figure. With a scream of pain and rage, the image of Mace dissolved.

At the same time, the womanly figure, whose hand she had used to grab the star, slowly faded. Silmariae gradually reappeared, Gill's fingers still around the hilt. The sword glowed fiercely; the castle courtyard was lit as if it were noon on a cloudless day. Gill sheathed the sword. Night fell again; she heard awed murmuring around her as her eyes adjusted. Turning, she saw Rowan standing one step behind her.

"I was afraid for a moment you might topple over, but you held on without any help," she said admiringly. "That was quite a spectacle!"

Gill smiled, feeling warmed by Rowan's attentiveness. She looked around for Eminric, and spotted him sitting with his back against the castle wall. Collin hovered over him. Allard, who held a box, stood nearby; Saris looked on with concern.

Gill walked over to the group. "Are you all right?" she asked Eminric, turning to Collin for confirmation before Eminric could reply.

Collin nodded. "He'll be fine. He took a shock, but I stabilized him."

Eminric stared up at Gill, wide-eyed. "Silmariae never did that before."

"That was Varantia," added Collin.

"Do you know how you did that?" Eminric asked.

"No; I just did as the sword directed me."

"Directed you?" Eminric asked. "You didn't call up that image?"

"No, I even forgot I had the sword with me."

Eminric exchanged a look with Rowan and Saris. Eminric said, "She let the sword control her. A novel idea."

Rowan shook her head in disbelief. "And here we always thought the keeper should control the sword at all times."

"Could that be what Mother did wrong?" Saris speculated.

"We learn by experience," Eminric said.

"Are you hurt?" Collin asked Gill.

"No."

"Tired?"

Gill shook her head.

Collin held out his hands. "Would you let me touch you?"

"Of course."

Collin placed his hands on Gill's arms, but drew back sharply with a startled gasp. He turned to Eminric. "She feels like Varantia; not human at all."

Gill lowered her eyebrows. How could that be? "*I* don't feel any different."

"But she *is* human, isn't she?" Rowan asked Collin.

"No question," Collin answered. He turned to Gill. "Did you feel another presence while you were using the sword?"

Gill considered. "I didn't sense any other thoughts or feelings, but there was a strange sort of...doubling, as if there were two of me, and we were helping each other."

"Something of Varantia was in you," Collin said. "I'm not sure what it was, but if it happens again, tell me."

"I think I can stand now," Eminric announced, holding up his hands. Collin and Rowan pulled him to his feet. Nodding his thanks, he asked Gill, "How did it feel to defend against Mace like that?"

Gill shrugged. "It was mostly like leaning hard against a door to keep someone outside from breaking in."

"I'd wager the sword fed her the energy," Rowan said. "It did that to Silmariae all the time. She had incredible stamina."

"How did you think of the orbital?" Collin asked.

"Orbital?" Gill asked.

"When we first came here," Eminric explained, "we left satellites in orbit. Somehow you brought one down and managed to aim an energy beam at Mace's fortress."

"I don't know...I just had the thought to use a star." She shrugged. "Maybe that was some part of Varantia guiding me."

"Possible," Collin said. "If you scored a direct hit, and I think you did, Mace won't be in any condition to attack Maclin again for some days while he's healing himself. That at least gives us a respite."

"Good," Eminric said, rubbing his neck.

Gill heard the sound of many voices and looked down to the streets. They were filled with people. A woman in an elegant dress walked slowly up the stairs toward her. When she reached the step below Gill, the woman knelt and looked up.

"I have been sent by a delegation of the leading women of the city. Will you take the crown?"

At first, Gill could only stare. "How could you offer it to me? You hardly know me."

She indicated the sword. "We heard that Silmariae had returned. The sword has never selected anyone who was hard of heart or mean of spirit. You just demonstrated you were willing to defend us, and that you had the strength to do so. There is no one else we would consider."

At her side, Allard opened the box he was holding and took out a crown. He gave it to the woman.

Gill looked from the woman to Allard. "I'd like to think about this, first."

Eminric stepped forward. "Let us have just a moment," he said kindly to the woman. He drew Gill away from the edge of the steps and gestured for Allard to join them.

Allard said, "She's right; as long as you're alive, they'll never consider anyone else for queen."

"But I'm going out to defeat Mace. I might not even be alive a month from now."

"It doesn't matter to them how long you wear the crown," Allard answered.

"Think of it this way," Eminric volunteered. "If you're queen, you can overrule Rowan in everything—win all the arguments." He smiled. "That's partly why Silmariae took the crown."

Allard put a hand on her arm. "It's not an easy step, I know. Not many feel adequate to the task. But there are advisors to help you, I can help you...you'll manage."

"It would be to your advantage in defeating Mace," Eminric added. "You would be in charge; you could ask for anything you need, anyone you need, and no one would refuse you."

Gill turned and gestured to Rowan. When she came over, Gill asked, "What do you think about this?"

"Accept the crown," Rowan said.

"Even though that means you'll be taking my orders?"

"How would this be different from when Silmariae was queen and I was taking hers? Besides," Rowan added with a wry grin, "if you don't accept, I may have to find another job."

Gill turned and gestured to Saris. When she arrived, Gill asked, "Do you think I ought to be queen?"

"Yes."

"But didn't you want the sword?"

Saris sighed and looked away for a moment. She turned back to Gill and said, "Yes. Because I had read the books, I thought no one could be more qualified than I...especially since it had been my mother's. But I saw what you just did, and you couldn't have done that if you weren't suited to the sword. I'm not sure that I could have done that; mother didn't, and until this night no one believed anyone could wield the sword better than she did. My mother said it's the sword that makes you queen. Now I know what she meant: the sword reads the heart and the mind and selects only the best."

"Did you want to be queen after your mother?"

Saris shook her head and smiled slightly. "I'll admit I've had fantasies about taking the sword ever since I was a child, but queen...no, I never expected to be queen...never wanted to be, to tell the truth."

Gill sighed and turned back to the crowd. She saw many expectant faces illuminated by the streetlights. The woman who held the crown turned to her with a look of compassion and confidence. In that moment it seemed to Gill as if it would be unforgivably petty to refuse and walk away. "What do I do?" she said to Allard.

Allard smiled and nodded toward the assembly. "They can appoint you queen right now by acclamation. All they have to do is put the crown on your head, and then I administer an oath in which you pledge to protect the kingdom and respect the rights of its people. If I may give you some advice...we have a tradition that you can change your name when you take the crown. I'd say take the crown as Queen Silmariae. They're going to call you that anyway, as long as you have the sword."

And so it was done. The people cheered her for a long time. She waved and smiled, not wishing to appear ungrateful despite her lingering doubts. Still, the confidence and encouragement they imparted was invigorating. As the event sank in, she realized that all along, she had thought no farther than taking the sword and going north, as the instructions had said. Even after arriving here, a part of her still held out the possibility that someone else, the Wye perhaps, would take primary responsibility for defeating Mace, and she would go back to Somerlie and live out a quiet life. But in accepting the crown, she had taken an irrevocable step. The responsibility was hers, and hers alone, to defeat Mace, and the responsibility toward her people was hers until death. That realization set in her the determination that whatever sacrifice was required of her, whatever strength it took from her, that she would succeed.

The next morning, someone brought breakfast to her room. After eating, she put on one of the dresses that Rowan had brought the day before. She reached for the sword, paused, and drew back her hand when she realized the sword had initiated the action. Smiling, she again extended her hand, took the sword, and strapped it on of her own volition. She went first to Allard's audience chamber, but no one was there, so she headed for the castle entrance. On the ground floor, she heard Eminric's voice and turned toward that room.

Inside, she saw a table stacked with supplies. Eminric and Leni packed the items in sturdy cloth bags as Allard looked on. Gill wondered when Leni had returned to Maclin from Eldswold; she had not remembered seeing him the day before.

Allard took a step toward the Wye. "I'm sorry to see you go, Eminric. I would prefer to have you here in case Mace attacks again."

"You saw how effective I was against him," Eminric answered. He shrugged a shoulder in Gill's direction as she crossed the floor to the table. "It is the duty of your queen to protect Asquith now; or, if need be, you can send to Eldswold for more aid."

"You're leaving?" Gill asked, astonished.

"Yes," Eminric said. "Somerlie is much nearer to Mace than Asquith is. He might put it into his mind to savage that realm. I may not be able to protect Arcacia as you did Maclin, but without me, they have no means of resisting him whatsoever."

"And I'll help!" added Leni brightly.

Collin came into the room, went to Leni, and embraced him in a hug. "How are you today, Leni?"

When Collin released him, Leni answered, "Fine. I saw Eldswold. Everything's fine there. The houses are set up again. But there's nothing for me to do. They said I was in the way. So I came here to see if I could help. I saw Mace last night."

"We all did, Leni," Collin said warmly.

"Eminric said I could come with him." Leni smiled.

Gill realized that although Collin was the youngest of the Wye in the room, Leni was the one with the mind of a child.

"I could use the company," Eminric confirmed.

"Listen," Gill said. "If you're going to Somerlie, you might as well stay in Alia's house. My grandmother has a key. I'll write a note and she'll give it to you."

Eminric paused in his packing. "That would be helpful. Thank you."

Allard gestured to a small knot of young men and women at the other door to the room. One rushed away for an instant, and came back with pen and paper, laying them on the table. Gill picked up the pen, wondering where the jar of ink was.

"The ink's in it," Eminric said. "Just write."

Slowly at first, Gill wrote a note to her grandmother, implying, but not stating, that she was in the south, and that she wanted Eminric to look after the house in her absence. She gave it to him, finding the ink already dry. He placed it in one of his packs.

"One thing I need to warn you about," Gill added. "Telford, the ice man, is an agent of Mace."

"I know," Eminric said soberly as he took some of the packs. Leni lifted some of the others; the pages by the door came to help with the remainder. Gill, Collin, and Allard followed them out and stood at the top of the stairs as the two Wye walked to the street and loaded a wagon drawn by a greathorse.

As they waved goodbye and drove away, Gill turned to Collin. "What's wrong with Leni?"

"Oh," Collin said. "He was one of those who went mad on the journey here. The flight took years, and not everyone can adapt to such an enclosed space for that length of time."

"Is he dangerous?"

Collin shook his head. "Not any more than you or I, and probably less so. But he has a diminished mental and magical capacity. He's also never made a magical artifact to enhance his powers." He turned to Gill. "If I'm going with you, I'd better start getting my things together."

Gill nodded. Collin walked away in the direction of what Silmariae's memory knew to be a side entrance. Gill turned back to the main entrance and found Rowan standing there.

"And how may I aid you today, majesty?" Rowan asked eagerly.

Gill shook her head slightly. "You needn't be so formal; I strongly sense that you weren't when with Silmariae." When Rowan grinned, she added, "I have to sit somewhere and think of how I'm going to defeat Mace."

"You don't have to think of that at all," Rowan said.

"Don't start."

Rowan sighed. "All right. The queen has an audience room. Silmariae used it all the time. It has a large bay window and a view of the city. It still has a lot of Silmariae's things in it. You might find some of them useful."

The audience room had a large central upholstered chair, as well as several smaller chairs and tables. Gill also saw a desk and shelves full of books. "Is there a map?" she asked.

Rowan went to the shelves and brought out an enormous book. One of the pages lingering in the hallway pushed a table next to the upholstered chair. Gill sat while Rowan placed the book on the table and opened it.

"Ah," said Gill, pointing. "Here's Maclin, and here's Mace."

"I take for granted we can get there," Rowan observed.

Gill looked up at her. "Are you always this helpful?"

"In making 'plans,' yes," she said unapologetically.

Gill sighed and turned back to the map.

An afternoon of thought did not bring Gill any nearer to a strategy for them to follow. Rowan maintained they did not need a plan, and was no help. Gill wished she had Eminric to consult, though Rowan did not think that he would be of any help if he were there, either. Gill asked if other Wye might be summoned to help, and was told that it would be unlikely for her to get a volunteer besides Collin. The Wye remaining at Eldswold were architects, builders, planners, artists, farmers, breeders of animals...no warriors. The entire Wye army, except Eminric, had been killed by Mace in the earlier conflict.

That evening, when she was in bed, asleep, a knock on the door awakened her. She reached for Silmariae on her own, grabbed the sword by the scabbard, and crept to the door. "Who is it?" she asked at the crack.

"It's Bryce. May I speak to you, majesty?"

Gill opened the door. Bryce stood there, wearing a lightweight robe belted around the waist.

"My bed is whispering to me," he said, somewhat apologetically.

"Uh...wouldn't Saris or Collin be better at helping you?"

He glanced sideways for an instant, as if thinking, and said, "You know, I guess you're right. For some odd reason, I thought of you first. Sorry to disturb you." He started back down the hall.

Gill leaned around the doorframe. "Wait. If there's magic at work, and it suggested that you come for me, maybe I'd better come. We can always send for Saris or Collin later."

She grabbed a surcoat and put it on over her nightgown. She took Silmariae, too. He led her to his room, which, though ample, was smaller than hers, and brightly illuminated by the ceiling. He had thrown back the covers; she could see the wrinkles where he had lain.

"Where did the sound come from?" she asked.

"I'm not sure. At first it sounded as if it came from the headboard, but when I sat up it sounded as if it came from under the bed. Then when I stood, it sounded as if it were inside the mattress."

She bent and put her hand on the mattress. "Did the bed make any threatening moves?" She hoped she did not sound ridiculous asking that.

"No," he answered seriously.

Gill straightened. The sword was quiet in her free hand, too, which she hoped was a favorable sign. "Good. But stand guard, just in case."

"At your service, majesty." When Gill continued to examine the bedding, he added, "You can get into the bed if you wish, majesty. There's nothing to worry about; I'm a lover of men."

She lay on the floor and slid under the bed. "I'm not worried about my reputation. I just feel awkward climbing onto other people's beds, no matter who their lovers are." She reached for Silmariae, unsheathed it, and used it as a lamp to check the bed supports.

"Fair enough, majesty."

She slid out again and sat up. "Nothing underneath."

"Yes, majesty."

She stood. "Do you have to call me that even when no one else is around?"

"Uh, no...."

Taking Silmariae by the hilt, she pointed it at the bed and slowly moved it back and forth. She felt a slight tug toward the headboard, so she brought the sword nearer. It aggressively sought one of the bedposts. All four were thick and rectangular; Silmariae's point slipped into a crack and Gill heard a click. Sheathing the sword, she ran her hand over the crack.

"Seems as if your first guess was right, Bryce. Is the bed an heirloom of your family?"

"Since you mention it, yes."

She found an opening and pulled back a door. It looked as if a box had been built into the bedpost. Inside the box was a glowing globe.

He bent down next to her. "What is it?"

"I was hoping you could tell me. Any missing family heirlooms you know of?"

"No."

Gill took the globe out. "This looks like Sloan's globe, so it could be Nils, or another of Von's missing globes."

"How can we be sure?"

"I don't know. Do you know where Collin's room is? We could ask him."

He led the way to a door. A light could be seen under it.

"He may still be awake," Bryce said.

"How can you tell? He glows in the dark."

The door opened. "I'm awake," Collin said. He had on the same clothes he had worn earlier in the evening.

"Good." She held up the globe. "We have something to show you."

Collin ushered them to a small table. Each of them took a chair around it; Gill set the globe in the middle. "Could this be Nils?"

"Can I pick it up?" Collin asked.

"Please," Bryce said.

Collin examined it closely for some time, turning it. He set it back on the table.

"Well?" Gill asked.

"I haven't any idea."

"You're a great help. I thought you said you knew magic beyond the healing arts."

He smiled. "Then I'll be happy to explain. Each of us has a general magical ability, and a unique magical ability. General magic is common to all of us; most of us can do the same things. In addition to that, we each have a magical ability that no one else can duplicate. Mine is in healing—over and above the general magical abilities to heal. Von's globes were his, and neither I nor Eminric nor anyone else could tell you exactly how they work."

Gill picked up the globe. "Thanks," she said sarcastically.

Collin was unflustered. "Anytime. Are you thinking of taking in the memories?" he asked Bryce.

"I don't know."

"Well, there could be a danger."

Gill frowned. Danger? Was there something the books had not told her?

Bryce leaned toward Collin as well, an intent expression on his face.

"Von was what you humans call a 'hoarder.'"

Gill rolled her eyes and moaned.

"I'm serious. He collected everything. You could hardly walk through his rooms, there was such a mess."

Bryce looked puzzled, but Gill broke in. "He's teasing you, Bryce. I took on Sloan, and I've developed no such urges."

Bryce let out a breath.

Collin chuckled. "I suppose that's why he gave Von only his memories, and not his personality."

Gill stood and tugged at Bryce's arm. They walked out of the room.

"I'd be happy to be of more help anytime," he called after them.

Gill paused and turned back. Two could play at this needling game. "You know, if you're a healer, I'd hate to be under your care, with your sense of humor."

Collin smiled. "You should see me around someone who's ill or injured. I'm positively grim."

Gill threw him a skeptical look and followed Bryce.

The next day, Gill, Bryce, and Saris sat in the audience room around a table.

Saris held the globe in her hands and turned it over. "I think Collin was right. We really can't tell what this is. It resembles pictures of Von's globes that Wye have given me, but there's no way to know for certain unless we try it." She put it down. "Even if it is one of Von's globes, we can't tell if it's Rhys, Frank, Edgar, or Nils."

"Does it make a difference?" Gill asked.

Saris shook her head. "I don't think so. Von made duplicates in case one or more were lost, so I presume they're much the same. He named them after human friends knowing that if he died, they would have to be given to humans. Other Wye couldn't use his unique magical creations."

Bryce fingered the globe gingerly and looked up at Gill. "But you think it's Nils."

Gill nodded. "I think it's Nils." She spread her hands. "Just a feeling. I can't define it."

"Maybe the sword is suggesting the identity to you," Saris said.

"That's always possible," Gill said.

"Why would it start whispering to me now? I've had the bed since I was a child, and others of my family before me."

"I don't know," Saris answered. "Maybe all that magical activity the night before it awakened. These magical artifacts seem to lie dormant unless they're needed, and then they seem to draw attention to themselves."

He blew out a breath and sat back in the chair. "I was thinking of asking to go with you to defeat Mace. I was a bodyguard in my younger days, and I think I'm still a fair strategist, if not a fair fighter. I hadn't been active for years before the war with Mace; they said I was too out of practice to go with the human division of the army. But maybe I'd be more valuable if I took on Nils, here."

"I'm not sure how to advise you," Gill said. "It's quite a sacrifice. Eminric said that I should have been able to control Sloan after the first couple of hours, but it was days before I had any control at all. You won't be able to feel emotion, which is both an advantage and a disadvantage."

"But the purpose is to be a spy, yes? I could walk into Mace's fortress and be welcome."

Gill remembered that Mace had been hoping Nils would come back. "Without a doubt."

Rowan walked into the room. "What's that?" she asked curiously.

"We think it's Nils," said Gill and Bryce at the same time.

Rowan took a chair and joined them at the table.

Gill looked over the globe again. "What it does to Bryce depends on whose memories are stored there."

"Von's, assuredly," Saris said. "But it may have no other memories. Sloan's is the only one we know has been used before. Maybe the others were hidden and never used."

As they talked, Bryce picked up the globe and put it in his lap. "You know, I feel drawn to it," he mused. "I'm tempted to open it up."

Gill and Saris quickly reached over the table and put their hands on the globe. "Not right now," Gill insisted.

Bryce nodded and placed the globe back on the table. Gill and Saris slowly resumed their seats. "I think it will be safe enough," he added.

"I suppose if it's calling you, that could be a good sign," Gill said.

"Generally, it is," Saris suggested.

"You said I would be controlling it?" he asked.

"You would," Saris assured him.

"That's what Eminric said," Gill answered. "But as I said, that wasn't my experience. On the other hand, he said it wouldn't do anything that you wouldn't want to do, and that *was* my experience."

They sat staring at it for some minutes more. Bryce put a hand under his beardless chin, stroking it thoughtfully. At last, he said, "My best advice as a strategist, majesty?"

"By all means."

"I take on Nils today and head toward Mace's as soon as I'm supplied. You follow at a slower pace. I spy out his fortress, then meet you at a designated spot outside. I should be able to tell you what he's doing so that you have the information on how to confront him."

Gill reached out and put a hand over his, overjoyed, at last, to have a plan to follow. "When can you start?"

Chapter 10

Bryce asked to be alone when he opened the globe. Gill granted the request but stood outside his door with Rowan and Collin and Saris. After an hour of listening to movements inside, wondering what might be happening, the four of them watched in anticipation as the door opened.

Bryce stood in the doorway. He had changed from his usual outfit to sturdy traveling clothes. He still had straight, short blond hair, but Gill thought his face had changed—slightly altered.

"Bryce?" Collin asked.

He turned to Collin but did not answer.

"Nils?" Gill ventured.

"Yes," Bryce said plainly. The voice was different, too.

"Looks like a cross between Von and Bryce," Collin said to the others.

For Gill, with the echoes of Sloan's memories still in her mind, seeing Nils was like meeting an old friend again after many years. It occurred to her that Mace probably had felt the same upon seeing Sloan. "Come with me," Gill said to Nils. "I need to show you something."

"Will it take long? I need to be going," Nils answered.

"Not long." Gill gestured to one of the pages. Silmariae's memory provided the correct phrasing. "See if it is convenient for King Allard to join us in the audience room."

Once inside the audience room, Gill pulled out the map book and spread it out. As she was doing so, Allard entered. "You asked for me?"

Gill motioned him over. "Yes, there's something I need to show you." She nodded to Bryce. "By the way, Bryce is Nils now."

Allard looked over to Bryce. "So you found Nils."

"Bryce did, anyway. It was a family heirloom unknown to him before last night." Gill leaned over the map. "I want you all to see the ring of Tashtalon." She put a finger on the map and traced it out. "For a human to cross the ring in either direction is death. I have a charm that protects me, but I wouldn't recommend any other human cross this." She turned to Allard. "You'll have to warn anyone who goes outside the city about this."

Allard nodded. "We may send to Eldswold to see if someone can make a charm for us."

"Maybe Mace isn't strong enough to maintain the ring now," Collin said.

"I wouldn't count on it," Gill said. She looked up to Nils. "This means you need to get to Mace's fortress without crossing the ring."

Collin traced a line on the map. "There's a road that goes to Mace's without going near the ring." He looked up. "But who knows what shape it's in after five hundred years?"

"I can manage," Nils said.

"Do you need help packing?" Gill asked.

"No; I know what I need and where to get it."

"I'll go with you," Collin said. "I need some items from the storage rooms myself."

"Wait a minute; you mean he's coming with us?" asked Rowan of Gill.

"Yes," Gill said. She met Rowan's eye to communicate that the decision had been made and that there was to be no argument.

Rowan shrugged. "Then as long as we're raiding the supply rooms, I should go along and get what I need, too."

The three of them left the room, but Collin and Rowan stopped when Saris announced, "I'm coming too."

Gill took a breath.

Saris drew herself up to her full height. "I know what you're going to say; I heard it all from my mother before she left."

"Did you hear your mother say that Mace tortures those he captures?" Rowan said.

"Yes, I heard," Saris said firmly.

Gill waved a hand. "The question, Saris, is not whether you have the courage to go. It's a question of putting the minimal number of people in harm's way, no matter what their talents are. I had originally thought of going alone, to tell you the truth."

"You can't go alone," Allard said. "We have the sword now only because Estes was there to retrieve it when Silmariae died. But I agree that you can take only a very few. We made the mistake of insisting on sending Silmariae out with a queen's escort. Mace's forces spotted them easily, long before they reached his fortress. Most of those in the queen's escort were slaughtered, as Rowan can tell you; she was one of the few who survived. Only Silmariae and two of her daughters were able to go on."

"That's precisely why Saris should stay here," Rowan said. "She doesn't have the skills to survive out in the wild by herself, especially if she's injured on the way."

"Oh, stop!" Saris answered. "I've heard this all my life and I'm sick of it." She waved her arm in an arc. "You and almost everyone in this city seem to think that if you're not a warrior, you're worthless. You can't handle a sword, you can't do anything. That's nonsense! All of you made Collin and me stay here because you simply *presumed*," here she waved both arms, "that we'd be a drag on all you sturdy warriors. But you never gave us a chance to try."

"That's because we couldn't afford to fail," Rowan countered.

"But you did anyway, didn't you? Maybe you wouldn't have if Collin and I had been along."

Rowan opened her mouth to answer, but Allard said quietly, "She has a point."

Rowan's mouth dropped open; she shut it again. "You can't be serious."

"I'm quite serious," Allard said. "Saris is right; we tried defeating Mace by force before and we lost. Perhaps it is time to use our heads, instead. There is no one on this planet more knowledgeable in the ways of magic than Saris; her advice could make the difference between success and failure."

Gill turned to Saris. She looked her in the eye; Saris did not waver. "Two conditions. First: the books stay here. We can't have Mace getting them."

Collin and Saris exchanged a glance. "They can't be taken out of the castle," Collin said.

"There's an anchor spell on them; I couldn't remove them if I tried," Saris explained.

"Second: you have to take orders from me."

Saris held her head up proudly. "I'm the daughter of a queen. I can do what I'm told."

"In that case, you're coming." Gill nodded toward the door. "Go get what you need."

"Gill!" Rowan protested.

Gill turned to her with a fixed stare. "I'm the queen; I just gave an order. You get to hear and obey."

Allard put a hand to his face to hide a smile.

Rowan bowed slightly. "May I ask her majesty the reason for her decision?" There was mild sarcasm in Rowan's voice.

"Yes. I've thought for some time that we *might* need Saris for her knowledge of magical techniques. Allard has convinced me that we *do*."

Saris's face broke out in a wide smile.

"You're all dismissed," Gill said casually. She shooed them toward the door. "Go."

Allard cleared his throat. "Perhaps, since her majesty is going, Saris could show her the storerooms so she can get what she needs, too."

Gill nodded. "Good idea." She walked past Saris, Rowan, and Collin, then turned back when she realized they were not following. "Are we going or aren't we?"

The basement had a number of storerooms. Rowan disappeared into one; Collin disappeared into another; Saris guided Gill to still others. Once inside, Saris pulled things that Gill could not identify off walls and shelves, and which Silmariae's memory gave her only vague recognition of. She pushed some items into Gill's arms, insisting Gill would need them; since they were small and few in number, Gill accepted them.

When she was back in her own room, pulling out her saddlebags and packing them, she heard a knock and turned. Nils stood in the open doorway.

"I thought I should tell you before I go that I have gained control of Nils," Bryce said.

Gill stopped her packing and sat in a chair. She nodded.

"It's very strange," Bryce went on. "I feel as if I'm living in the back of my mind instead of at the front, but that the front is empty."

Gill smiled. "I know."

"The first time you saw me in the room with the map, Nils was entirely in control. I couldn't move a finger."

Gill took a breath. "You're doing better than I did."

"I hope I don't slip up. You seemed to have given Sloan control all the time. I'm thinking I'd better let Nils do the traveling and the talking with Mace."

"That would be a good idea." A thought occurred to Gill, and she added, "You ought to know that at the time I left Mace, his slaves were angry at me because Mace considered me a favorite. You could be in danger there, even more quickly than I was."

"I can handle the situation." When Gill nodded in reply, Bryce added, "Nils said that."

She smiled. "Strangely enough, I could tell."

"I hope Mace can't."

"He won't," Nils and Gill said at the same time.

Bryce put a hand to his mouth. "I suppose I'd better stop arguing with myself and go."

"May luck go with you," Gill said.

"Wait at the Clearwater Pond for me. You saw it on the map."

"We'll be there."

When Gill had finished packing, she went to see how the others were doing. Collin's door was open, so she strolled in. She did not recognize any of the paraphernalia that he had scattered on his bed, dressers, tables, chairs, and even the floor.

He looked up when she crossed the threshold. Seeing her expression, he remarked, "I'm not like your ancestors, who crossed light years of space so they could seek a simpler life and recreate what they called 'the good old days.' If I'm leaving home, I'm bringing the comforts of home with me."

A shiny cylinder with handholds and levers, resting on a table, caught her eye. "What's this?"

He walked over and touched the indicators. "This is an energy weapon. This is the safety, which is on, and prevents the weapon from being discharged accidentally. This setting, the lowest, is for stunning one person; the next one is for stunning a group of people; the next one will kill a person; the next will kill a group of people; the next will bore a hole through a wall of stone; the highest setting will dissolve a stone wall."

"Great Tashtalon's knees!" she exclaimed. "Why didn't you just take several of these weapons over to Mace's fortress and use those on him!"

He turned to her and said calmly, "We tried that." At her puzzled expression, he added, "The war with Mace would have been over long ago if it were simply a matter of who had the most powerful weapons. The reason Mace is so difficult to defeat is that he has powerful and intricate magic. That's why we need Silmariae to defeat him."

"Then why bring this, if it's useless?"

"It might not be. I may have to blast through a wall so that you can get to Mace."

Rowan came in, scanning all the artifacts. She turned to Gill. "Oh, here you are."

"My bodyguard doesn't need to be with me all the time, does she?" Gill teased.

"No, I came to talk about Saris."

Gill resumed examining Collin's implements. "She's going."

"Very well, she's going. Can I say my piece anyway?"

Gill turned back to her. "Certainly. I took an oath to uphold freedom of speech."

Rowan inclined her head. "Thanks," she said dryly.

"What's the objection, then? I'm curious now."

Rowan put her hands on her hips and took a deep breath. "She's 19 years old! She hardly knows what Mace is, except as some vague malevolent force. The first time she comes across the ugly reality, she'll freeze, or panic, or fall to the ground retching. Then one of the rest of us will have to be occupied with helping her, rather than helping you."

"You think so?" Collin said.

She turned to him. "Yes, I think so. I've known her all her life."

"So have I. She never struck me as the panicking sort."

"She's no different than anyone else her age, and believe me, I've seen plenty of youngsters her age fall apart at less."

"I never found her to be typical of her age. She's solid and dependable, and has a lot of energy. Those may be qualities we need."

"I'm not saying that she doesn't have character; I'm saying that she's not mature enough for a task like this."

"She's Silmariae's daughter," Collin said, "and has Silmariae's sense of duty. I think if she were tempted to panic, that sense of duty would override any other instinct."

Rowan sighed.

"Think of it this way," Gill said. "I'm going, and she's only four years younger than I am...."

"Minus some five centuries," Collin murmured.

"That four years makes a lot of difference at your age, Gill. Besides, you have Silmariae's memories, and the experience from Von."

"But I would never have gotten those in the first place if I hadn't been responsible already. I'm not sure four years in my case would have made that much of a difference."

"Silmariae didn't take her," Rowan insisted.

"I'm not Silmariae."

"You'll get no argument from me on that." She shook her head and left.

The next morning, before the city was fully awake, Gill, Rowan, Collin, and Saris gathered at the stables to start their journey. Gill saddled Kiri; the others also loaded their packs on greathorses. Except for the stable grooms, only Allard was there to see them off.

Gill noticed that all of her fellow travelers wore sensible clothes: shirts, pants, boots. The women's clothes were muted tones of black, gray, brown, or blue. Collin, however, wore yellow and green. Rowan, as usual, let her thick arms go bare, though she had riding gloves, and a vest of the same lightweight Wye armor that Gill had. Gill also had taken the necklace allowing her to cross the ring of Tashtalon. Even though their route did not take them though it, she felt it better to be prepared for anything.

When they were mounted and ready to go, Allard called out, "Use your caution, as well as your courage."

Saris bent down and handed him a tiny box. "You can find out how we are at any time."

Allard held it in his hand as if loath to touch it and quickly deposited it in a pocket. "I don't think it's wise for us to call you."

"What's that?" Gill asked.

"A way to talk over long distances," Saris explained.

Rowan rolled her eyes. "Do we really need those?"

"You don't have to have one if you don't want one," Saris said.

"I don't," Rowan confirmed.

"I have one," Collin said.

"I gave Gill one, too," Saris said.

"You'll have to show me how to use it," Gill said.

"We will. It will give us something to do on the journey," Saris said.

"All right." Gill looked around. "Let's go then." She led the way through mostly empty city streets. As they came to the city gate, now cleared of vegetation, it opened for them of itself, and then closed behind.

"Magic?" Gill asked.

"Electric eye," Saris answered.

Gill did not bother to ask.

The road Collin had pointed out ran westward from the city gate. Collin cleared the heavy undergrowth in front of them by magic as they rode. By midday, they reached the River Silver. A stone bridge spanned the water; Saris dismounted, inspected it, and pronounced it sound. On the other side, the overgrowth was normal; Collin barely had to use his magic to brush it away.

"Eminric outdid himself in hiding the city behind such thick vegetation," Collin remarked.

When dusk came, Collin cleared an area by the side of the road. They had made stops during the day to eat, or to take care of physical needs—Saris had brought a box which somehow processed and disposed of the waste matter. Now Collin and Saris went about setting up a camp. Each of them removed material from a small cylinder and shook it out as if it were a blanket. Suddenly, tents took shape. Collin and Saris secured them to the ground.

Rowan sighed and shook her head. "Not for me," she said, removing a bedroll from her saddle.

"Suit yourself," Saris answered. "I gave you a tent, too," she said to Gill. At Gill's puzzled expression, Saris found and removed a cylinder from her saddlebags, and set it up as she had set up her own.

Meanwhile, Collin searched through his bags, bringing out various gadgets. "A hot meal tonight," he said.

"I could just make a fire," Rowan volunteered, straightening out her bedroll and setting up her camp.

"That might draw undue attention," Collin said. "My body can provide enough light for us."

"And that *won't* draw undue attention?" Rowan snorted.

"My tent was made for Wye. When I crawl into it to sleep, I won't be visible to outside eyes," Collin answered tolerantly.

While Gill watched, Rowan took out a knife and peeled some fruit. Saris and Collin sat in low canvas chairs and set up their gadgets. They cooked a tasty meal of noodles, vegetables, and meat, which they shared with Rowan and Gill. The cleanup, too, took minutes.

As Rowan and Saris bent to pick up scraps, Gill eyed them curiously. "Did you two do something different to yourselves? You didn't find another globe, did you?"

The two women exchanged glances with Collin. Rowan shrugged. "I asked Collin to reduce my breasts, close my birth canal, and stop my monthly flow for now in case we were captured. It's done sometimes before going out to fight."

"I would have recommended it for you except for Silmariae," Saris added. "The sword wouldn't let Mother handle it when she was altered by Sloan."

"I know; I was simply curious."

Rowan said goodnight and crawled into her bedroll. Saris and Collin crawled into their tents; Gill imitated them. She found a padded floor inside, and shiny blankets which were thin but warm. She snuggled into them and fell asleep quickly.

The next morning, eating breakfast and breaking camp, again, were accomplished quickly and neatly. "Sleep well?" Collin asked Rowan as his tent flattened and rolled up by itself.

"Extremely well, thank you," Rowan said with a triumphant grin.

They had not ridden far when the greathorses suddenly balked at going any farther.

"What is it?" Rowan asked.

"Some magic; let me check." Collin dismounted and walked ahead. Abruptly, he drew back as if he had bumped into a wall.

"Are you all right?" Gill called.

"Unharmed—but I think there's a barrier here." He tentatively reached out a hand, and "felt" along air for several paces in each direction.

"Can we get across?" Saris asked.

"It's going to take some energy to get through. This could be a trap set by Mace for us, or simply a general precaution."

"Nils obviously got through," Saris said.

"Or passed by before Mace set it up." Collin walked back to his horse but did not climb into the saddle.

"Let's see." Saris took out a box and spoke into it. "Bryce."

"That's not going to give him away, is it?" Rowan asked.

Saris shook her head. "He can't be inside Mace's fortress yet, even if he rode at a greathorse's pace since he left the castle. If he is in any danger, though, he'll put the silencer on. The transmitter will simply vibrate and he won't have to answer it."

Saris had barely finished speaking when Bryce's voice came out of the box. "Who's calling?"

Saris spoke into the box again. "Saris. Can you talk?"

"Yes. Is there a problem?"

"We've run into a barrier. Did you run into any?"

"No, but then again, Nils spent his first few minutes taking various charms out of hidden spaces in the bed frame, so I may have been protected."

"All right. We'll see what we can do here."

"Don't call back anytime soon. I can see the fortress spires in the distance."

"Understood." Saris pressed a button on the box and put it away.

Gill swung a leg across her saddle. "Shall I see what Silmariae can do?"

"I can probably disperse it, for that matter," Collin said. "The question is, if we tamper with the barrier, will that make Mace aware of us and bring on an attack?"

"Why not just see if we can go around it?" Rowan suggested. "The worst that will happen is that we'll find we'll have to try something else."

Collin felt his way westward for some paces, then found he was turning northwards, the way they came. "That's no good."

"Let me try eastward, then," Gill said. She swung her leg back and urged Kiri in that direction. Every so often she would try to turn Kiri south, but the horse would resist, and she would go on. Soon, she saw the River Silver ahead, and then, a body on the forest floor. She turned abruptly and screamed, "Stop!"

"What?" Collin asked, urging his horse forward.

Gill held out an arm to Rowan and Saris. "Don't move forward another step."

"Why?" Rowan asked, after she and Saris had reined in their horses.

Collin looked down. "These are old remains. They can't have been killed by this barrier."

"This is the edge of the ring of Tashtalon. Rowan and Saris could be killed."

"They could?" He patted his greathorse and slowly rode forward, until they were in a field of remains. The greathorse whinnied softly. He looked up. "It's true; this is quite deadly. An impressive work of magic."

"I'm impressed," Rowan said dryly.

Collin turned to her. "I didn't say I approved. But it does show how strong Mace's magic is."

"What do we do now?" Saris asked.

"Let's see if I can get through the barrier first." Collin turned his horse, waded into the river, and rode southward. "This works."

"Then I can ride through the barrier," Gill said. "Once I'm past that and the ring of Tashtalon, Collin can bring back the charm to Saris, she can come around...."

"I follow," Rowan said. "Let's get started."

When Gill was on the other side of the barrier, and back on the road, she removed the necklace and gave it to Collin. He brought it to Saris. Gill noted she stiffened and looked straight ahead to avoid glimpsing all the bodies. "Are you all right?" she asked as Saris drew even with her and gave up the charm to Collin.

Saris nodded and swallowed. "I just haven't seen that much death before. I mean, when my grandmother died, I saw her body laid out, but that wasn't anything like this."

They sat quietly as Collin and Rowan approached. Rowan took off the charm and passed it to Gill, but spoke to Saris. "Maybe now you can forgive your mother for not bringing you," she said sharply.

Saris bowed her head. Collin reached over and patted her on the back.

"You know," Rowan said, "we can still send you back across the barrier and you can ride home if you want. Because you're going to see a lot worse than this before we're done, and we can't have you coming apart on us."

"I think she did rather well," Collin said.

Saris took a deep breath and lifted her chin. "I'm coming with you, whatever happens."

Rowan turned to Gill.

"Let's go," she said simply, and urged Kiri forward.

Chapter 11

They arrived at Clearwater Pond in the late afternoon. The water lived up to its name—Gill could see all the way to the bottom. Collin again cleared a space for a camp and set minor magical barriers to keep out insects and small animals. Although the water appeared wholesome enough, Saris insisted on straining the drinking water through a filter pot.

Gill knew how far they were from Mace's fortress based on the map, but still she looked for landmarks. The ash hills were not yet visible above the treetops. The trees here were spaced several paces apart; the grasses barely reached to the tops of her boots. Forest flowers sprouted here and there, birds and fluttering insects flew from tree to tree. Rowan tied the greathorses within reach of water.

Instead of a campfire, their tents were centered around a nest of gadgets and devices that Saris and Collin set up. When it came time to eat dinner, Rowan sat on the ground on one side of the nest, supported by her rolled-up bed; Saris, Collin, and Gill sat on the other side in their foldable canvas chairs.

After sunset, when Collin's glow became noticeable, he put on gloves, a thick cloak, and a hat with a veil resembling a beekeeper's. They sat back after Saris cleaned up the supper debris. She had no sooner resumed her seat when Gill heard a beep.

Saris pulled her small palm-sized box out of a shirt pocket and spoke into it. "Saris. Go ahead."

"This is Bryce."

Gill and Collin moved their chairs next to Saris; the three huddled together while Rowan looked on.

"Are you sure you won't be interrupted?" Collin asked.

"Positive. Mace has gone to his magic laboratory, and gave orders that I was not to be disturbed, so I could sleep well. No one is even to go into the hallway outside my room. In fact, everyone around here is all but kissing my feet."

"You're getting a better reception than I did," Gill said.

"I would say things are a lot different now than when you were here, majesty. Mace is terrifying. If it weren't for Nils, I would have bolted from the fortress, screaming, soon after I arrived."

"I thought everyone was kissing your feet," Collin teased.

"They are. Mace embraced me like a long-lost cousin come back from the wilderness. He wept on my shoulder, which I found unexpected, though Nils took it in stride."

"Any chance you can put a knife through his ribs if he does it again?" Rowan asked.

"No chance at all. One of the captives here snapped and tried to stab him with a knife. The knife dissolved into dust and so did the man. The malice, the power, coming from him is intense. You can feel the fear from the captives. They seem glad I'm here because when I'm around, they're out from under his gaze."

"I'm not surprised," Gill replied.

"Mace himself is raving," Bryce continued. "He goes on and on about the injustice of the Wye; how all they had to do was leave him alone, and why do they keep bothering him. How the humans are such ingrates because he gives care and food to these puny short-lived creatures and all they want to do is destroy him. Most of all, he goes on about how women want to get him under their control and he wishes he could wipe them from the face of the planet."

"How much of an effect did the encounter with Varantia have?" Collin asked.

"It seriously wounded him," Bryce answered. "Even with all the magical protection about him, her majesty scored a direct hit with the energy beam from the orbital. It sapped his strength. I gather he tried to attack both Eldswold and Arcacia later anyway, and was repulsed at both sites. He's recovering quickly, though."

"So Eminric was right," Collin said.

"He knows that Silmariae is coming to him, and that someone's out to kill him. But he's confident that he'll destroy the sword this time."

"What's he planning to do?" Gill asked.

"He hasn't told me his plans, but he did tell me Silmariae's mistake: she used it as a sword."

"What do you mean, that was a mistake?" Rowan asked. "It *is* a sword. What does he think it is, a rock?"

"That's what we humans think of it," Bryce explained. "It's a magical artifact, shaped like a sword. Yes, it has a blade and can be used as a sword, but that's unrelated to its magical abilities. I remember Silmariae saying that she worked hard to control the sword and be the best swordfighter she could. But that's the wrong approach. It's not that sword won't let you use other swords when it's around because it's *jealous*--it won't let you use any other swords because they're a distraction to its real use."

"Which is?" Rowan asked.

"I'm not sure. But trying to cut off Mace's head isn't going to work. That's what Silmariae tried. Mace is most uncomfortable with the appearance of Varantia. That surprised him. That's supposed to mean something, though I don't know what, and shows that her majesty is on the right track, but Mace hopes Varantia's earlier appearance was a lucky chance. He thinks her majesty is going to come storming in here, sword in hand, to try to cut off his head, and so he's rid of her, too. This time, he says, he's going to make sure that even if he's weakened by the sword, which Silmariae did do, temporarily, no one else will be able to take advantage of that to retrieve the sword and hide it from him again."

"Anything else you can tell us that might help?" Gill asked.

"No, that's all I know, and I'm telling you this now for a reason— Mace isn't going to let me leave here."

"I thought you were his long-lost cousin?" Collin asked.

"That's why he's not going to let me leave. You see, after supper, he put Nils to sleep and carried him here. I was still awake, but I didn't open my eyes until after he left. He talked to himself when he thought I was asleep, though, saying that he would be sure I never went away again. I don't know what that means, but he's in his magic laboratory now, preparing something."

Gill grabbed Saris's wrist and held the box to her mouth. "Get out of there! Now!"

Collin put a hand to her shoulder and gently pulled her back.

Rowan crawled over to Saris's spot, disengaged Gill's hand, and took the box herself. "You realize that if he tampers with you, the next time we see you, we'll have to presume you're an adversary."

"I understand."

"He's not going to be an adversary, because he's leaving," Gill insisted.

Rowan turned to Gill. "I know how you feel, but you must have realized that the reason we're here with you is to enable you to defeat Mace, even if it means *our* lives. You can't save our lives at the expense of that goal."

Gill set her jaw. "He took an oath to obey the crown."

"Yes, I did," Bryce's voice said from the box, "but I also took an oath to protect the crown with my life. Through the years, there's been a lot of philosophical debate as to what to do when those two orders come into conflict. My own commander, who trained me, advised me to do whatever I would be willing to be responsible for. And, under that standard, I'd rather be responsible for disobeying the crown than for abandoning the objective."

"He has to stay," Collin told Gill. "I don't like it, either, but he has to stay."

Gill sighed, bowed her head, and ran a hand through her hair.

Collin leaned forward and spoke into the box. "Hide the transmitter, in case he searches you. I suspect if he found it he would think it was just a way to reach Asquith, but you never know."

"I'll do it."

"He's not going to kill you," Collin reassured him, "and since he can't read your mind without killing you, you don't have to worry about betraying the fact that you're spying on him for us. He thinks you're a clone of Von, something Von made so that he would survive after his physical death. Nils won't give him any other impression."

"I understand."

"Stay well," Collin said. He reached over, turned off the transmitter, and gave it back to Saris.

Gill leaned back against Collin and sighed.

Collin put an arm around her. "Remember, whatever Mace does, Bryce won't feel any pain or fear."

"Which is far better than what will happen to us if we ever fall into his hands," Rowan said.

"What does that mean, Mace will make sure he doesn't leave?" Saris asked. "A binding spell? An anchor spell?"

"So that Bryce can't go farther than a certain distance from Mace?" Rowan speculated. "Don't those sorts of spells cease when the creator of the spell dies?"

"They do," Collin confirmed.

"But if he's working all night, I would think it would be more serious than a mere binding spell," Saris mused.

Gill rubbed her face with a hand and sat up. "What if we were to ride through the night? Could we get to Mace's fortress by morning?"

Rowan leaned over and put a hand on Gill's arm. "Gill, I told you, we can't go and rescue him."

"We wouldn't make it, anyway," Collin added.

Saris reached over and touched Gill's sleeve. "Majesty...."

"Gill," she corrected.

"Gill," Saris repeated. "The best way for us to rescue Bryce is to destroy Mace, as we planned. So when you find Mace, don't use Silmariae as a weapon."

"What else is she supposed to do?" Rowan said. "I can't believe we've been using it wrong all these years."

"Perhaps not wrong," Collin interjected. "Varantia must have shaped the artifact into a sword for a reason."

"Could be symbolic somehow," Saris speculated.

"But it has a blade," Rowan protested.

Saris shrugged. "I don't know. I do know that Mother always said she had to struggle with it, bring it under her control."

"And she used it quite effectively, too," Rowan said. "Silmariae never lost a contest until she saw Mace."

"Until she saw Mace, she only had human opponents," Collin pointed out. "Besides, if you recall, Varantia appeared in Maclin precisely because Gill did *not* try to control the sword."

Rowan scratched her neck. "I can't argue with that."

Saris leaned over. "Gill, when you see Mace, try to do what you did in Maclin."

Rowan shifted her weight back and forth uncomfortably. "That's great in theory, but very likely when Gill finally sees Mace, it's not going to be a clean one-on-one fight. Mace is going to use all of his magic and influence to persuade Gill to do what he wants, to get her in danger, and she'll find it hard to resist. Besides which, if Mace or anyone else for that matter runs up to Gill aiming to hack her arm off, her instinctual response is not going to be to lean back and let the sword tell her what to do."

Saris put a hand on Gill's shoulder. "Pretend the sword is Sloan."

Gill turned to her. "What?"

"Pretend the sword is Sloan. Let it take the lead."

"What if it does nothing?" Rowan asked.

"I would presume that if Varantia made it especially to challenge Mace, it wouldn't fail to act in his presence. It did in Maclin."

Gill rubbed her chin, thinking. "He certainly won't fail to notice *it*. Everyone in Maclin recognized it on first sight."

Saris smiled. "He won't notice it until you draw it."

Gill stared at her, confused.

"It has a spell of non-noticeability keyed to Mace. It's one of the last things Mother transmitted to us before she died. She and Estes had entered the fortress by stealth. The sword was so anxious to get to Mace that it ripped off her belt and flew right into Mace's path. Mother hid and watched as Mace picked it up by the sheath and tossed it aside. She couldn't believe it. But there are such spells in the books."

"I've woven one or two of them myself," Collin volunteered. "It's the small spells that you have no defenses against."

"Since everyone else in Mace's mansion is from Somerlie; they have no knowledge of Silmariae and won't notice the plain sheath and hilt," Rowan added.

Saris again caught Gill's attention. "Another thing that could help us: do you know what Mace's artifact is?"

Gill stared at her.

"The focus of his power."

"Um...when I was injured, Mace carried me to a hidden room with a lot of objects, took some wristbands from a box, and put them on."

"Those must be his artifacts, if he kept them hidden and used them to enhance his power," Collin said. "Destroying them would weaken his magic."

"He probably never takes them off now," Saris said.

Gill thought for a moment, looking at Collin in the dim starlight and his diminished glow. "By the way, what's your artifact? I presume you have one."

"He won't tell," Rowan blurted out.

"Gives me an air of mystery," Collin said proudly. "Healers need that."

Rowan snorted.

Saris looked around. "The original plan was to stay here until Bryce came with news. Now that he's not coming, what do we do?"

Rowan stood and walked to her bedroll. "I'm getting some sleep."

Saris leaned toward Gill. "How do we get into the fortress? Ciernan helped Mother get in; we can't duplicate his spell."

Gill shrugged. "Unless we take Collin's energy weapon and blast a hole through the wall, we have to go in through the front gate—which is watched day and night."

"How about the hills?" Collin asked.

"They're not solid; they're ash. We'd be buried if we tried to climb them," Gill answered. "What about magic?"

Collin let out a breath. "As she said, I can't duplicate Ciernan's spell. There's no magic to make us invisible, if that's what you mean."

"I brought some charms, but they won't help," Saris said.

"What did you bring?" Collin asked.

"A language charm, since Eminric told me the language of Somerlie has changed; an oblivion charm, so my mind will go blank in case I'm tortured; and a warding charm, to absorb the force of a magical blow."

"I take it that won't help you if someone comes at you with a sword," Gill said.

Saris nodded and sighed. "Maybe Rowan is right. Maybe we should go to bed and think about what to do in the morning."

The next morning, as they ate breakfast, Gill proposed that they simply ride within sight of Mace's fortress and then think about how to get in. This spur-of-the-moment non-plan greatly appealed to Rowan; since Collin and Saris could not think of any alternatives, they broke camp after breakfast and rode south.

Before noon, Collin reined in his horse and looked up.

"What is it?" Gill asked.

"There's a spell spreading over us," he said.

Gill put a hand on Silmariae's hilt and looked around. "Is Mace trying to find us?"

Before Collin could answer, Saris pointed to the ground. "Look."

As they watched, they saw grass growing up, even between the stones in the road.

"Mace is trying to enclose his fortress with vegetation, just as Eminric protected Maclin," Collin said.

"Let's go before we're completely blocked," Rowan said, and urged her greathorse forward.

As the day wore on, travel became increasingly difficult. All Collin could do without using a spell strong enough to attract Mace's attention was to open a narrow lane through which they passed single file. When the shadows lengthened, Gill wondered if they would have to spend the night walled in by plants. Suddenly, they broke out into a clearing.

"What did he do," Rowan asked, emerging from the undergrowth, "stop the spell?"

Gill looked around and pointed. "See that intersecting road over there? That's the road that goes to Arcacia in Somerlie. He needs to keep that clear so he can continue to import workers."

Collin slumped in the saddle. "Let's make camp. I'm tired."

They made a cold hasty supper out of their supplies and went to sleep shortly after sunset. In the night, Silmariae pushed against Gill's leg. She bolted from the tent, to find Rowan already on her feet and facing south.

"Lights," Rowan whispered.

"Hold a minute," Gill whispered back. She rummaged in her saddlebags and took out her spyglass. She stood next to Rowan and extended it. "They're bringing in more workers from Somerlie."

"Will they come in this direction?" Rowan asked.

Gill put the spyglass down. "No. They're so tired by now they won't notice anything, except...." She had a sudden thought and ran to Collin's tent. "Don't come out," she said at the entrance. "Mace's men are passing by."

"I was just about to come and see what was going on," said Collin from inside.

"Just stay there," Gill ordered. Without waiting for a reply, she walked over to Saris's tent, nearly colliding with her as the younger woman emerged.

Gill quickly put a finger to Saris's lips. "Mace's men are passing by," Gill whispered.

Saris nodded; Gill took her hand away. Gill sighed and walked back toward Rowan, thinking in relief she had averted a disaster. As she opened her mouth to whisper to Rowan, something slammed into her.

She raised her arms to protect her head. A wind stronger than any she had ever imagined hurled her against a tree. The air beat at her like a fist. If this were a storm, it was a worse storm than Gill had ever experienced—and completely dry, besides. Silmariae pounded at her leg.

She drew the sword. Gasping, she felt an immediate respite. Gill blinked the dust from her eyes. She could hardly see an arm's length away because of the dust, leaves, and debris. Around her, the storm continued to howl with a thundering noise much like the hoofbeats of a hundred greathorses.

The tempest raged for some time, then halted as suddenly as it began. Gill sheathed the sword. She could see nothing. Immediately, she drew the sword again and saw in the glow that the dust was thick, suspended in the air, but settling even as she watched.

Another glow caught her eye; she saw Collin approaching. "Is that you, Gill?" he asked.

"It's me...or, rather, Silmariae."

Collin waved his arms. The dust around them flew away. "Are you injured?"

"I'm fine. Have you seen Saris or Rowan?"

He shook his head. "But dawn will come soon, and when the dust settles, we can search."

Gill nodded. "Now I understand how Mace must have attacked Eminric's group at that last battle." She bit her lip. "Horrible thing."

"The storm Mace unleashed against the Wye army *was* horrible," Collin agreed. "But it was nothing like the storm we just weathered. Any well-trained youth among our people could have made that. The assault on the army of Eldswold was a hundred times stronger, I assure you."

Gill inhaled sharply. "I can hardly imagine."

Collin nodded. "If Eminric's battle group hadn't passed their strength to him, I doubt if he would have survived."

"Then what was that?" Gill asked. "Mace having a temper tantrum?"

"I don't think that was Mace, at least not directly," Collin said. "You see, Mace has kept a tight control on the weather here for centuries. Our weather-watchers tell us that when that happens, once in a while the atmosphere will break out in a sudden squall, as a sort of safety valve. It probably happens here every few years."

"I see." Gill noticed the sky brightening in the east. She turned a circle, slowly. "No sign of Saris or Rowan. Where could they *be*?"

Collin pointed. "At least the greathorses were massive enough to resist the storm."

Gill walked over to Kiri and examined him. The coat was covered with dust and pieces of leaves. For all that, the greathorse was uninjured; all she saw were some scratches. She patted his coat, letting off a puff of dust. She took a curry comb out of the saddlebags and began brushing his coat.

"The wind blew our tents and supplies away," Collin added as she worked. "They're probably stuck in that mass of vegetation to the north."

"Or blown into the river." Gill sighed. "This means that in order to get food, we have to go into the fortress."

"I haven't seen a lot of fruit trees around here," Collin agreed.

Gill gestured southward. "Let's take the road, then. Maybe we'll find Saris or Rowan on the way."

After quickly grooming the horses, they walked down the road together—leaving the greathorses at the pond—and took the turn west. Gill worriedly kept an eye out for Rowan or Saris, looking right and left as she strolled on. What had happened? Had Mace captured them? Were they being tortured? Had Mace read their minds as he had read Bruno's? Did he know that Gill and Silmariae were just down the way?

Collin stopped and pointed. "Look."

Off the path lay a broken cart. They tread carefully in the grasses and weeds, examining the splintered wood, but saw no sign of human remains. They went back to the road.

When they reached the edge of the clearing with the gardens, they stopped in a glade of thick vegetation where they could observe unseen. Everything looked the same as when Gill first had seen it as Sloan: men tending the gardens, the gate open. No one was visibly standing guard, though she knew that someone kept watch constantly.

"Looks like the storm we felt didn't reach here," Gill said.

"Those things *are* generally localized."

"No sign of Saris or Rowan...if they're anywhere inside, they're probably dead already."

"Not necessarily." When she drew breath to ask what that meant, he continued, "Remember, I altered them before they left. I even placed cysts in strategic places to suggest male equipment. It's possible they could be mistaken as male...or at least hermaphrodites. Mace may assume they're from Somerlie and simply put them with the slaves, in that case."

"In that case, they'd be tortured."

Collin drew a breath. "If they're still alive after we defeat Mace, I can heal their bodies and much of the trauma, as well."

"That is, if *you're* alive."

"There is that," Collin admitted.

She turned to the fortress. "What now? Any suggestions?"

He looked at the sword. "Is Silmariae telling you anything?"

"Nothing now, no. I don't think it would be a good idea to just walk in."

"That depends."

She turned to him. "On what? You said there were no spells to make one invisible."

"That non-noticeability spell that Saris talked about might serve. The spell works this way: others will see you, but the effect is as if they passed you on the street. They'd know you're there, but they wouldn't give you much attention unless you did something to draw it."

She nodded. "I wonder how long before that happened, though."

"It isn't perfect, that's true." He paused, then pointed. "Here's another idea: see where the edge of the fortress wall meets the forest?"

"Yes."

"If we went back and found the energy weapon, we could outline a block of stone. Take the block out, go in, and replace the block. I presume there are a lot of chambers in there where one could hide."

"That's assuming we could go back and find it before we starved."

As Gill spoke, Collin wrenched his head around. His gaze riveted on a spot on the wall. He flung out a restraining arm.

"What is it?" she whispered.

"Mace is throwing out a tracer spell," he murmured. "He's searching to see if Silmariae is near."

Gill touched the sword. "It isn't giving any sign. Can you protect us from Mace's spell?"

"No, but I can have it catch me instead." He reached into a pocket, brought out a transmitter box, and put it in her hand. "Stay here. Don't do anything until Silmariae directs you. And don't try to rescue me or any of the others, if you see us."

Before Gill could utter another word, he had stepped out onto the road. He strode past the gardening areas, through the gate, and disappeared.

She was alone.

Chapter 12

Gill waited, without moving, for some time. She wondered what she should do. Should she hide, in case Mace or his men came storming out of the fortress after her? Should she try to go in? No outcry or sign of violence came from within the enclosure; she found this lack of activity maddening. She would rather do something, take the sword and fight someone, anything but this.

She did not know how long she had been staring when she heard an unnatural chirp. She looked up and around, listened for the sound of humans moving through the brush, but there was only the beep. Then she remembered the transmitter, which Collin had given her and which she had put in her pocket.

She drew it out and held it up to her lips. "Yes?" she said cautiously.

"Gill. It's Bryce. It's safe for me to talk. How about you?"

"I'm fine. How are you?"

"In good health. Mace didn't harm me. He did something, though. I'm not sure how to describe it...you know how you felt there was a wall in your mind between you and Sloan?"

"Yes."

"There's no wall between me and Nils now. I feel as if I'm fully occupying my mind, but I feel Nils, too."

"Is that uncomfortable?"

"Not really, but it is strange. I'm getting used to it."

"Is Nils still keeping you out of danger?"

"Very much so. Whatever the effect is, Mace is pleased. Since we're about the same size, he's even given me some of his clothes. A bit archaic in style, though."

"Saris said he might have put a binding spell on you, so that you couldn't go more than a certain distance away from him."

"If he did, I don't know about it. But it doesn't matter. I'm staying until either I or Mace is dead, and I'm still here to help you any way I can."

"Rowan said you weren't to be trusted after Mace affected you."

"That's a good precaution. It's policy among anyone trained as a guard, not to trust anyone who might have been tampered by an opponent. You can choose to trust me or not."

Gill sighed. "I don't see why I can't talk to you."

"Good. I'm calling to tell you Collin is here."

"Is he alive?"

"For the moment. He made what was probably a wise move. He changed his shape to look more like Von. Mace thinks he's Rhys."

"One of the other globes."

"Yes. But he can't hide his true nature from Mace for long. If Mace touches him, even brushes against him accidentally, he'll know Collin is Wye."

"What do you think he'll do?"

"I honestly don't know, and neither does Nils. Mace is getting desperate to find Silmariae."

Gill thought about that for a moment. "Does Nils have any advice for me?"

There was a brief silence, followed by, "None. Sorry."

"Have you seen Rowan or Saris?"

"I think I saw Saris. She came in with the last batch. Some sort of disaster overtook the caravan on the way here and they were scattered."

"But no sign of Rowan?"

"Sorry, no. The man who I think is Saris came in with some stragglers. The net flew off them, the wagon they were on broke, and they had to walk in. We had small groups of men trickling in for some time."

Gill bit her lip before speaking again. "I know we aren't supposed to look out for each other, but see what you can do."

"There's no rule saying you can't watch out for each other as long as it doesn't interfere with the objective. I'm seeing what I can do to get her into the household. They're tortured less, but they get work no one else wants to do. Still, Saris isn't afraid of hard work, so she would probably approve of the tradeoff."

"Good. Where are you, by the way?"

"The green room."

"I know which one that is."

"I knew you would. Is there anything else I can do for you?"

"Not at present, but I know how to reach you."

"Be cautious. I wouldn't be able to answer if I were with Mace."

"I understand."

"May luck go with you."

"And with you."

She put the device back in her pocket. Her stomach reminded her that it expected a meal. She stood, facing the fortress, thinking, and had just concluded that she ought to go back to the campsite to see if she could find the food when Silmariae let out a low hum. Gill drew it and held it up to her face so that she was staring into the sword's runes. She felt energy course from her hands to her arms, and up her neck to her head. Her face seemed to shrivel. The energy went to her chest; her breasts shrunk. She expected the transformation to continue to her genitals, but the force spread no further. She remembered Saris advising her to let the sword take the lead, as Sloan had. Well, she thought, it seemed to be doing that. She hoped it was a good sign.

Gill turned toward the fortress. She went up the road between the garden areas, but none of the humans looked up or showed that they took any notice of her.

When she was through the gate, she saw men running from the mansion. Unafraid, she walked straight to the front door and proceeded in, up the staircase, and to the hall outside one of Mace's rooms.

The air was close and crackling. She heard voices clearly from inside.

"I smashed an entire army from Eldswold." The menace in Mace's voice was almost palpable. "Did you think you could resist me?"

"No," Collin answered calmly, "but now you have magical spells over the whole of Somerlie. If you fought me, I would lose, but I would fight back, and that would weaken you at a time that you need all your strength. I don't think you will risk that."

"All I need is enough magic to capture you." Mace said in chilling tones.

"That you already seem to have done." Collin still sounded unruffled.

Gill was distracted by footsteps approaching. She turned and saw Bryce walk up to her. He looked into her face; his expression showed astonishment and recognition. He took her arm and whispered, "Not now. Find something to do and I'll come for you later."

She nodded, walked down the stairs, and left the mansion. In the yard, again, no one took much notice of her. She surveyed all the areas, seeing that little had changed since she had last been there. At the end of her tour, she paused by the booth that the supervisors used to torture the younger men. The booth was not in use, but she saw Saris scrubbing blood and filth from the last session. Saris's hair had been cut very short, and roughly—she could very well pass as a man. She also—already—had fresh scars and bruises on her face and neck. She paused in her work, caught Gill's eye for an instant with an expression of both recognition and grim determination, and went back to her task.

At that moment, when Gill felt neither pity nor empathy, she realized she was in the grip of another entity. She remembered she had not felt fear toward Mace, either. But it was not the emptiness that she had experienced with Sloan—it was as if a will stronger and infinitely more mature than hers was gently reining in her emotions as Gill herself might have directed Kiri along the road.

As she stood there, pondering, Bryce walked up to her. He nodded to Saris and took Gill by the arm. "Come with me."

When they were back inside the mansion, Gill gently removed his grip and placed a strong hand on his. She guided him to Mace's library and shut the door behind him.

Before Bryce could say anything, Gill found herself walking to the shelves. "I presume you're taking me to Mace. Good. Tell him that he must set a barrier against Silmariae." She took a book from the shelf and opened it. Paging through, she found a particular section and put a finger on it. "Here." Bryce edged closer and looked over her arm. "Suggest the Phi technique. He'll think Von provided you with the information. I'm sure that Nils can sound convincing."

Bryce marked the place with his finger and closed the book. "Yes... Varantia?"

"Correct, but be careful where you speak my name. It may be overheard."

"Agreed. What else?"

"Continue with your plan and I'll continue with mine."

Bryce led the way out of the library and up the stairs to Mace's rooms. Bryce knocked with a deliberate pattern. Mace answered cordially. "Come in, my friend."

Bryce stepped in first and gestured Gill to follow. She looked humbly at the floor, but in her peripheral vision she could still see most of Mace, who sat in his chair at his desk.

"Since I'm to stay, my lord, I was wondering if I could have a man to take care of my needs. Galt, here, came in from those last captured. I think he will serve."

Mace's eyes passed over her quickly. "One is as good as another, I suppose." He turned to Nils. "Can you be sure of his reliability?"

"If he is at my sole disposal, I can ensure his complete loyalty."

Gill realized Nils was asking Mace not to torture her, and hinting that he could put some sort of binding spell on her.

"Very well," Mace answered. "Show him to Rand, so that the supervisors know he is yours."

Bryce stepped forward with the book. "The situation with the prisoner reminded me of something." He opened the book in front of Mace. "I think you should set a barrier against Silmariae, since we know the humans will try to send it here. The Phi technique may be best."

Mace took the book, read it, and scratched his chin. She noticed he wore the wristbands. "I don't know...I've used the Tra techniques exclusively for centuries, and they've worked well for me."

"It is only my purpose to put your mind at rest, my lord," Nils volunteered. "Perhaps it is time to try another technique? It may confound your enemies, and certainly prevent Silmariae from crossing your borders. Once that is done, you would have no need to concern yourself about what the humans of Maclin or the Wye of Eldswold might do. You can go back to living as you wish."

Mace nodded slowly. "Yes, we can set a barrier right at our borders; Silmariae will never get in. Very good, Nils. I think we shall get along well indeed." He gestured toward Gill. "Take your man; I will see to the spell."

Next, Bryce ushered her into Rand's room. He barely glanced at her and promised Bryce to speak to the supervisors. Bryce asked that Gill be given a room in the mansion; Rand told him to use the small room next to his, which was empty at the time and had a connecting door that Bryce could unseal.

From there, they went to Bryce's room. Gill walked in first. As Bryce closed the door, the mirror caught her attention. Looking into it, she saw a different face—heavily scarred, nose out of joint. She put a hand to her cheeks.

Bryce stepped up behind her. "At least the others will think you've already been tortured."

Gill put her hand down and sighed. "I suppose that was the idea."

"You're there, too, Gill? Both Varantia and Gill at the same time?" He paused. "Like me."

She turned to him. "It's very different from having Sloan. Sloan was an accumulation of memories and experience from different minds. This is more than a mind; this is a personality. I have feelings; she has feelings. They are different from mine, but compatible."

"That was a very impressive display in the library," Bryce said. "Nils knew Varantia; or, rather, Von did, and for Nils, the experience was just like talking to the live Varantia."

"Get used to it, there's more," Varantia advised.

Bryce stared at her in awe. "How are you doing that?

"It was difficult at first. When I sensed Mace back in Maclin, Gill was in a receptive frame of mind, so I let myself out with a powerful surge. I occupied Gill briefly after that, experiencing events through her senses, and then was able to put myself back into the sword. When we neared Mace again, I was able to control my release back into Gill. I think that now I will be able to flow back and forth more naturally."

Bryce nodded. "Do you want to know what happened to Collin?"

"Yes."

The voice resonated as Varantia added hers to Gill's. Gill turned to Bryce and smiled sheepishly.

"Mace put Collin in a room in the castle wall. Third door from the southwest corner on the lower level. He immobilized him; Collin can't get loose. Mace is leaving him there to die of starvation, or thirst. He can't remedy those by magic."

"I'll go."

"Shall I go with you?"

"No. If anyone sees me, they'll think that you sent me on an errand. That is, if they notice me, and you probably discovered I'm not very noticeable."

"Yes, Mace and Rand barely looked at you. I was surprised."

"There's an old saying from Wik: 'It's the smallest spells that are the most effective.'"

As before, Gill found the corridors within the walls empty of traffic. They were dimly illuminated from the ceiling; the cold stone reflected nothing and added to the gloomy atmosphere. Nothing in the rooms would interest a human; with Mace's magic laboratory carefully concealed, there was no reason for any human to come here, or linger here if sent.

Collin's room was not even locked. Gill opened the door and found the room comfortably lit. The room was small, and almost filled by a table with a marble top and stone legs. One end jutted into the wall to the left of the door. At a glance, Gill could see Collin lying naked on the table; his arms held in place above his head by cuffs at his wrists; his legs similarly restrained at his ankles. She quickly closed the door and walked to a spot at his waist, where his lower body was out of view.

Collin faced away from her, staring at a blank wall. Gill felt changes in her shape again. Gently, she placed a hand on his arm. Slowly, he turned to her, gasped in astonishment, and fixed his eyes on her.

Varantia smiled. "Hello, Collin."

"Varantia," he whispered.

A nearby shelf caught her eye. Collin's clothes lay there, neatly folded. Varantia reached up and took a downy blue blanket. "I remember when you used to drag this around as a toddler. You or your parents must have put a spell of permanency on it; it still looks new." She looked at him. "It's your artifact, isn't it?"

"I don't tell that to just anybody."

"You can tell your secret to a dead person, I would think."

"Are you dead?"

She carefully folded the blanket and put it back. "Oh, yes. I can assure you I'm not one of those who can't accept the fact. I'm here long enough to deal with my beloved. When I've accomplished my task, I'm gone."

"You still love him."

Varantia said wistfully, "Enough to give my life to stop him."

"So you did commit suicide to give power to the sword? You knew if you did that, only a human could use it?"

She smiled. "These humans are exciting, aren't they? They've greatly extended the range of our magic."

"In which way?"

"I know the sort of magic you specialized in doesn't lend itself to such applications, but think of it—humans are entirely empty of magic, so they can be filled to the brim. Von realized that when he made his globes. I got the idea of Silmariae from him, though I took the idea a step further. We would have never invented such magic had there not been humans around to use it."

"So...you've been waiting for a proper human to come along."

"I knew that if enough time passed, someone would allow me to surface."

"You should have left instructions. We were guessing for a long time."

She took a breath. "Believe me, I would have left instructions if I had had the time. But things happened so quickly...I was dead almost before I knew it. On the other hand, time has little meaning for the dead, so the wait was not uncomfortable or frustrating."

"Even so, the wait *has* made things more complicated."

She nodded soberly. "I know. That will be amended." She moved closer to Collin's head to look into his eyes. "Collin, defeating Mace is going to take time. Gill, here, is anxious to get to work and be done with it, but it can't be accomplished that quickly...I wish it could. Mace is simply too strong. I'll accomplish my task with all deliberate speed, but...you might not be alive by the time I'm done."

"I understand."

She put a hand to the sword. "It's senseless. Silmariae could release you in an instant. But if I do that, I risk draining the sword's full strength or drawing Mace's attention."

"I don't expect you to do that. Just let me know if I can be of help."

"Alive or dead, I'll free you once I'm able to put an end to Mace's magic. I wish I could at least bring you food or water, or cover you, but someone would notice. My plan critically depends on Mace feeling secure right now, and he won't if he thinks you're free or strong and can threaten him. I'm sorry."

"I understand. Don't apologize."

Varantia nodded and turned to leave. Gill felt her face shriveling again as she opened the door.

To keep up the appearance that she was Bryce's slave, Gill brought Bryce his midday meal, and they ate in his rooms. They unsealed the inside door and Gill settled in the adjoining room.

When Gill took the trays to carry them back to the kitchen, Bryce said, "When you're done with those, meet me in the torture chamber. I've asked the supervisors to send Saris there. That will do several things for us: first, it will make Mace more comfortable with me if he thinks I'm torturing someone; second, it will do you and Saris good if the others think you're being tortured; third, it will give us a private place to talk at length."

"What if Mace walks in and wants to observe?"

"He's still in his magic laboratory setting the Phi spell. Besides, there are times of day when I know he doesn't want to be disturbed. We can use those times ourselves. If he changes his schedule, we'll just have to improvise."

When Gill went into the torture chamber, she found Saris on the table, naked, blindfolded, and restrained. A supervisor and his assistant stood nearby.

Nils turned to them. "I can manage from here. There's no need to prepare him after this. I take pleasure in the preparation, as well."

The supervisor nodded and ushered the assistant out ahead of him. Gill closed the door behind them and secured it.

Nils took off the blindfold and restraints. "Go and get your clothes."

Saris leaned over to the shelf where the clothes lay, but paused. "What if Mace or someone else wants to come in? Shouldn't I stay here to keep up appearances?"

"Neither Mace nor anyone else will disturb us today," Nils reassured her.

When Saris was dressed, she sat on the edge of the table. Gill sat next to her. Nils took the only chair in the room—a high stool.

Bryce turned to Saris. "I got you reassigned to the house. When you go back, the supervisors will tell you that you're coming here. You'll have a very tiny room in the mansion cellar with all the other house slaves, and you'll be assigned to scrub up this room and anyplace else where Mace leaves a mess."

Saris nodded.

Bryce indicated her scars. "Sorry I couldn't get you before you were tortured the first time."

"I wasn't tortured," Saris said. "When I was first given other clothes and told to dress, one of the other newcomers saw me and said I was a freak. He and some other newcomers started beating me. The supervisors broke it up, saying that no human was to kill another except in the fighting ring, or if someone died under authorized torture. Then they put me to cleaning the torture room; I guess no one else wants to do that."

"You could have fought back, couldn't you?" Gill asked.

"Oh, yes, I know how to throw a punch. But I thought worse might come to me if I did, so I dropped to the ground, curled up, and protected myself with my arms the best I could."

"How are you holding up?" Gill asked again.

Saris took a breath, swallowed, and nodded. "It's hard. Harder than I thought when we left Maclin. But Rowan said that we would see worse, and I said that I would do what I could, and I will."

Gill patted Saris on the back.

Bryce looked from Saris to Gill and back again. "Saris, Gill has taken Varantia now. That is how we are going to defeat Mace."

Saris stared at Gill in awe. "No wonder the sword refused Mother when she was wearing Sloan. Sloan was Von's artifact, and Varantia can't use Von's artifact."

Varantia turned to Bryce. "I have already told Collin that this will take time. Collin may die before my plan has any effect."

"Where's Collin? What happened?" Saris asked.

"Collin came in disguised, but Mace found him out fairly quickly," Nils explained. "Mace knew he would only weaken himself if he fought Collin by magic, so he has Collin restrained in one of the rooms in the fortress wall, until he starves or dies of thirst."

"Can't we bring him anything?" Saris asked.

"Mace would notice," Nils and Varantia said at the same time.

Saris let out a long breath.

Varantia turned to Bryce. "What I'm planning to do is to reduce Mace's magical abilities until he has none."

Saris whistled softly. "A huge undertaking. I've read it in the books. It's only been done once or twice before...Telnurian, Wendimere...."

Varantia stared at Saris in amazement.

"Ciernan gave her the forbidden books," Bryce explained.

Varantia nodded. "It is said that it takes an outside observer to get a complete perspective."

"If you don't mind my asking," Saris said curiously, "are you alive or dead, and if you're dead, can you weave spells as well as when you were alive?"

"An excellent question," Varantia answered. "It could also be asked if I can be as effective inhabiting a human body rather than my natural one. But I have my artifact." She touched Silmariae. "And I've had no trouble weaving spells so far."

"So, how can we help you?" Bryce asked.

"I don't know yet. My plans are laid as branches in a tree. If I try something and it works, I go on to the next branch. If I try something and it doesn't work, I take another branch and follow that until I'm blocked. But all the branches have an end, and if I can remain that long, we shall get there."

"Right now, then, we need to help in keeping Gill alive," Bryce said.

"Which you have done well so far...you and Nils," Varantia said. "It may be that I will require additional help," she nodded to Bryce and Saris, "for one task or another, but I won't be able to ask until it happens." She slipped off the table. "One thing I must do now, however, is to add some scars to Saris and myself." She put a hand on Saris. "This won't hurt, but it will feel strange."

"I know. Go ahead." As Varantia worked, Saris added, "This is more complicated than I ever imagined...I thought all we needed to do was confront Mace and kill him."

Gill broke in with her voice. "So did I, Saris...so did I."

"And both of you would have been as dead as Saris's mother if you had tried," Nils added.

Chapter 13

After taking their evening meal in the kitchen, Gill and Bryce walked back to his room. As they neared the staircase, Gill saw Mace at the top, leaning on the balustrade, looking down. The hungry expression on his face chilled her. She and Bryce stopped to follow his gaze. Six men carried a sturdy man, naked, blindfolded, and gagged. Though he was heavily bound, the victim struggled in the grip of his captors.

"A pretty fish," Mace said eagerly. "One that thrashes around after it is caught." He grinned at Nils. "But I will take the fight out of it."

"I'm sure you will, my lord," Nils said, "and savor the pleasure of it."

By this time, the bearers had reached the top of the stairs. Mace threw a gleeful look to Nils and followed them to the torture chamber.

Gill saw that Mace no longer wore his wristbands. When the party had disappeared and the door was shut, she whispered to Bryce, "Time for the next step. I'll be back later."

Bryce turned to her. "Do you need help?" he murmured.

"Not for this." Gill walked out of the mansion to the gate and slipped in through one of the doors to the inside of the fortress wall.

Seeing no one there, she went directly to Mace's magic laboratory, passing the barriers. Gill had to give all control to Varantia; she herself had no idea what to do next. But Varantia's plan seemed to be well-plotted; she did not hesitate, though Gill knew Varantia needed Gill's memory to tell her where everything was.

She found the wristbands in their case, took them out, and laid them on a bench. From another shelf, she took a bottle and sprinkled what appeared to be powder on them. The powder disappeared on contact. She held them in her hands, closed her eyes, and took a long breath. Gill could feel the movement of some sort of energy, but nothing else. Varantia released the breath, and, apparently satisfied, returned the wristbands to the case. Varantia shared the thought with Gill that the powder, reinforced by magic, would cause the wristband material to start decaying.

Varantia walked around the room, sprinkling powder on other objects. She handled them, or manipulated them, or examined them. When she was finished, she set the powder back on the shelf, and replaced everything exactly as she had found it. Nothing was even a hair's-breadth out of place.

That done, she left the laboratory and walked to the top of the wall. Broken clouds obscured most of the stars. A warm breeze blew. After looking around and seeing no one else, Varantia took the transmitter box out of Gill's inner pocket.

"Eminric," she called, using Gill's voice.

"Eminric," came the response.

"Can you talk?"

"I'm the only one awake in the city. The sleep of Tashtalon still takes hold here. Where are you?"

"In Mace's fortress."

"Is it safe for *you* to talk?"

"Quite safe. Everything is going well, but I have a request."

"Name it."

"I want you to contact Eldswold and Maclin and order them not to send anyone else here."

"Why?"

"Because my plan depends on Mace feeling safe, secure, and unthreatened."

"You wouldn't mind giving me any details on your plan?"

Now Varantia used her own voice. "Come, Eminric, you know that I know what I'm doing."

"Varantia...," he breathed.

"We're on the same side, or at least we were when we last talked. I presume you haven't changed your mind."

"Not I. But are you the same?"

Gill broke in with her own voice. "She and I are literally of one mind on this, Eminric. If you won't trust her, trust me."

"Besides," Varantia added. "You lose nothing by complying. If Mace attacks Somerlie or Maclin or Eldswold again, you'll know that we failed, and you can use whatever means you have left."

"In that case, I can comply with your request. Silmariae has never bowed to Mace, and I know that this, at least, is tied to you both. But there is still a problem."

"What's that?"

"Leni. Tashtalon took a number of men from the city the night before we came, and Leni went after them."

"Creator of the Universe!" Varantia exclaimed. "Why didn't you stop him?"

"I thought I had. He must have waited until I was asleep and then gone, because he wasn't here in the morning, and I wasn't about to leave Somerlie undefended to find him. Mace tried to make an assault on Arcacia, which I repelled—he was weaker after the assault on Maclin. The citizens here thought they were seeing a vision of the god. They're frightened; especially with the raid taking place about the same time. The Lord Protector is hard pressed to keep order. I'm doing what I can to calm them, as well as I can unobserved."

"Best stay where you are, then." Varantia took a breath. "We haven't seen Leni, but if Mace finds him, he's dead. He's already taken Collin and is restraining him until he starves to death, but he did that because fighting Collin would have drained his strength. Leni he could squash like an insect."

"That's what I'm afraid of."

Varantia sighed. "As much as I would want to, I can't save him if doing so interferes with my plan."

"Don't even try to save him if it keeps you from defeating Mace."

"Still, Mace has created a new barrier around the fortress. Let's hope Leni finds that and goes home."

"A new barrier?"

"A Phi technique."

"Nasty."

"And a further drain on Mace's power, I hope."

"As they say around here, luck go with you."

"And with you. Good night."

Gill stayed for a time, trying to spot stars, but the clouds did not yield, so she went back to the mansion. As she walked up the stairs, she saw Saris come out of the torture chamber, arms full of bloody rags and other cleaning supplies. Her expression was grim; her jaw set. She made eye contact with Gill, nodded briefly, and went on her way.

Gill returned to her room. The door to Bryce's room was open; he was awake and alone, standing at the window and looking up at the sky. Gill went in and sat on the bed.

"Progress?" he asked.

"Yes. I've set a spell on Mace's main artifact and most of his stronger magical charms. The spell is slow-acting; in five to ten days they should fall apart."

Bryce took a chair, set it opposite Gill, and sat. "Will he notice?"

"Because I used a slow-acting spell, he won't notice the deterioration unless he goes to the magic laboratory and handles the items. We have to keep him out of there until the spell works to its end."

"Won't he notice his power waning?"

"Not unless he exercises it. We have to make sure he does nothing that requires more than a routine use of magic."

"Such as turning someone into dust?"

Varantia nodded.

"I'll do everything in my power," Nils said.

"Good. I have some suggestions."

"Please."

"The way Mace welcomed Sloan, and then you—and especially his using his strongest magic to bind you to him—tells me he is desperately in need of companionship. I want you to distract him by keeping him busy, doing things with him."

"The only thing that seems to give him pleasure is to torture people," Bryce said. "To join him in that raises certain ethical and practical dilemmas."

She waved a hand. "No, I'm not asking you to join him in that. Let me rephrase: you remind Mace of his old pastimes with his old friends. He didn't torture people then. He was as normal as Eminric or Collin until he became obsessed with power, and even that process took a century or two." She sighed. "Then his mind became warped. I believe you humans say, 'Absolute power corrupts absolutely?'"

Bryce nodded.

"His friends started to leave him until only a handful were left. I couldn't stay any longer, either. But I think he misses those days.... He may have turned to torture as a macabre way of establishing rapport and dominance with people he felt were his inferiors."

"That had never occurred to me," Bryce answered, "but it makes sense, in a twisted sort of way."

"What I want you to do is to reintroduce him to his old pastimes. Perhaps one will capture his attention for as long as we need. If he starts getting bored with one, switch to another."

Bryce rubbed his chin thoughtfully. "Any suggestions as to where to start?"

"He used to take pride in gardening. The library downstairs reflects a former love of reading—I can direct you to his favorite novelists. He's also interested in drawing or painting, working with clay, horses—I presume you saw how well he maintains the stables--music, astronomy—he used to have quite a powerful telescope and I wonder if he brought it with him."

Bryce nodded. "That gives me a start."

"I should be able to help you feel him out as to when he's bored, and guide you on how to maintain his interest in something once you've captured it. The less he uses his inborn magic, the less he will feel the need to use an artifact or charm, and the faster the disintegrating spell will work."

"What if the worst happens and he does try to exercise a more powerful spell, and finds he has weakened?"

"He shouldn't need to use anything above routine magic if you occupy him. If that fails...," she took a breath, "...we'll have to deal with what happens."

"Not that I think we don't have a good chance, but I presume that you have an alternate plan in case he finds the disintegrating spell and reverses it?"

"Yes, but this is the fastest and most direct method. The others will be slower and more difficult. And the longer we stay here, the more we risk Mace or Rand or someone else discovering our true intentions."

"Then I shall make this work," Nils said confidently.

The next morning, Gill was awakened by Mace's voice in the next room. She put her ear to the adjoining door, which was shut, and found that Nils and Mace were talking companionably. Quickly, she dressed and went to the kitchen, directing the workers to put certain foods on two trays. Saris was in the kitchen, eating her own breakfast; Gill enlisted her to take a tray and they knocked at Bryce's door. At Bryce's invitation, they came in and set the trays at the table where Mace and Bryce sat. Saris bowed and backed out of the room; Gill closed the door behind her and remained there, assuming a humble posture.

Mace looked over his tray, turned to Gill, and then turned to Bryce. "Amazing. My favorite breakfast, prepared exactly to my taste." He took a fork and sampled. "Excellent." He stole another glance at Gill. "Your man is very good."

"All I know about directing others I learned from you, my lord," Nils replied. "And I do so not half as well as you."

Mace settled back into his chair and continued eating. "I could show you some techniques." He smiled. "The man last night, that you saw, I tamed him, tamed him well. The next time I call him, he will come without hesitation."

Nils put a hand on his chest and bowed his head briefly. "My lord, such a generous offer, but you are such a great artist, and I, such a beginner, that the contrast would be so great...after you, what could I do to compare?"

Mace nodded. "You must control your man your own way...and he does come without hesitation when you call?"

"He does. And that's what matters, I'm sure we agree." Nils turned to Gill. "You may go get your own breakfast; I don't wish to hear your stomach rumbling all morning."

Gill bowed and left for the kitchen. When she returned, she saw Mace and Nils standing on the balcony. She took the empty breakfast trays, cleaned off the table, and returned to the kitchen. Once more going back to Bryce's room, she found the two still there.

"Carmanicil may have been the one to fashion the greathorses from the humans' horses, but I have made them into a superior breed," Mace said to Nils. "Let me show you."

Gill followed both to the stables. The grooms, mostly younger men, bowed and stepped back as far as distance allowed when Mace came in. An older man, apparently a supervisor, asked Mace if he could do anything. Mace dismissed the man and told him to go back to his work.

Mace then went from stall to stall, showing off each individual horse and its characteristics. There were long pauses when Mace simply admired and petted the creatures. Preoccupied with his boasting, Mace did not notice, when he entered a stall, that he slammed the door on Bryce's hand. Nils immediately put his hand behind his back.

Mace turned. "What was that?"

"My knuckles cracked, my lord."

Gill could see that the hand was badly injured and had started to swell. She quickly looked around; all the grooms and the supervisor were out of sight, presumably they had hid to keep Mace from turning his attention on them. She knew that Mace would blame her—and torture her—for Bryce's injury if he knew, but she was more afraid that Mace would take Nils to his magic laboratory to heal it.

"Are you coming in?" Mace asked Nils.

"Your pardon, my lord; I need to go relieve myself. And I want my man to get me some liquid refreshment; my throat is rather dry."

Mace turned his attention to the greathorse in front of him. "By all means. Come back when you're ready."

"I will, my lord."

Gill walked behind Nils, shielding his hand from sight. They went directly to the tunnel and took a door to the rooms inside the wall. Finding the corridors, as usual, empty, they hurried straight to Collin's room.

Collin turned his head toward them as they entered.

Nils held up his injured hand. "Mace slammed a stall door on it."

"I see. Gill, take the blanket from the shelf and put it under my head. Bryce, take your hand and put it on one of mine."

They both complied. Collin closed his eyes.

"Don't you need to see...," Gill began, but Collin interrupted.

"Hush," he said, softly but firmly.

As Gill watched, the swelling subsided almost immediately. Nils made a move to pull it away, but Collin spoke again. "Not yet. I have to get the internal injuries under control and strengthen the tendons."

Nils put his hand back. Soon, Collin opened his eyes.

"How does that feel?"

Bryce flexed it. "It feels normal. It never really hurt, though."

"I'm not surprised, with Nils inside you," Collin replied.

"How are you doing?" Gill asked Collin.

"Very well, though if Mace were to come in, I could do an imitation of someone weakened by hunger or thirst. He won't be able to see past the deception; my sort of magic is not his specialty."

"You're fine even though you haven't had any food or water?" Gill asked.

"Oh, I've had some. Leni and Rowan fed me."

"What?" Gill exclaimed despite herself.

"Remember the storm? That was generated by Leni, trying to free the prisoners. He found Rowan, who had been blown in his direction, and they went back and searched the undergrowth, finding a lot of our supplies and the energy weapon. They used it last night to drill a rectangle in the outer wall and remove a stone to get in. Leni found me right away. They shared their food and water with me."

"Where are they now?" she asked.

"They went outside again before daybreak. They said they'd come again this evening."

Gill caught Bryce's eye and sighed. "I have several questions I want to ask them, but we don't have time to talk to them now."

Bryce nodded. "I'll tell you when Mace is occupied. You can come back and talk to them then."

Gill gently lifted Collin's head, took the blanket from under it, and set his head back on the table. She placed the blanket on the shelf. "If they come back before we do, tell them not to go into the yard or mansion."

"I think they know that," Collin answered. As they turned to go, he called, "Varantia?"

She turned back. "Yes?"

"I know you didn't develop any healing magic after you tried to replace your mother's dislocated hip and failed, but really, you should be able to take care of any routine cuts or breaks. Most of our people do. Coming to me for any little item is risky."

Nils said, "In her defense, once Mace notices an injury, it can't appear to heal any faster than is natural; but with this one, Mace hadn't seen it yet, and I think it was more than routine."

Collin nodded. "This time, yes. But I wanted to underscore the point while it was fresh in everyone's mind."

Varantia sighed. "I can heal myself fairly well, but I admit I am skittish about anyone else."

"Just remember you aren't necessarily helpless in these situations. That's all I ask," Collin said.

"I'll keep it in mind," Varantia answered.

When Gill and Bryce were out in the corridor again, Bryce turned to Gill. "The baby blanket is his artifact?"

"Don't spread it around."

"I won't, but now I know why he never told anyone."

Mace was still preoccupied with the horse when Bryce and Gill returned. When he finally noticed Bryce, he ordered two of the great-horses saddled. He and Nils rode them out into the yard, where they did some elementary but well-executed dressage. The humans in the yard gave them ample room to exercise the horses, and many of the men stole interested glances at the performance—even the men chained to the carousel turned their heads when the disk spun around.

Suddenly, Mace reined in his greathorse and cheerfully challenged Nils to a race. Gill remained quiet despite her panic: the length needed to challenge a greathorse would take them beyond Mace's new Phi barrier; Mace would have to exercise his magic in order for Nils to cross. Would he sense a slight weakness in his magic, giving them away?

Gill felt her heart pounding as Nils and Mace lined up. At Mace's signal, he took off, and Nils never caught up. She watched as they galloped through the tunnel. At the end of the gardens, Mace turned—and came back. He laughed as he reached the starting point and stopped, about three greathorse lengths ahead of Nils. When Nils caught up, Mace dismounted and took his greathorse by the reins. Nils did the same, and they walked the horses back to the stables. Gill let out a breath and followed.

"Again, you are unexcelled, my lord," Nils began. "I could not help but notice the herb section of the garden as we rode out. The hybrids look robust."

"Those are my work, too," he said proudly. He threw the reins to a groom who had come out, barely paying attention to the young man, or to the next youth who took the reins of Bryce's horse, "I would be happy to show you. But first, I am in the mood for a meal and a good soak in a tub." He put a hand to his chest. "Even though it takes only an insect's effort to keep clean by magic, there is nothing like the feel of hot water."

"I cannot but agree, my lord."

He glanced at Gill. "I might get myself a body, too, now that I think of it." He pointed a finger at Gill. "You might take a moment or two to practice yourself."

"I may well do so," Nils replied.

Mace turned his attention back toward Bryce. "I will send for you when I am ready, and I can take you on a tour through the gardens."

"I would greatly enjoy that, my lord."

They separated at the top of the stairs. Bryce wanted a bath himself; Gill busied herself with fetching their midday meals while he ran a tub, then took his clothes to the laundry when she returned the trays to the kitchen. The laundry, too, had machines that were beyond Gill's knowledge, though Saris seemed familiar with them. She was there when Gill entered, grimly washing her cleaning materials. All Gill had to do was give Bryce's clothes to a worker.

As arranged, she next met Bryce in the torture chamber. Varantia added a few more scars as they sat to talk.

"This is harder than I thought," Bryce said, "though Nils is confident and throwing himself into the act with abandon."

"Eminric told me that Von came to turn Mace around," Gill said. "Maybe he made those globes with that intent, and Nils is fulfilling his ultimate purpose."

"I'm not sure whether to be grateful or concerned that Leni and Rowan have shown up."

She nodded. "On one hand, they'll be able to keep Collin alive without us having to sneak food from the kitchen or stores, which we know we can't do without drawing Mace's or Rand's attention. Collin, as you saw, we may need...healthy."

"Agreed."

"On the other hand, the more of us there are, the greater the chances of one of us making a fatal error or being discovered."

"Also agreed."

She sighed. "I'll have to talk to Rowan and Leni."

"Once we're out in the garden, you'll probably have all the time you want."

Both Gill and Nils knew the expected length of a torture session. They moved some of the instruments out of place, and used the hose both on the table and some of the instruments, to make it appear as if Nils had forced Gill to clean up the mess, which was sometimes done and also made summoning Saris unnecessary.

With so much on her mind, it was not difficult for Gill to leave the chamber with a sober expression and a slow gait. As they reached Bryce's room, they turned to see one of the humans come up the stairs and enter the chamber, followed by Mace and a couple of attendants.

Gill remained in her room with the doors shut until Mace and Nils had gone to the gardens. Then she returned to Collin's room. When she entered, Collin called out, "Don't worry; it's Gill."

Gill heard noises and crouched. Leni crawled into the room from a square hole in the wall under the table; Rowan followed.

"Leni set a warning spell at the outside doors," Collin explained. "When you came in, we heard a chime."

"The rooms next door have cabinets large enough and empty enough to hide in," Rowan said as she stood and brushed herself off.

Leni spread a sheet over Collin, covering him decently.

"I thought you weren't going to be back until this evening," Gill said.

"Mace was walking in the gardens," Rowan explained. "We were afraid that he'd step into the surrounding brush and find us."

Leni put a curious but gentle hand up to Gill's face and felt along the ridges of the scars there. "Varantia."

"Hello, Leni. I'm glad you're well."

Rowan started. "Collin told us, but I couldn't quite believe it...."

Gill turned to Rowan. "I'm glad you're alive, Rowan, but you and Leni being here makes matters more complicated."

"I can hide!" Leni said brightly. "I can hide better than anyone!"

"He can," Collin confirmed. "The spells he uses are so weak he can't make any alteration that would attract Mace's notice, and he's had hundreds of years of practice, haven't you, Leni?"

"I can tell when people are coming. I can know where they are all the time, if they get close enough for me to put a spell on them!"

Varantia put a hand on Leni's arm. "I know you can, Leni." She looked at Rowan, "As for you...."

"Put me to work. Switch me with Saris."

"Impossible."

"You can't leave Saris in there. She won't survive, and there's the danger she'll give us away."

"She's already there and taking her out would draw more attention than we need right now. She's adapting, just as all the other nineteen-year-olds in there are—and the eighteen-year-olds, and sixteen-year-olds."

Rowan sighed. "Then let me join her."

Gill shook her head. "The time is past for adding more people. Mace surrounded the immediate area with an impenetrable barrier; someone coming from outside will make him think the barrier has been breached."

"Can't you just let me mingle with the others?"

"Rand, if not Mace, knows every single human in there, by face if not by name. You'd be noticed immediately."

As Rowan opened her mouth to answer, a chime sounded.

"We hide!" Leni said. He pulled the sheet off Collin and ducked under the table.

"Were you followed?" Rowan asked as she crouched behind him.

"Not a chance," Gill said.

"You'd better go," Collin advised.

"I will, but I don't have to hide in a cabinet. If I'm seen next door, they'll just think I'm on an errand from Nils." She followed Rowan quickly, ducking under the table and crawling through the hole in the wall. Once Gill had followed her inside the other room, Rowan hurried toward a cabinet; Leni slid the missing panel silently back into place and found a cabinet of his own.

Varantia took out a charm, held it to her ear, and leaned toward the wall. She heard a door open.

"I'm Rand; Mace's overseer here," a voice announced to Collin.

Chapter 14

Gill could hear Rand pacing, one footfall heavier than another because of his limp.

"So you're one of Mace's people," Rand said.

"I am." Collin's voice was low, but clear.

"If I didn't know better, I would think that you're human."

"Although we look similar, there are still significant differences between us."

"The way you say words is strange."

"Languages change in 500 years. But I'm quickly learning the differences."

"Magic?"

"Language adaptation is one of the most elementary skills."

"You can still do magic?"

"Simple things, such as keeping myself clean. But the spell restraining me is so strong it would seriously weaken or kill me if I tried to break free."

"Good."

"You don't approve of me?"

"You? You're nothing. But you came here to get Mace, and I'm glad he got you first. I'd thrash you myself, but Mace gets mad if anyone does his business for him."

"Wouldn't you like the torture to stop?"

Gill could hear that Rand had stopped pacing. His voice came closer to the wall.

"I'll tell you what I want. This is my home now. I have a place here. I'm looked up to, and I mostly get what I want. A lot of the supervisors, the men who have been here the longest, feel the same way. We get enough food to eat and a decent place to sleep. We don't need anyone coming in and upsetting things."

"I understand."

"Do you?"

"Yes, I do."

"Then you know why I'm leaving you here. I hope you die slowly in a lot of pain."

"I expected you would."

A long silence followed. Eventually, Rand limped away, closing the door behind him. Gill crept to the wall next to the hallway and again listened as Rand's footsteps became fainter, and the outer door opened and closed.

Another chime sounded. Leni and Rowan stepped out of their respective cabinets.

"Any idea who the visitor was?" Rowan asked.

Varantia nodded. "I'll explain when we're back with Collin."

The three of them returned to Collin's room, and Leni covered him again. Varantia turned from Rowan to Collin. "Rand just reminded us of another reason why we can't put Rowan in with the others—her language would sound archaic to the others."

"Who's Rand?" Rowan asked.

"The one who was just here; he's overseer of the humans, Mace's second-in-command of the compound, and a very dangerous man," Varantia answered.

"What about Saris speaking the language?" Rowan protested.

"She has a language charm on her," Collin said.

"...and is probably learning the language quickly, as Nils did," Varantia added.

"So what do I do?"

"I'd say do as Leni does and hide."

She put her hands on her hips. "Meaning I'm useless and ought to have stayed in Maclin?"

"Not at all," Varantia said. "Once Mace finds out his magic is reduced, we may need a skilled fighter. Rand's speech to Collin just now was a reminder that if anything threatens Mace's supremacy, we'll have angry humans to contend with."

"You mean they don't want to be free of that monster?" Rowan said.

"It's very much the same reason why Somerlie didn't revolt over 500 years of Mace's tyranny," Collin said. "You become so afraid of the tyrant's power, and you get so used to it, that you don't know or don't remember what normal life is. Many people, when given a choice, will keep on living a life they're used to, even if it's a hard life."

Rowan shook her head. "I'll never understand it."

Collin turned to Varantia. "You're trying to rob him of his magic?"

Gill realized that Collin—and Leni and Rowan, for that matter—had not yet been told of the plan. "Yes. If we can keep him distracted over the next four to nine days, so that he doesn't feel a need to use more than elementary spells, his artifact and his charms should disintegrate. He'll be left with less magic than Leni." She turned to him. "Sorry, Leni."

"I don't mind."

"You're not going to kill him?" Rowan demanded.

"One step at a time," Varantia said calmly. "We can't do *any*thing to him until his magic has been reduced. Then we shall see. Perhaps Collin could make his mind well again."

Collin blew out a breath. "Maybe. But living so dysfunctionally over this long, his very brain matter has changed, and the behavior may be locked in. I could turn that back to normal, but he would be a very different person, almost an entirely new person—and I could not do it without his cooperation, which he may never give."

Rowan and Varantia stood across the table from each other; now Rowan walked around the table to face Varantia directly. "Look, I realize he used to be your mate and all, but I've known people like Mace, and once they've crossed a line, as he certainly has, they don't change back."

"You're talking about humans."

"I've noticed you're not that much different from us."

Varantia raised an eyebrow. "I'm not sure you realize the extent to which we all changed to make living with you comfortable."

Rowan made no reply.

"Let me put it this way," Varantia offered. "How successful were you when you tried to kill Mace before?"

Rowan looked away uncomfortably.

"Then let's try it my way." Varantia said. "I assure you, whatever needs to be done to stop him, I will do."

Rowan touched the sheath. "You must have made your artifact into a sword for a reason."

"I know Mace. What better way to communicate that my intentions were, as you humans say, deadly serious?"

"Wouldn't it have been better to disguise your motives?" Collin asked.

"As I'm sure Rowan can confirm, there's something to be said for making your opponent consider you a threat before you ever see each other."

That evening, after supper, Nils summoned Saris to the torture chamber to let her know about Leni and Rowan.

"Leni says he'll help you distract Mace," Gill said to Bryce. "He asked Varantia about Mace's interests while we were talking with Collin earlier. He says he's explored the storage rooms and knows what's in them. He claims he can plant things of interest that you can use if Mace's attention flags."

"I think he already *has* done something," Bryce said. "This afternoon, when Mace and I were touring the gardens, Mace seemed to suddenly find a wildflower of interest, or an unusual plant."

"Easy for a Wye to get a random seed to sprout quickly, or change the shape of a plant," Saris said.

"Saris," Gill said, "we need to keep an eye on the humans. If Mace is weakened, or it comes to a confrontation, some of them are going to come to Mace's defense."

Saris nodded. "I'm getting to know some of them. I overhear a lot of talk if I'm outside cleaning."

"Rand sends you on tasks?" Bryce asked.

"Yes. I'm getting a reputation as a thorough cleaner," Saris shifted her weight uncomfortably.

"Can you keep it up?" Gill asked.

"Oh, yes. I'm learning a lot, though not the sort of things I really wanted to learn."

"I know," Gill and Bryce said at the same time.

She smiled feebly. "I suppose it's easy to forget that it's hard for you, too."

"It's hard for everyone," Gill added.

The next day, the instant it became clear that Mace was not interested in touring the gardens again, Nils steered him to the library, pretending he needed to look up something there. When they entered, Mace immediately spotted an open book on a table and went to it. He picked it up and paged through it.

He turned toward Nils, ignoring Gill, who stood a pace behind. "I had forgotten I had brought all these books from Wik. I thought I would read them on the journey, and never got around to it. Once I built this place and stacked them, I forgot all about them." He smiled. "My favorite novelist."

"By all means, my lord, sit and read. I'll find something and join you."

The table where Mace found the book stood next to a richly upholstered and overstuffed high-backed chair, situated perfectly to catch the light from the windows. Mace settled in with a sigh and began reading. Nils found a book also and sat in a slightly smaller chair at right angles to Mace's.

Gill spoke briefly in Bryce's ear. Bryce nodded and waved her off. Gill knew from her explorations as Sloan that there was a wine cellar of sorts; Varantia knew exactly which sort of wine Mace preferred while reading and went to Leni to enhance it to his precise tastes.

"He found the book," she said to Leni.

Leni smiled. "Good."

Gill went to the kitchen for glasses and Mace's favorite finger foods. She set them on the table at Mace's elbow and continued to wait on Nils and Mace throughout the day, serving them the midday meal when Mace showed no signs of movement.

As Gill went back and forth carrying things, she felt Varantia draining from her back into the sword whenever she walked into the library. It was a prudent precaution, Gill knew, because if Mace touched her while Varantia was inside her, he would sense Varantia immediately.

In the afternoon, as Gill stood by Bryce's chair, waiting further instructions, Mace closed the book and turned to Nils. "He writes women well."

"My lord?"

"Have you ever noticed how women talk? 'No. Stop. Do not do that.' The most frequent words in their vocabulary. My father would always let me do what I wanted. My mother always tried to stop me. Then there was Varantia. Oh, she was fine for a while, and then settled into her women's habits. I should not do this. Please do not do that." He grinned. "No need to worry about them here."

"You are a veritable terror to women, my lord."

Mace grinned at Nils. Gill thought to herself that she never hated Mace more than in that instant. He pointed to her. "Get me the red-bound book, second shelf from the top, south end."

Gill quickly complied, holding the book carefully and presenting it to Mace with a bow. Unexpectedly, he grabbed her arm and pulled her roughly to him. He said something, but Gill was so startled and horrified that she could not make out the words. She kept her composure and looked into his face. Clearly, he expected an answer...now.

"As you say, my lord," she said steadily.

Mace chuckled, pushed her away, and released her. He turned to Nils. "Good to know that your man would be as obedient to me as he is to you."

"Naturally, I have taught him that, my lord."

He waved an arm. "Do not worry. I keep my word. He is at your sole disposal."

Nils nodded solemnly.

"Though if he had refused me, I would have had to take him."

"By all means, my lord."

Slowly, Gill walked backwards to where Nils was. He motioned for her to bend down and whispered in her ear, "I think we can do without you for now."

Gill nodded and left the room, realizing that Mace had asked her if he could torture her. She sighed and sat on the bottom step of the staircase, marveling that she had remained calm in Mace's grip without the help of Sloan or Silmariae or Varantia. With this procession of alien thoughts in her mind, it was easy for her to forget that she alone was in charge. Varantia could use her, but not against her will. Varantia could create the plan, and set the spells, but once magic had done all it could, it was her responsibility to see that Mace was defeated.

She stood and touched Silmariae. Once more, she felt energy flow through her and Varantia's thoughts settled in her mind. She smiled, welcoming back her ally, whose first thought was that Mace's interpretation of the novelist's portrayal of women was not accurate.

For the sake of appearances, Gill served supper to Mace and Nils. This time, Mace did not even look up from his book as Gill refreshed his drink and left the bottle. Nils waved her away; she found the two equally absorbed when she came later to take their empty trays. After quickly checking on Collin, Leni, and Rowan, Varantia peeked into the magic laboratory. She saw the beginnings of corrosion on the objects. Satisfied, she returned to her room.

Late in the evening, after Gill had gone to bed, Bryce returned and knocked on the open door between their rooms. Gill, in bedclothes, sat up in the bed. Bryce was outlined in the light of his own room.

"Nils took Mace grabbing you in stride, but I don't mind telling you if it weren't for him, I would have been frightened out of my wits."

"I was petrified," Gill confirmed.

"You didn't show it. Varantia? Sloan?"

"No, surprisingly, that was me."

"I'm impressed."

"I guess I've been around Mace long enough to know better."

Bryce leaned against the door wearily. "Don't take this as a slight, but sometimes I think Saris and Collin are braver than we are, facing all of this horror without any aids."

"I was thinking the same thing. Without Sloan, I would have run in terror several times when I was here before."

"I suppose eventually we'll adjust?"

"Yes. But think of this: no one, not even Rand, has as much direct contact with Mace as we do. Perhaps if they had done as we did without our aids, Saris or Collin, brave as they are, might have eventually snapped. We've seen some of the humans, with much less exposure to Mace, do that. So maybe you and I aren't any more or less brave than any of the others."

"You have a point."

"I know even Eminric wouldn't necessarily exchange places with us, and he's the most powerful Wye alive, after Mace."

Bryce nodded. "Nothing left to do but go to bed and see what tomorrow brings. Goodnight."

Gill was awakened by Mace's voice in the next room.

"I did not know you sketched, Nils."

Because the adjoining door was open, she saw Nils climb out of bed and look at an easel, which faced away from her. "As you can see, my lord," Nils said, "I'm not very good. Just something to keep my hands busy and relax my mind for bed. That one I did last evening."

Out of sight of the two men, she slipped out of bed and dressed as quickly as possible.

"You know," Mace continued, "I was quite a dabbler in my youth. There was so much I was interested in, I never had the time to develop all my talents to their fullest."

"Your modesty becomes you, my lord. I'm sure you excel at everything."

"You think so?" Mace lifted the easel. "We used to do a lot of nudes in our tutorials." Hands still full, he turned to Nils. "You know, we have many nudes, right in the yard." He shrugged towards the door.

Nils pulled at his nightshirt. "I need to get dressed, my lord."

"Follow when you can." He walked out, easel, pad, and all.

When he was safely away, Gill, now completely dressed, ducked into Bryce's room. "I'll bring your breakfast outside."

Bryce turned to her as he quickly pulled on a pair of pants. "Looks like Leni doodled on the pad. Nice doodles, by the way, but not a professional still life. I wonder how he got it up here without anyone seeing him."

"He said he was good at hiding."

Again, Gill was able to enlist Saris as well as other kitchen workers to bring out trays, and supports for them, to Mace and Nils. Mace ordered the carousel stopped and set up the easel right in the yard. Five men were chained there, erratically spaced, with fresh lash marks, old lash marks, or both. Mace picked out a particular man and had one of the supervisors pose him, back to Mace. His model ready, he alternated between sketching and eating. Nils was not obligated to join Mace in his sketching; but was expected to give artistic praise, which he did lavishly.

Once Mace's attention was occupied, Gill was able to get some breakfast for herself and Saris, and clear the other trays when they were done. The two women returned the trays to the kitchen; Saris was sent to cleaning duties around the yard. Her expression had changed in past days from grim to determined. Other than the scars Varantia had added for show, Saris had no other marks and her face had healed from the initial beating. Despite the hard work, she appeared healthy and more confident than in the first days she had been there.

When Gill returned to the yard, she saw two men come from the barracks with pads and writing tools. With a cautious look toward Mace, each of them sat and began to sketch also, several paces from the easel. She had no idea whether Mace had invited them or whether they had risked coming out on their own. Mace ignored them, or seemed to, and the supervisors left them alone.

She hovered around Mace and Nils, but paced long distances behind them. When she came close enough behind Mace, she saw an impressive drawing. Either Mace did have talent, or he was using magical ability to enhance it. Varantia thought it was a little of both. At the end of her pacing, she also peered at the other two artists. The papers seemed torn from some sort of record book, but this did not deter the artists, who showed talent. One used dots of various sizes close together to make his portrait; the other had some sort of charcoal and did a lot of blending. They used trays in their laps as easels.

Before midday, Mace had the basic form outlined, and had started to add details. Gill walked around the carousel to catch a glance at the model from the front. His face was rigid, his teeth clenched from having to remain so still for such a long time. The other men on the carousel at least had the luxury of moving as much as the chains allowed to relieve cramps. At last, though, the model could take it no longer and twitched. Mace roared with rage. He tore the page from the easel and crumpled it in one hand; with the other, he pointed to a supervisor and then to his model. The supervisor nodded and proceeded to apply a lash to the victim.

Mace turned to Nils. "He ruined my sketch!"

Nils spread his hands. "A study, my lord, a study. From a model unworthy of your talents. There are others to choose from."

Mace turned, and for the first time, it seemed, noticed the other two men sketching. He pointed. "You!"

The two men turned, their expressions grim.

"Are yours ruined, too?"

Feebly, each of them gestured to another man on the carousel.

Nils leaned toward Mace. "Naturally, they would chose easier subjects, my lord."

Mace nodded. He enlisted another supervisor to position one of the remaining men for him. He threw the ball of paper in his hand to the ground and began sketching with more concentration. The two human artists, seeing that they were not to be tortured, at least not then, returned to their works.

As the sun rose higher, Gill fetched a midday meal for Mace and Nils. Other men in the yard, as they went back and forth from their work, would pause and look—at a safe distance—at one or all three of the sketches. Rand came out and inspected each one, but showed no more than mild interest. Mace did not appear to notice him. Gill thought that Rand's curiosity must be burning if he had walked so far, having to conceal his limp, when he did not have to. But he gave no orders and made no comments; Gill presumed he was satisfied that order in the yard was being preserved and work was not being unduly interrupted.

Just as Gill started to think she ought to go to the kitchen and get supper, Mace completed his sketch. He leaned back with a satisfied "ah!" and gestured Nils closer to comment. With Mace's eyes off him, the model relaxed with a sigh.

Nils made a show of examining the sketch. "Magnificent, my lord. Magnificent."

If Gill leaned to one side, she could see the sketch in its entirety. It was quite good; very technically correct.

Mace put down his writing instrument. "Let's see how the other students are doing." He walked over to the first artist, Nils and Gill in tow. The artist looked up at him questioningly. Mace leaned over, waved at the picture, and spoke to Nils. "I never could see a reason to use dots. Makes the eyes cross."

"Lesser artists must do what they can, my lord."

Gill thought the portrait was outstanding. It captured not only the details, but the passion, pain, and sadness of the scene.

Mace simply nodded at Nils and walked to the next artist. Once out of Mace's field of vision, the first artist gathered his materials and hurried back to the barracks as fast as dignity would allow.

The next artist, also showed outstanding talent. He too had captured the nuances of the scene. Mace simply clicked his tongue. "Smudged," he said to Nils.

Once Mace had turned his back, the second artist scrambled after the first.

Nils let out an exaggerated sigh. "These humans simply cannot be expected to equal your talent, my lord." He put a hand on Mace's shoulder and guided him back to the easel. "We must preserve your sketch before the sun fades it."

"Yes. You can put it in your room. My gift to you."

"I'm not worthy of the gesture, my lord. Surely you would want it in your study."

"I insist."

"In that case, my lord, I'm honored."

They packed the easel and strolled back to the mansion. Mace was oblivious to the change in the yard, and Nils showed no sign of noticing it, but it was plain to Gill and every other human: two humans had indulged in a simple human activity, and had not been punished. It was as if a collective sigh blew through the enclosure.

That night, when Bryce and Gill were alone in Bryce's room, they stood in front of Mace's sketch on the wall. Every scar, every bruise, every gash, had been set in meticulous detail.

"I'm keeping it," Bryce said to Gill. "If I ever forget why we're here, all I have to do is look at this."

She nodded. "Those human artists...they must have been desperate to recapture a moment of normal life to risk themselves like that."

"I think that we just prevented two deaths...that if they hadn't had that outlet, they would have snapped and attacked Mace. Did you feel the tension dissolve—it was like someone had cut a restraining band."

She considered before answering. "I think you just cleared up a mystery. Did you see Rand come out?"

"Yes."

"He must have come to the same conclusion. With the barrier in place, there may be no more caravans to Somerlie for a long while, so they have to preserve the humans they have. Mace won't care if the humans dwindle—he'll just work the ones that are left twice as hard. But Rand can't afford to have his workload, or the workload of the other supervisors, increase. So if letting a couple of humans draw pictures keeps them from lashing out and getting killed, Rand and the supervisors will excuse them from work for that long."

Bryce turned to her and held up a finger. "Let me build on that. I would wager that in the barracks, those two have several drawings already. They let them do those things as long as it's hidden from Mace."

"That makes sense. I haven't been in the barracks. Have you?"

"No, but Saris has, and she's got an ear out. Next time we see her, maybe we can ask."

She inhaled sharply.

"What?" he asked.

"Saris knows where Leni is. Maybe she did see sketches in the barracks, talked to Leni about them, and that's why Leni put the easel in your room."

Bryce assumed a thoughtful expression. "May I speak plainly to you?"

"Please do."

"Do you remember saying that you wanted to come here with Silmariae alone?"

"I do." She smiled. "And yes, Bryce, I see now that that would have been a mistake."

The next morning Gill was awakened by a knock on Bryce's door. Through the opening between the rooms, she saw Bryce get out of his bed, put a robe over his bedclothes, and open the door. Because of the angle of the door, she could not see who was in the hall.

"Mace is not here?" Rand's voice came.

"No. Is he missing?"

"No one has seen him since last night."

"I haven't seen him," Nils said. "Shall I send a message to you when I do?"

"No, he's done this before. I thought he might be here, that's all."

Bryce nodded and shut the door. Gill felt chilled. She hurried into Bryce's room.

"You don't suppose he's gone to his magic laboratory?"

Bryce answered her with a look of horror.

Chapter 15

Gill and Bryce dressed quickly and went to the tunnel. The household and the yard appeared normal. Varantia reached the entrance to the laboratory and stood outside. After standing still for a few moments, she shook her head.

"He's not in there. I could feel the power if he were."

"That's a relief. But where is he?"

Leni stepped out from behind a door. "Have you checked the cellar where Saris sleeps?"

She gasped. "Leni! You didn't put Mace in with Saris?"

"No, Gill," he said innocently. "But Saris found a pottery wheel in an unused room where she is. We think maybe someone many years ago made one for himself and hid it from Mace. Rowan and I went outside the wall and dug up some clay. I cleaned and kneaded it and we put it there."

"How did you get Mace in there?" Bryce asked.

"I made him hungry for mushrooms," Leni said proudly. "I made sure he was so hungry he would want them right away, and get them himself. There's a mushroom farm in a room in the cellar. I left the pottery room open, and he went in there. Saris saw him."

Gill had slumped, leaning against the wall, in relief. Now Varantia straightened and put a hand on Leni's arm. "You did well, Leni, but please don't try to put a spell on Mace again, at least not until it gets to a point where we're fighting him."

"He didn't feel it. I made sure."

She removed her hand and looked into his eye. "I know, Leni. But we never know when he'll get suspicious and start questioning anything out of the ordinary."

"I won't do it any more, then, Varantia."

"How's Collin?" Gill asked.

"Oh, he's good. If he thinks you're someone else coming in, he looks real sick. But when he knows it's you, he looks better."

Bryce put a hand on Leni's shoulder. "You're doing real well, Leni."

"Collin and Rowan and Saris tell me what to do sometimes."

Gill nodded. "Keep listening to them."

Bryce and Gill turned and walked away. Leni called after them. "Mace is getting weaker. I can feel it."

Gill glanced back. "Let's hope so."

The cellar under the mansion was adequately lit and well-ventilated, but the hallways were narrow and the rooms numerous and small. All the workers were at their tasks elsewhere; Bryce and Gill saw no one as they wove their way through the passages until they found a room with an open door. They could see Mace within, playing with the clay. A bowl half-full of mushrooms sat on the floor at his side.

Nils paused at the threshold. "How may I serve you today, my lord?"

Mace paused and gestured with a muddy hand. "Come in, come in. Look at this. I haven't done this since I was quite young."

Nils stepped inside and sat on a low stool opposite Mace. "Now that your abilities are fully mature, my lord, I'm sure you can work wonders." Behind his back, he gestured at Gill to leave.

Her responsibilities, again, were limited to bringing food and cleaning up after them. As Mace's experimentation in pottery and sculpture proceeded, however, the room became so messy he sent for Saris. When she went inside, Gill hovered anxiously at a spot in the hall within sight of the room. Mace had promised not to torture Gill, but he had made no such promise about Saris, and Gill knew that Mace would torture whoever was at hand when the mood struck.

The sound of steps made her turn. The rhythm of the limp told her Rand was coming down the stairs. Knowing that loitering would draw suspicion, she walked into the room, thinking to simply ask Nils if she could be of service. She felt Varantia drain from her when she crossed the threshold.

Saris was scrubbing clay remnants under Mace's pottery wheel. Mace, with a grin, held up a neatly formed vase for Nils to inspect.

"Dazzling, my lord. A match for any of the ceramics in your mansion."

Mace heard Rand at the door and turned. "Take this and have it fired." He held out the vase.

As Rand stepped forward to take it, Gill thought that with such a variety of men kidnapped over the years, finding someone who knew how to fire a clay pot would be possible for Rand once he made inquiries.

Mace stood and brushed at his clay-spattered clothes. "There was a saying back home: 'The larger the mess, the greater the artist.'"

"Then you are, undoubtedly, a magnificent one," Nils said.

Mace sighed. "I am feeling so good I think I will indulge myself with a body for a while." He bent toward Saris and touched her arm. "Prepare yourself."

Saris compliantly stood to follow Mace, but something in Gill's mind screamed, "No!" She reached for Silmariae and took a step forward. Nils appeared in front of her, stuck her hard on the face, put hands on her shoulders and shoved her against the wall.

"What is this?" Mace demanded. "Is your man rebelling against you?"

"He simply faltered in attending me, my lord. I have corrected the situation."

"Perhaps you had better follow me," Mace suggested. "We can discipline them both."

Nils held a finger up to Gill's face, warning her not to move. Gill was still stunned by the blow; she could not disobey if she wished. Nils walked over to Mace. Though he whispered, Gill's excellent hearing picked up every word.

"My lord, if he sees you work, he'll know that I'm not the artist that you are, and he will be even harder to control."

Mace nodded. "I understand. Let me handle this." He signaled Rand, who had not yet left the room, to take Saris in hand. Suddenly, he stood in front of Gill and hit her stomach with such a force she almost retched. "So!" Mace demanded. "You think you can go your own way here." He hit her again, found his blow muffled by her belt, and took it off. He held the sword by the scabbard for in instant, then tossed it aside. "You fancy yourself a fighter, do you? I will show you what," he hit her on the side, cracking ribs, "a fighter," he hit her on the other side, with the same result, "is." He pummeled her back, sending her sprawling on the floor.

Gill lay on the floor with her mouth open, in such pain she was unable to utter a sound. She heard Mace say, "Rand, do you have a shocker on you?"

Rand handed the vase to Nils and pulled a device from a pocket. Mace took it, bent down, and applied it to Gill's aching side. The pain was excruciating. She convulsed and moaned.

Mace straightened up and kicked her. "Silence!"

With immense effort, Gill managed to restrain another groan.

Mace handed the shocker back to Rand. Rand took back the vase in one hand, while still holding Saris, who had kept her face blank, in the other.

Nils said to Mace, "I may have to find and train another man, my lord."

Mace took a towel and wiped his hands. "Trust me, my friend. This is how I trained Rand, and you can see that he is alive and obedient to me. Your man will recover, and you will see that he has changed for the better. He will never disobey you again." He nodded at Rand, whose face showed he was pleased with the demonstration, and gestured at Saris, who maintained a bland expression. They left. He threw down the towel and called to Gill. "Get on your feet, you are not that injured."

Gritting her teeth, knowing any display of pain could bring on more violence, she slowly rose. When she had her feet under her again, Mace pointed a warning finger at her, "I do not want to see you limping or holding your arms abnormally either." He nodded and winked at Nils, turned on his heel, and left.

When his footsteps had faded away, Gill let out an enormous moan and slumped forward. Nils caught her and helped her to the floor. He found Silmariae and put the hilt into her hand. When her fingers closed around it, Varantia surged back into her.

"Only heal the internal injuries," Nils reminded her urgently.

"I know," Varantia said.

Slowly, she felt her body healing. When she felt well enough, she held up a hand. Nils helped her to her feet.

"Can you walk?" he asked solicitously.

"Yes," Gill breathed. "I feel stiff, slow, and worn out, but I can make it."

Nils let her go and took a step back. "It's best that you are, or Mace would be suspicious."

Gill nodded. "I think we need to talk to Collin."

"So do I. Let me lead the way."

When they opened the door to Collin's room, everyone turned toward Gill. She saw their expressions of horror and heard their gasps of surprise.

"What happened?" Rowan said, moving toward her.

"Mace did a bad thing again," Leni said, apparently to answer Rowan.

"Let me get a look at those," Collin said.

Instead of moving toward Collin, Gill fell into Rowan's arms and buried her face in her shoulder. Rowan embraced her; Gill hissed and winced. Rowan released her and put arms around Gill's uninjured shoulders, carefully. Gill sobbed. Her imagination ran wild, picturing what Mace could be doing to Saris at that very moment. She shuddered...and winced again, when even that small motion aggravated her injuries.

Rowan gently pushed Gill within reach of Collin. He touched her arm, concentrated, and said, "I take it Varantia took care of the internal injuries. The external ones aren't life-threatening, fortunately."

Rowan embraced Gill again, gingerly. "What's going on?"

Bryce folded his arms across his chest. "Mace took Saris to his torture chamber."

"Didn't I tell you we shouldn't take her?"

"She has a charm of oblivion," Collin reminded her. "She won't tell Mace anything and she'll have little memory of the event."

"Won't Mace notice?" Rowan asked.

"No, she'll appear to have gone into shock. Mace probably sees this all the time. He won't think anything of it, and it's too small a spell for him to detect."

Bryce leaned back against the door and shook his head. "Saris isn't the problem."

"Then what is?" Rowan asked, puzzled.

Bryce nodded to Gill.

Gill pulled away from Rowan, stepped to the far wall, and lowered herself to the floor, sitting with knees up, shivering. Leni got a cup of water from the water jug and offered it to Gill. As she sipped, Leni came up with a large, thick blanket and tenderly put it around Gill.

"May I speak freely, majesty?" Bryce said to Gill.

Gill nodded. With the water and the warmth, as well as the care received from the others, her agitation began to subside.

"You nearly got yourself killed today," Bryce said firmly. "You cannot allow that to happen."

"I can see she's been in a fight," Rowan said.

Bryce turned to her. "Yes. Mace beat her when she moved to rescue Saris from him. It was all Nils could do to cover for her."

Collin moaned.

"You're not injured, too, are you?" Bryce asked.

"No. It's Von again." Collin looked despairingly at Gill.

"Von?" Bryce asked.

"Or, rather, his creation. It's not Gill's fault. Silmariae's reaction to seeing her youngest child being carried away by Mace must have been instinctive and powerful."

Bryce looked from Collin to Gill. "Majesty, I know it's a great responsibility to carry Silmariae—the sword and the memories. Not to mention Varantia and Sloan. But it is your *duty* to keep them under control. I would do it for you, if I could, but I can't. We escaped detection this time only by a hair."

"Did I do this by making Mace hungry?" Leni asked nervously. "I won't do it again, I promise."

Gill looked up at him. "No, Leni, you did nothing wrong. I did."

"It was a mistake, that's all," Collin said.

"We can't afford to make mistakes, not like this one. We've made too many of them. Silmariae died from some mistake we don't even know about!" Bryce held out a hand, showing a space between his forefinger and thumb. "We are *this close* to our objective. If Varantia is right, the day after tomorrow, Mace will be done for. And I, for one, will be glad, because I've had my fill of this palace of death." His voice broke; he bowed his head.

Rowan walked over and put an arm around his shoulders. "I know," she said. "It's hard on all of us."

Bryce composed himself and turned to Gill. "Majesty, you *must* understand; you cannot endanger yourself to save *any* of us."

Gill nodded. "I know," she said grimly.

In the silence that followed, Leni said meekly, "I have another idea for Mace."

* * *

They knew that Mace might try to find them after he had tortured Saris, so Bryce and Gill returned to Bryce's rooms. When it was clear that Mace was going to spend some time, Bryce sent Gill for dinner. As she walked stiffly through the hallways and into the kitchen, other workers winked or nodded at her. All she could think was that word had gotten around that Mace had beaten her himself, and that she was now considered one of them because of it.

Bryce and Gill started dinner in silence. About midway through the meal, Bryce said, "I'm sorry, majesty."

"Don't be," Gill answered. "You were right."

He sighed. "I wish we knew how Silmariae died."

"I don't know," Varantia said. "She never allowed me to emerge, which was mistake enough, so I do not know what happened. But I say you are right, too. If Gill does anything to suppress or overwhelm me, I can't aid you. If she continues to allow me the freedom I have had these past days, then it may be possible, even if she dies, for me to act."

When they finished their dinner, and Mace still had not shown up, Bryce said, "Go see if Leni is ready with his latest plan."

Gill went to the top of the wall. The sky was partly cloudy, but as she looked on, the clouds seemed to scramble away. At first, she thought that was odd because there was no wind on the ground. Then she remembered it was part of Leni's plan. As she walked westward, she saw an object blocking her path. It appeared to be a huge black barrel, mounted on stilts, with a spyglass fastened on the side. As she bent to examine the curious thing, she heard voices behind her.

"Your man has found my telescope," Mace said jovially.

As quickly as she could, Gill knelt and bowed her head.

"You see," Mace said to Nils as he passed her, "his manner is much improved."

"You have worked wonders, my lord," Nils answered.

Gill rose slowly after they walked by. Mace commandeered the apparatus. As Nils and Mace talked, pointing at objects in the sky, and looking through the barrel, she slowly realized that the barrel was a huge spyglass, and that they were seeing stars and other magnificent sights up close.

At first, watching the two at the apparatus, Gill felt a longing, then a lust. Once she realized her feelings, she suppressed them, knowing it would be dangerous if Mace noticed her looking at the apparatus too hungrily. She consoled herself by thinking that if she ever left Mace's fortress alive, she would ask around for one of these things, so she could look at everything. Eminric or one of the Wye of Eldswold must know how to make one, she thought.

Mace became bored with stargazing sooner than Gill expected. Again, she made haste to kneel and bow her head as they walked by. She saw Mace's boots stop in front of her; Nils stood beside him.

"I think, my friend, that now would be an excellent time to demonstrate your authority to this man. I will have the cleaner sent, too. I found him too shallow for my taste, but I understand that you take them as a pair."

"I do, my lord. A most excellent suggestion."

To keep up appearances, Gill had to undress and lie on the table in the torture chamber. She shivered, but not from the cold. Lying there naked, looking at the ceiling, knowing there were instruments nearby that could rip her apart, she had an idea of the fear the others must feel when they were in the room. When they heard a knock at the door, Bryce stood in front of Gill to shield her private parts from view. Saris entered, pale and walking slowly. Once the door was shut again, Gill stiffly sat up and reached for her clothes, feeling a wave of relief that Saris was at least sound enough to come there unassisted.

"I'm glad you're alive," Saris said weakly.

"I'm glad to see you, too," Gill said as she dressed.

When they were all seated, Saris added, "I'm sorry, Gill. I feel this was my fault."

Gill shook her head. "It wasn't."

"That was Mother taking control of you, and she wouldn't have if it hadn't been me."

"If it hadn't been that," Gill said, "it would have been something else."

Bryce put a hand on Saris's shoulder. "We want to know how you are."

"Pretty numb. I activated the charm of oblivion," she indicated a ring on her finger, "before Rand took me out of the pottery room. Until Mace let me go, I wasn't aware of much of anything. I must not have provided sufficient amusement; he released me after about an hour and had the attendants get someone else for him. I learned about Gill mostly from overhearing Rand talking about it in the kitchen."

Varantia said, "Where are you injured? I may be able to do something."

Saris shook her head. "I looked myself over, and the cuts and bruises were pretty minimal. I have burn spots here and there; the kitchen workers gave me some ointment that seems to work. They told me that Mace must have used shockers on me, and that it was normal not to remember much. Mostly, I feel pretty washed out."

Gill sighed. "I'm glad it wasn't worse."

Saris nodded. "I discovered something."

"What?" Gill asked.

"Why Mace tortures people. I remember when Mother came back after wearing Sloan, she told us that Mace had started to torture people on a regular basis. He was taking prisoners from the army of

Somerlie and Asquith. Everyone thought he simply had gone mad...
but there's another reason." Saris took a breath.

Bryce patted her back. "Take your time."

A few moments later, Saris continued, "When he tried to kill everyone on Wik, and absorbed the magic from the ones he did kill...he liked it. He can't get magic from humans, but in torturing them, he draws from their suffering. He likes that, too. It's addictive for him."

Varantia bowed her head.

"Are you all right?" Bryce asked gently.

Varantia looked up sadly. "I'll have to kill him," she said softly.

"Wasn't that inevitable?" Saris asked.

Varantia sighed. "I had hoped there was a chance we could save him. But Rowan was right...in a way. His system has changed. He's a feeder. He can't live without feeding now. That's why he kept Somerlie's population alive all these years. He needs others to feed off, or he dies."

"Can't we just deprive him, then?" Bryce asked.

"No," Saris answered for Varantia. "He'll just gather a desperate surge of strength and kill everyone nearby...including Gill." She turned to Varantia. "My guess is that's how Von and his last remaining friends died. Mace got angry and suspicious, yes, but I would wager he was angry and suspicious because he was deprived. He had to feed on something and they happened to be nearby."

Varantia sighed. "He can't be cured. Not even by Collin."

Bryce bent down toward her. "But the disintegration spell will still work, won't it? Deprive him of his magic? Make him vulnerable?"

Varantia nodded.

"Then we must be do everything possible to be sure the disintegration spell works," Bryce said grimly.

Mace did not come to Bryce's room the next morning. Gill rose after Bryce and dressed herself. When she went into Bryce's room, she found him examining a stack of games on the table.

"Leni's latest suggestion?" Gill asked.

"Apparently so," Bryce said. "Something in Von's memory tells me that these will keep Mace occupied for days."

"I think they will," Varantia said hopefully.

As they sorted through the stack, trying to select ones that would interest Mace the longest, Bryce asked, "Isn't today the first possible day the artifacts should start turning to dust?"

Varantia nodded. "Depending on how resistant the artifact materials are, they may last until tomorrow, or another few days, before they are all completely gone."

"Can you tell when his main artifact crumbles?"

"Not unless I go and look. I could do that, I suppose, if Mace were distracted."

"More to the point, will Mace be able to tell when it crumbles?"

"He won't be able to tell anything unless he tries to work a strong spell. As of today, though, if he does, he'll be aware of the decay immediately."

"And where does that put us?"

"He'll still be quite strong, but nowhere near his full strength. He couldn't, for instance, destroy the entire army of Eldswold, if they still existed."

"But enough to destroy us?"

"If the artifact is intact, he can, and all at once. If the artifact is destroyed, he can kill us singly, but only with a great effort."

Bryce took a long breath. "Let's get on with the work of distracting him, then."

Gill carried the games to Mace's study. There, Nils and Mace played through three meals and a late evening snack. Nils waved Gill off to bed well after nightfall. Gill took the opportunity to find Saris. She was already in her tiny room, preparing to go to bed. Gill motioned her to get dressed and come.

Varantia led Saris to Mace's magical laboratory and guided her through the illusion of a wall. Nothing had been disturbed, but there was a musty odor.

Saris looked around. "Mace certainly accumulated a lot of charms and minor artifacts."

"It's his main one I'm concerned with." She walked over to the cabinet and opened it. She took out Mace's wristbands, and weighed each of them in a hand. They seemed fragile. On impulse, she grasped them with her fingers and crumbled them like crackers.

Saris inhaled appreciatively. "That was his main artifact?"

Varantia dusted off her hands. "Yes." She turned around. "All the rest of these are ready to crumble as well. If Mace makes any move, reduce the room to dust, so he can't attempt to reassemble or restore them. Leni and Rowan, I believe, have the energy weapon."

"I can use it," Saris volunteered.

"Good. Let's see how the others are doing."

They found Collin straining to pull away from the wall, while Leni and Rowan looked on. "Hold on that, Collin," Varantia said.

"I'm just about loose," Collin said.

"Wait until morning and it will be easier," Varantia said. "I just crumbled Mace's artifact."

Rowan turned to her. "Then he's powerless," she said hopefully.

"Not quite. With the artifact gone, his power will diminish in the next several hours until it's at Leni's level. But he's weak enough now so we can make plans to bring this to a conclusion."

"And he can't tell his artifact was destroyed?" Rowan asked.

"Not unless he tries to draw on it for his magic," Varantia said. "He hasn't since we've started this operation."

"He would have to be in actual contact with it to use his full magical abilities, anyway," Saris added, "which is impossible now."

"So, what next?" Rowan asked.

"Leave Mace to me." She nodded at Saris. "I want you to stay around here from now on. Have Collin heal any wounds you have left from Mace, and give Rowan your language charm in case she needs to go into the yard. Do you have a transmitter?"

She shook her head.

Rowan jerked a thumb toward the wall. "All our things are next door. There's one there."

"Good. At my signal, or when you sense any sort of disturbance, or if Mace shows up, destroy the laboratory, and anything else around here that looks as if Mace could use it."

Rowan waved her hand. "Leni and I have found a lot of contraptions in this area. We don't know what they're for, but they don't look beneficial."

"All technology looks threatening to you, Rowan," Saris said.

"This time I agree with Rowan. Destroy it anyway."

Saris nodded.

"Can I use magic on Mace now?" Leni asked shyly.

Varantia thought about it, then put a hand on Leni's shoulder. "Wait until one of us tells you we're fighting Mace; then you can use all the magic you want."

"You think he'll fight?" Rowan asked.

"He'll certainly resist me taking him," Varantia said. "Now that Saris has told us he's a feeder, I don't doubt he'll try to restore his magic by killing Collin or even Leni, or try to use some implements or charms that he's hidden somewhere."

"You think there are others?" Saris asked.

Varantia nodded. "I know Mace."

"Where exactly are you taking him to?" Rowan asked.

"To oblivion; where he and I should properly be."

Chapter 16

Gill went to her room to sleep. Saris, she knew, would not be missed until morning, and it would be easy for Nils to say he had sent her somewhere if anyone asked. When she put on her nightshirt, she looked in the mirror and saw the bruises disappear as Varantia restored her already healing body to normal.

In the morning, Gill put on the Wye armor under her clothes before getting breakfast. After eating her meal, she brought food to Mace's room. As she placed breakfast plates on a table, Mace turned to Nils.

"Playing these games has given me an idea. Do you remember the orbitals we placed when we came here?"

"Yes, my lord," Nils answered. "But Eldswold placed even more of them. A war of orbitals might be amusing, but would get us nowhere."

Mace smiled, shook his head, and held up a hand. "No, my friend. You see, I planted yet another device, in case the army of Eldswold ever cornered me, so that I could tell them that they must let me live, or I would destroy this world. It was so long ago—and of course I have not needed it these past centuries—I had forgotten about it until these games reminded me."

Gill finished placing the plates and knelt, listening.

"A wise precaution," Nils said.

"Yes. The locks on the control panel are tied to my magical artifact, which only I can use."

Gill prevented herself from breathing a sigh of relief. With the artifact dust, the control panel could be destroyed. But she needed to know more and kept silent.

"Forgive me, my lord," Nils said humbly, "your intelligence so greatly surpasses mine that I do not quite comprehend. I presume you would not want to destroy the planet now, so, how would it be used?"

"Ah!" Mace said, leaning back in his chair. "But we can combine these with magic. Like making a new artifact. With our new artifact, we direct the energy not to destroying the planet, but destroying

Eldswold and Asquith." He sighed. "Somerlie we would have to leave.
We do need slaves to do the work."

"Naturally, my lord."

Mace was not looking at her. He swiveled the chair back and forth,
a smile on his face, a finger on his lips. Gill rose, straightened to her
full height, and took out the transmitter.

"Saris."

"Yes?"

"Now."

She pocketed the transmitter. Mace stared at her in astonishment—or, not her, but Varantia, who had formed an image around
her.

As Mace lifted himself out of the chair and opened his mouth, a
deafening noise shattered the air. At the same time, a bright light,
overwhelming the sunlight, flashed through the windows. A tremen-
dous shock, like an earthquake, shook the house. Nils was thrown
against a couch; Mace and Varantia held on to opposite sides of the
table to keep their balance. As the echoes died away, Mace and Varantia were face to face across the table.

An expression of hatred distorted Mace's face. "You cannot defeat
me."

They heard a boom as if lightning struck nearby.

"I just did. Your artifacts and the control room for your doomsday
devices are now dust."

"Impossible!" He slammed a fist on the table and looked up into
her face. His body shook as if he were straining himself. Varantia
looked on calmly as he tried, and failed, to summon enough magic
to break hers. She extended a hand. "Come, Mace. It's time."

"Never! I will kill you, and I will punish this traitor, too!" He swung
savagely on Nils. As Varantia moved to take Mace, he sent out a pum-
meling blast of air, similar to the one Leni had used on the caravan,
which slammed her to the floor. The squall lasted only for several
seconds. Even as Varantia gathered enough magic to resist and walk
through it, it died away. Mace and Nils were gone.

Drawing Silmariae, Gill bolted into the hall. No one was to be
seen to the right or left, but looking down the stairs, she could see
a shadow near the opening to the portico. She sheathed the sword
and hurried that way.

She stopped short at the door. At the end of the portico stood Leni.
At Leni's feet lay Mace, caught in a net of sleep. Bryce stood nearby.
Collin and Rowan walked toward them from the wall, both wearing
Wye armor.

Leni smiled proudly. "I waited on top of the wall until he came
and threw it on him."

Rowan stepped forward and nudged the net with the tip of her
sword. "Caught in his own net; how poetic."

Gill turned to Bryce. "Are you all right?"

He took a breath. "Startled, but sound."

Saris emerged from the tunnel with the energy weapon. The butt of the weapon lay in her hands; the nozzle rested on her shoulder.

Gill called to her. "I presume you got the magical laboratory and control room?"

Saris nodded.

Rowan said, "We cleared out anything else that looked suspicious, too."

"Maybe I should check to see if anything is left," Bryce said.

"I think I got anything important, but you never know," Saris said.

Gill nodded at Bryce; he walked away. A noise in the yard drew her attention there. The men were gathering in a large assembly. Others were joining from the barracks. Gill had never seen all the men in one place, and had not realized until then how many there were.

"Any suggestions as to how to handle this mob?" Rowan said in her ear.

Gill's eyebrows lifted. "There are many expert swordfighters among them."

"Just our luck."

The men advanced with increasing determination and at a quicker pace, as Gill went through various escape plans in her mind.

Saris unshouldered the weapon. "Stand back. I'll take care of this."

"What are you going to do?" Gill asked.

"Don't worry; I won't harm a hair on their tortured heads." She moved the settings, aimed, and fired. An amber light filled the yard, accompanied by a high-pitched whine. All the men collapsed.

Saris turned to Gill. "They're alive. They can see and hear us, but they won't be able to do anything much more strenuous than lift a fork to feed themselves until evening."

"Hello," Collin said, looking beyond Gill.

Gill turned her head to see who Collin might be talking to, and felt a tickle on her back. She spotted Rand; he apparently had come outside though the kitchen door and around the mansion. He held a broken knife in his hand.

"Oh, were you trying to kill me?" Gill mocked.

With a roar, Rand lurched forward, trying to thrust the shattered blade into her face. But age and torture had taken the edge out of his strength and coordination. Gill disarmed him easily, grabbed him by the hair, and pressed his face against one of the column supports.

"It's over," she roared. "No more Mace, no more torture, no more thrashing anyone anytime you feel they deserve it. You're no longer in charge here. You're just the same as everyone else."

"Kill me," he spat out, "I'd rather be dead."

"Oh, no," Gill said. "I want you to spend the rest of your miserable life as a nobody, with no power, no influence. I want you to watch as others who have no interest in torturing people rise to rule over you. I want you to feel the frustration of knowing that you won't ever, ever, be allowed to thrash anyone who frustrates you again."

"Who do you think you are, female scum?"

She spun him around. "Believe it or not, I was once Sloan. But as far as you're concerned, I'm your granddaughter, you puddle of slime."

She heard gasps behind her and realized she had not told this to her companions.

He hawked his throat and spat, but missed his mark due to a tortured and misshapen mouth and tongue.

Looking past him, Gill saw another man. He seemed familiar; then she recognized him as the "fish" that Mace had tied up and tortured soon after she and Nils arrived. He must not have been with the others when Saris stunned them; he looked to be on the edge of collapse. Collin walked out and reached to steady him, but the man swerved away and plunged a knife into Rand's ribcage.

Gill grabbed the attacker and pulled him roughly away. Collin eased a gasping Rand to the ground, straddled him, and put his hands on Rand's sides.

"He deserves to die," the man said.

Gill turned to him. "And what about you, murderer?"

The man stammered, apparently not able to find words to answer. She gestured to Saris. "Tie him up, immobilize him, do something."

Saris took the weapon from her shoulder, adjusted the settings, and shot. A beam the width of a finger came out; the man fell back to the ground in a sitting position. Saris nodded at Gill and resumed her stance.

Gill turned to Collin and Rand. Rand's eyes were now closed; he appeared to be unconscious. Collin's face showed intense concentration. He shook his head slowly. "There's a lot of injury here."

"What about his mind?" Gill asked.

"Behavior is part brain structure; part habit. Since he's human, he can't resist if I put the brain structure back to normal, but the habits may never be unlearned."

"Try it anyway."

Collin nodded; Gill watched as Rand's external scars and deformities slowly disappeared. She heard a movement behind her and swiveled around quickly, sword at hand, unwilling to tolerate any more backstabbers.

Saris held out a hand. "Relax. They're just getting over the first shock. All these men are going to do is sit up. It'll take every bit of energy they have right now."

Gill sighed with relief.

"I'm going to search the yard to see if there are any others unaccounted for." Rowan shook her head. "Some bodyguard I am. First I miss Silmariae's killer, and then I miss Rand trying to stab you."

"What's armor for?" Gill said indulgently.

"I'll go with you," Saris called to Rowan, unshouldering her weapon and following.

Behind her, Gill heard a noise, and saw one of the younger men raise a finger to her. "Uh...if you're his granddaughter, does that mean you've come to take us home?"

Gill looked around and found other hopeful faces among the assembly. She raised her voice and said, "Let me tell all of you why you're here...and why most of you will remain here. It's because most of you believe that if someone offends you, they deserve to suffer. It's because you acted that way that you were taken in the first place, and it's all you've known since you've been here. But I'm here to tell you that's not the way most of the rest of the world thinks. Not in Somerlie, not anywhere else but right within these walls." She gestured around the periphery. "And all of you are going to stay here until you give up the notion that you're somehow entitled to hurt, torture, or otherwise make life miserable for anyone who does something that you don't like."

She looked around at the assembly, seeing many confused expressions or open mouths. She had voiced a completely alien concept to them.

"That's easy for you to say," said one of the older men, but no one Gill recognized as a supervisor. "Mace never did anything to you."

Gill leaned down and spoke savagely. "Mace butchered my best friend." She gestured to Saris and Rowan, who were coming back. "He murdered her mother and father, her best friend, and their..." Gill tried to think of a phrase to describe Silmariae that they would understand, "...Lord Protector." She swept her arm back to Collin and Leni. "He turned hundreds of their friends and relatives into dust. So don't say that Mace never did anything to us. Compared to that, what did he ever do to *you*?" She immediately knew what they *could* answer, but they remained silent.

She turned back to Collin, who had his hands on either side of Rand's head. Rand gasped and opened his eyes; Collin leaned back and rose to his feet.

Now the men stared wide-eyed at Collin. "You're greater than Tashtalon," one of them breathed.

Collin turned to them. "If you mean I don't waste my energy trying to destroy others, you're right."

"Shall I stun him?" Saris asked Collin.

Collin shook his head. "He's going to be weak enough for the next day or so."

"And that leaves...." Saris nodded to Mace.

Rowan gave the sleeping figure on the patio a nudge with her boot. "What do we do with this one?"

Varantia again formed around Gill. "I'll do this." She reached down, touched him, and drew back with a gasp. She looked up at the others. "This is Bryce!"

Chapter 17

"What?" Rowan said.

Slowly, the facial features became recognizably Bryce's. "Mace must have used what little magic he had left to change him," Saris said.

Gill sighed. "He must have switched jackets when he had me pinned down in his room." She turned to the stables. "If he'd taken a greathorse, we would have seen it. Unless he can fly, he must still be here someplace."

"We haven't had air travel for centuries," Collin volunteered.

Gill turned to him. "Can you do anything so Mace can't pull a switch on us again?"

"Yes, I can put a spell over the area."

"Then do it," Gill said. She looked around the yard. "He could be anywhere." She took a breath. "All right. Leni, you stay here and watch the humans. Take the net off Bryce; he'll help you when he wakes up. Saris and Rowan and I will search the wall."

"What about me?" Collin asked.

"I can't have Mace killing you to strengthen himself," Gill said. "You stay here, too."

"I could look through the mansion, just in case?"

Gill nodded. "I saw him go to the wall; it would be hard for him to come back without us seeing him, so go ahead, since he's probably not there. But if he is, call us immediately."

Collin took out a transmitter from a pocket. "I will."

When the women reached the wall, Gill said, "Here we split up. I'll check the lowermost level; Saris, take the middle; Rowan, take the top."

"I'm not leaving you," Rowan said.

Gill sighed. "Now's not the time to stick with me. If we don't find Mace fast, we may be all dead. Varantia believes he may have other things hidden. Now go, and meet back here."

When they met again, none had found any sign of Mace. Gill quickly walked through the tunnel and looked across the gardens into the woods. "I can't believe he would leave here."

"I don't, either," Rowan said as Gill returned to the yard.

Saris put the weapon on her shoulder again. "Let's think about this. We know we've removed everything from the rooms in the walls."

Gill nodded. "Sloan searched every one of them. There can't be anything he didn't see, and there's nothing left."

"But, Mace could have hiding places. A buried chest of minor artifacts or charms, for instance."

"That's possible," Gill admitted.

"And you said Sloan went through *every* room?" Saris prompted.

"Every room," Gill insisted. She paused; her expression changed. "Every room in the wall. Some in the mansion Sloan couldn't get into. Sloan told me those were Mace's private quarters." She turned to run back to the mansion; Saris pulled her back.

"Wait. Let's think first. What is there for Mace to use?"

"Nothing from the walls," Rowan said. "That's all dust."

"What if he had artifacts hidden in his rooms?"

"If he had artifacts hidden in his rooms, the vambraces would have been with the them, not in his laboratory," Varantia said. "He put them in his laboratory with the illusion of the door precisely because he wanted them out of reach of anyone who might come into the mansion."

"But what of the artifacts of his deceased friends? Where are they?"

Gill shrugged. "I don't know, but Mace couldn't use them."

Saris touched Gill's arm. "But you and I and everyone else can use the artifacts of the Wye because we're human."

"Yes?" Gill said.

"So...what if Mace let go of the last of his magic so he could use the artifacts of his friends?"

"No one would do that," Varantia said. "It would be as if a human cut off four healthy limbs."

"But it can be done; it's in the books."

"It would be simpler for him to kill Collin and strengthen whatever magic he had left," Varantia argued.

"But why wait in ambush for Collin, hoping he'd come by, and hoping he could kill him, when he can drain himself of magic and use the other artifacts without a doubt?"

"He'd do it," Rowan said. "Let's go."

They ran to the portico and stopped. "Has Collin come back yet?" Gill asked Leni and an awakened Bryce.

"Not yet." Bryce said. "Is something wrong?"

"Plenty," Gill said, and rushed in. Rowan and Saris were at her heels. Using Sloan's knowledge, she went straight to the first of the rooms he had not been able to enter. She drew Silmariae and put the other hand on the door latch. Glancing back to Rowan and Saris, she said, "This is my fight. There's nothing you can do except pick up the sword if I die and try to defeat Mace yourselves. So stay back."

"You don't mind if we thrash someone who might come up behind you while you're occupied with Mace?" Rowan asked.

Gill threw her an exasperated look.

"I just thought to remind you that's what we're here for."

Gill touched Silmariae to the latch to break any lingering lockout spell, and jerked the door open. She saw nothing except an elegantly furnished room. She stepped in, looked from side to side, saw nothing, and stepped back into the hall again.

"That was easy," Rowan remarked.

Gill nodded at Saris. "Search this room for artifacts; I'll try another."

There were only two other rooms to try. She opened the door to the second and immediately found herself enveloped in a rust-colored jelly. Rowan hurried to her aid, and as soon as she was opposite the door, she was enveloped as well. She fell to the floor with a thud. Silmariae melted the jelly surrounding Gill; it sloughed off into a puddle at Gill's feet. She reached out to do the same for Rowan, at the same time shouting, "Saris! Stay back!" Rowan punched fiercely from within the mass. In the next instant, Gill realized Rowan was not so much trying to free herself as she was urging Gill to go on without her. Gill remembered her task was to get Mace at all costs, even if the price was that of abandoning her friends. She set her jaw and took a step inside the room.

Immediately, she was surrounded again. This time Silmariae worked more quickly. The next barrage never reached her—Silmariae now acted as a shield.

Varantia formed again around Gill. "Enough of your games!"

She looked across the room to see Mace sitting in an elegantly-upholstered chair underneath a large window. His fist was extended in her direction, a thick black cord wound around the hand. He lowered it slightly. "So, you found a way to defeat the cord of Isalene."

"Isalene was a bumbler."

Mace frowned. "You never approved of my friends."

"On the contrary; I respected Von—too bad you killed him."

He surged to his feet. "Silence, woman! You don't understand... you never did."

"I understand too well."

"Do you? You thought you could defeat me by destroying my artifact and charms? I always have a plan, Varantia. No matter what happens, I will regain control. I have the eye of Kelric to keep you from me, and the armband of Galeron to protect me from harm. When I am finished with you and your traitors, then I shall take him," he nodded to the wall where Collin was stuck, eyes closed, within a mass of jelly, "replenish my magic, and everything will be as before. Except this time I *will* defeat Eldswold."

Varantia took a step back and checked Collin. "He's alive, Mace; he put himself in suspension. You can't absorb his magic while he's in suspension." Gill realized that without magic, the human Rowan must be dead now, suffocated. Her rage surged; she gripped the sword; Varantia wavered. Out of the corner of her eye, she saw Mace winding the cord for another attack. Gill gritted her teeth and smothered her anger. Varantia's image re-formed, clear and strong.

Mace gasped for an instant, then chuckled. "Your tricks cannot distract me. I *will* kill him; I *can* kill him while he is in suspension."

"You would have to give up those artifacts to absorb his magic."

"Once you are out of the way, I will not need them."

Varantia slowly walked toward him. "You cannot defeat me, Mace. You cannot kill me, because I am already dead. And my artifact is stronger than any artifact the Wye have ever made because I gave it my life energy."

"We shall see."

Gill felt Varantia drain from her into the sword. Mace seemed to sense the change. His arm flew backward and forward again. Something like an eye flashed in his hand.

Gill found herself caught in a nightmare. In Mace's place a thing of horror advanced on her, trying to kill her. It was incredibly massive and impossibly vast, stinking of malice and hatred. Her body felt leaden. A great effort of will only managed to lift her arm slightly. The monster's other hand brought forward another object, which appeared to be a thick-handled knife with a blade half the length of her smallest finger. The band encircling his upper arm gleamed as he hacked at her again and again. Terror screamed within her; pain multiplied inside her. Somewhere in Gill's mind a thought emerged, telling her she could save herself if she would only stop.

Against that thought, an image formed: the image of Alia, lying in blood on the floor of her house. Her imagination added Mace, hacking at Alia just as he now hacked at Gill. Through the agony, she turned her head to focus on the armband. Forcing her arm against the weight and the pain, she lifted Silmariae. The monster, intent on her torture and destruction, never saw. Gill felt herself weaken. If only she would die, a voice said in her mind, the pain would be gone. The terror would cease. Let the monster kill her.

The sword lifted higher. Blood started to dribble from the corner of Gill's mouth. Silmariae arced to the armband. Fluid streamed from Gill's nostrils. Gill's knees started to give way, but her will kept the sword going up. Her vision started to cloud. The sword continued on its true course. Gritting her teeth, a cry building in her throat, she leaned forward into her enemy's weapon. The sword smashed the armband.

Gill's chin nodded to her chest; she saw the knife hilt protruding from her ribs.

Chapter 18

Gill crumpled to the floor, landing on her right side. Every breath was agony. Looking up, through her foggy vision she saw the monster, now without the armband, stoop to finish her off.

Inside, she felt a tingle. Varantia was starting to heal her. *No!* Gill's mind screamed. *Let me go! Destroy him while you can!*

Out of the sword, the ghostly form of Varantia took shape. Rising above Gill, her spectral hands clutched the monster, which suddenly turned to the mortal Mace. He collapsed, lifeless, and turned to dust as his body hit the floor. Over the corpse, an image of Mace congealed. Varantia embraced the essence of her former spouse and they both faded, as if blown away by a wind unseen and unfelt.

With a shudder, Gill let out a blood-frothy breath and abandoned herself to painless oblivion.

Her first sensation was of sound: undistinguished voices. She wondered if this was what death was like. Just sound? Nothing else? She felt a hand on her arm. She realized she had an arm. Did the dead have arms? She had to see. She opened her eyes.

Collin stood above her, smiling at her. Bryce looked curiously at her around his shoulder.

"I'm glad you're awake," Collin said.

"Am I dead?"

Collin and Bryce exchanged a look. Collin turned back to her, took a breath, and let it out. "You *were* dead--but only for a brief time," he hastened to add. "Fortunately, Leni freed me from the amber and brought me out of suspension in time for me to save your life."

"Mace is gone," she said with relief.

Bryce nodded. "Most remarkable thing I ever saw."

"You saw it?"

Bryce appeared uneasy. "Leni and I thought you might need some help. We saw the whole battle from the doorway."

Gill gasped and tried to sit. "Rowan," she croaked weakly.

Collin moved his hand to her shoulder and gently pushed her back. "She's fine. Saris gave her the charm that wards off magical assault. It didn't keep her from being enveloped in the amber, and it didn't allow her to break through it, but it did give her enough of a pocket of air to give Leni time to dissolve it and free her."

Gill let out a breath.

Bryce said, "That was quite a fight you put up with Mace."

She snorted. "One stroke."

"Huh?" Bryce's brow furrowed.

Collin sat on the bed next to Gill. "Mace turned an artifact on you to distort your perceptions."

"I know. I could barely move."

"Barely move?" Bryce said.

"You were hacking away vigorously at the armband," Collin explained. "Mace looked astonished. He must have been convinced that with the armband to protect him, the artificial eye to distort your perceptions, and the blade artifact to torture you, that he was perfectly protected."

Bryce turned to Collin. "Didn't Leni say that no one had ever been able to harm Kelric when he had it on?"

Collin nodded. "Mace must have presumed that Silmariae, even with Varantia lending it her life power, could not shatter the armband. Fortunately for us, it did."

"I doubt, though, that any Wye will fortify an artifact like Silmariae again," Bryce mused.

Collin blew out a breath. "I certainly won't."

Gill said, "If Kelric was never harmed wearing the armband, how did Mace manage to kill him?"

"He separated the armband from Kelric first, of course." Collin again put his hand over hers. "You'll be weak for the next couple of days. Get a lot of rest." He nodded at Bryce. "Bryce will get you something to eat. I have to see to my other patients."

"Patients?"

"I'll explain," Bryce said. When Collin left, Bryce took a chair and sat by the bed. "Collin is busy healing the rest of the men. It's quite a task. There are 72 of them."

"Are they giving you any trouble?"

Bryce inclined his head from side to side. "We had to lock Rand up—comfortably, but he can't go anywhere. Most of the others are in awe of Collin and Leni. They don't know that Collin is less powerful than Mace was, and we aren't telling them."

"Good idea."

"They even think Leni is astonishing. Leni's the one who's keeping them in line. Still, it hasn't been easy. Collin's healing the worst off first, and those are mostly the supervisors, who have been here the longest. So the younger men complained we were favoring the supervisors."

"I can imagine."

"I don't think Collin and Leni realized that humans can get that hierarchical. Collin has lost his temper at them a couple of times, which has terrified some of them. Then they resist his coming to heal them, because they think he's going to hurt them."

"I see."

"Collin also gets exasperated because a couple of the men have died while he was resting or healing someone else. He's tried to explain that they should tell him or Leni when someone's seriously ill or on the brink of death, but I don't think they understand—they've been too far removed from normal human behavior for so long."

Gill sighed. "I don't know what we're going to do about that."

"Collin's already covered that," Bryce said. "He sent to Eldswold for a group of experienced counselors. They'll supervise the men here, evaluate them, teach them how to lead a normal life again, and release them if they think they'll do no harm to anyone. Meanwhile, their relatives in Somerlie can come here to visit them, if they wish."

"I guess that's the only way," Gill said.

"I'll get the food." Bryce disappeared out the door.

While he was gone, Gill looked around and found that someone had placed Silmariae, sheathed, next to her on the bed. She smiled, shakily lifted her arm—in so doing, she noted that her breasts had been restored—and patted the sheath with a hand. Varantia had gone, but her artifact remained to remember her by.

When Bryce returned, he put a tray—with soup and soft bread and butter—down on a table, found some pillows, and helped Gill into a sitting position. When she was settled, she asked, "Now that Mace is dead, you're freed from his binding spell, yes?"

Bryce rubbed his hands together. At her inquiring look he said, "Now that's a tale. You see, Mace couldn't affect Nils directly, because Nils was Von's artifact. So what he did was change me so that I could never give up Nils."

She gasped.

He smiled and reached out to steady her. "Don't worry. Collin changed me back. Nils is once again in the background of my mind. Collin said I was lucky; probably no one else but he could have changed me back. He said something interesting, too. When I was joined to Nils, I had the ability to feel emotion."

"You did?"

"Yes. Collin said that part of my brain was free when Nils settled into another part. He says after Mace merged us, that I remained calm because Nils had conditioned me to and that subconsciously I wanted to remain calm." He paused thoughtfully. "I guess I was braver than I thought."

She smiled at him. "I always knew you were." Then she remembered the incident with Mace. "What about the pain? Shouldn't you have felt pain when Mace slammed the stable door on your hand?"

He shrugged. "Collin says that Nils can still suppress pain, if I let him—and I certainly didn't want to show any then."

Gill blew out a breath. "That was a narrow escape."

He grinned weakly. "I knew when I said I would go with you that something might happen...that I might lose an arm, or a leg, or be permanently scarred...or die. As consequences go, I guess this wasn't too bad. I can put Nils back in his globe once we return to Maclin, and in the meantime, Collin made some sort of adjustment so that I can feel emotion until then."

Gill grinned suddenly.

"What?"

"I suppose we don't have to worry about Nils turning you into a hoarder, either?"

Bryce laughed. "It was always the case that Nils wouldn't do anything I wouldn't do."

Gill felt better after a light meal; Bryce helped her to her feet for a brief walk to the washroom. She settled back into bed for a nap, but woke to the sound of scraping outside her door.

The door opened. Rowan and Saris came in, carrying a small bed between them. Gill saw that their breasts had grown back, as well. Rowan said, "Now that you're awake, Saris and I are moving in." After she set it down, Rowan added, "After all, I *am* your bodyguard." They went out and brought in another bed. The room was large enough so that even with the additions, they were not crowded. When they put that one down, Saris added, "I'm just here for company. I hope you don't mind."

"Not at all," Gill said.

Saris sat on her bed; Rowan found a chair.

"You can take a nap if you want, or we can talk," Rowan said.

"I'm not sleepy right now," Gill said.

Saris sighed. When the other two turned to her, she said, "I understand now why you didn't want to bring me. After all that's happened, I think you should have left me home."

Rowan walked over to sit beside Saris. She rubbed Saris's back.

"I don't think we would have done as well without you," Gill said.

She shook her head. "Rowan or Leni could have done anything I did," she said softly.

Gill turned to her. "Mace tortured you. I'm sorry."

She shook her head again. "No, that wasn't the worst. I don't even remember much of it, except Mace glowing from the pleasure it gave him. That was terrible enough. It was feeling afraid...*all the time*, feeling afraid. Not knowing whether someone would suddenly kill me, or Mace would get angry for no reason and turn me to dust, and the cruelty, the *cruelty* of these men. I had no idea anyone could be so cruel to another person, and not even feel bad about it."

Rowan hugged her. "Should I send for Collin to help you again?"

Saris rubbed her forehead. "No. I think he's done all he can. At least I'm not having these intense memories come up out of nowhere."

"We call it battle shock," Rowan explained. "It doesn't even start until after the battle."

Saris nodded to Rowan and turned to Gill. "I guess if I had to do it over, I wouldn't have come."

"If I had to do it over, Saris," Gill said, "I'd take you again."

Saris grimaced.

"I'm sorry, Saris. I'm sorry for you, and me, and Rowan, and Bryce. I know exactly what you mean about the terror of this place. I felt it too."

"I know," Saris replied. "I'm sorry. You had it worse than I did. I guess you must think I'm silly."

"Not at all!" Rowan insisted.

"On the contrary," Gill said, "I understand completely why you wouldn't do it again. But I would—because it was the only way to defeat Mace. The only thing I would do different a second time, is that I would try to save Alia. Maybe I couldn't even have done that, knowing what I know now. Eminric couldn't, and he knew more than I did."

Saris licked her lips. "Still, I know why Mother left me behind."

"I'm glad you have forgiven her," Rowan said.

"Can you forgive me for letting you come?" Gill asked.

Saris pressed her lips together and nodded. "I guess if you hadn't had our help, you wouldn't have been able to do what you did. If Rowan or Leni or Collin or Bryce had died, you would have needed me even more. If you had failed, Mace would have come and killed me in Asquith, along with everyone else...and probably the last thing I would have thought is that I should have come."

Two days later, Gill felt strong enough to walk outside. At first glance, everything looked the same—men occupied with various tasks around the yard. But then she began to notice other differences as she strolled around. The booth where she had seen the supervisors torture men had been turned into a place to store ordinary repair tools. The chains on the carousel were gone; the carousel itself had been transformed into a plaything. Some of the younger men amused themselves by spinning on it. The men themselves appeared normal—no scars, no limps. She even spotted the man who had stabbed Rand. He looked whole now—she even saw him smile at a man who slapped his shoulder companionably.

"Are you Gill?"

She turned to see Lydia's son Owen talking to her. He held a chick in his hand, stroking it affectionately.

"I thought it was you," he continued. "The new gods say you're in charge."

"They're not gods," Gill corrected.

He bowed his head, and traced an arc with the toe of his boot. "That's what they say." He looked up. "But they changed me. One of them did, anyway. I don't feel the same as before."

"What do you feel?"

He continued to pet the chick. "It's hard to say. I feel...well...not angry as much. Not wanting to tear things apart."

Gill did not answer. She did not know if he was telling the truth, or just trying to impress her.

"They say I can't go home, at least not now. But can you say hello to my mother, tell her that I'm alive?"

Gill nodded. Owen shyly turned and walked away. Collin stepped up to her and touched her arm. "All the men have been healed."

"Good. I hope you aren't exhausted."

"Oh, no. I only had to pull a few from the brink of death. Besides, I have my artifact with me."

Gill nodded to Owen. "How can we tell if they're faking when they say they're reformed?"

"I can heal their brains, not read their minds." He took a breath. "Dianthe is in charge of the counselors coming here; her magical specialty is in behavior. She'll determine whether they're fit to rejoin civilization."

Gill looked around. "We'll have to make a list to take to Arcacia to notify the families of the survivors; then we can think about arranging visits from there to here."

"We already have a list, and yes, I'm sure Dianthe will want to allow visits."

Gill scanned the yard again. "Where's Rand?"

"Locked in the mansion. I'll show you."

Gill dressed in the Wye armor and strapped Silmariae at her side before going in to see Rand. Collin had determined that even with Varantia gone, Silmariae still had a strong magical charge and remained a potent weapon. Perhaps it was more than she needed to confront Rand in his current state, but Gill felt it would only be to her advantage to look as threatening as possible.

Collin had given her a magical key for the lock; she knocked once at the door and opened it. Rand stood next to a chest of drawers with a book in his hand. He looked up as she came in.

"So, you're my granddaughter." He closed the book and placed it on top of the chest of drawers.

"Yes." Gill examined him closely. Without scars, without the misshapen nose and mouth, he looked like a kindly old gray-haired man. Even the voice was gentler. She wondered if Mace had injured his vocal cords as well.

He scratched an eyebrow and turned away. "I'm not the same man. I suppose you know that."

"Yes." Collin had advised Gill not to press too hard, but she did hope to find out how much of a change Collin had made.

He walked to a chair and sat. "I don't know whether to be grateful or not. I'm free of a need that tortured me all of my life, but I don't know how to live without it." He shook his head.

"There are people coming who can teach you." Did he even want to live a normal life?

"Maybe that will help; maybe not. A man who has lost all that he's lived for should kill himself. I don't even have the desire to do that," he said sadly.

"Do you want to see the rest of your family? I could arrange that." Although she doubted that her grandmother and father would come to see him, she wanted to see what Rand would say.

"No. I still hate them," he said listlessly. "I don't even want to see you," he added without anger or annoyance.

She nodded. "That I can arrange." She left, and with a sigh, locked the door behind her. Whatever tenuous familial obligation she might have felt for Rand dissolved with his dismissal. She was free of him.

While Gill had been recovering, Leni and the others had brought Kiri and the other greathorses from Maclin back into the stables and gathered all of their gear. Collin advised them to be gone as soon as Dianthe and her team arrived; they packed and were ready to go when the line of greathorses and carts came through the tunnel.

Gill and Collin greeted Dianthe, a tall woman with a friendly face but a no-nonsense manner. The men in the yard paused and looked at them curiously.

Dianthe looked over the yard. "You told them I was coming?"

"Yes," said Collin. "They're all here, except Rand, the overseer, who's locked in the mansion." He handed her the key.

Gill scanned the expectant faces in the yard as well. "I don't know how they'll take to you. Everyone in Somerlie has been taught from infancy that a woman in authority is a bad thing."

"Well, if they're going to live in a kingdom governed by a queen as well as a king, they're going to have to learn to treat women with respect before they can leave here, and what better way to practice than with me?"

"May luck go with you, then," Gill said.

"You're the one who needs the luck," Dianthe said.

Gill frowned. "Why so?"

"We came through Somerlie. The humans there are very unsettled. Have you talked to Allard?"

Gill turned to the others. "We've tried, but haven't reached anyone in Maclin."

She nodded. "We had to physically send Wye there to tell them of your victory over Mace. But they should have convinced Allard to pick up a transmitter by now. Try it."

Gill shrugged, pulled it out, and spoke. "Allard."

"Congratulations, Queen Silmariae," Allard's voice said.

"I had a lot of help." Gill nodded to the others.

Although Allard could not see the gesture, he picked up on the implication. "We're planning a large victory celebration for you all when you return."

"I'll look forward to it," Gill said. "But I need to go to Somerlie first."

"Since you are personally acquainted with the Lord Protector," Allard said, "I think it would be best if you, and not I, present him with the news of Mace's defeat, and our desire for Asquith and Somerlie to be united once more."

"I had been thinking the same."

"Is there anything we can do for you here?" Allard asked.

"No, I think we have all we need. Thank you."

"My best to you all."

Gill pocketed the transmitter and turned back to Dianthe. "They're unsettled in Somerlie, you said?"

Dianthe nodded. "And you, your majesty, are the one whose duty it is to set things right again."

Gill nodded in reply and spoke to her companions. "Then it's time we got started."

Chapter 19

Gill noticed a difference in the area as soon as they left. Turning back to the fortress as they rode through the gardens, she saw that the wall—parts of which had been shattered when Saris had used the energy weapon—had been repaired. Leni volunteered that he had done the work. As they went on through the forest, and neared the river crossing with bodies on either side of the road, she had to remind herself that the ring of Tashtalon no longer existed.

Collin looked to one side. "We'll have to send word to Dianthe to assign some of her associates to take care of all these."

Gill nodded.

Once they were past Mace's territory, and on the road, they urged the greathorses to their natural pace, and managed to get halfway to Arcacia before sunset. They stopped at an inn, familiar to Gill from her previous travels as Sloan.

Between Gill and Leni, they came up with enough coin to pay for their rooms, plus an evening and morning meal. The innkeepers, a married couple, looked worn. The man held an infant in his arms. Gill realized that the sleep of Tashtalon had also vanished with his magic.

"New baby, I presume?" Rowan said sympathetically.

The woman sighed. "You don't know. He doesn't sleep through the night. He expects to be fed. And the little ones...they come into the bedroom when we do sleep, complaining they can't sleep, or want a drink of water."

Rowan smiled. "Sounds normal to me."

The innkeepers and Gill turned to her with expressions of confusion. "It does?" Gill asked.

Quickly, Bryce looked from one to the other and leaned forward. "She means it's normal that the little ones would want attention."

The man used his free hand to rub his eyes. "Hard to tell what anyone says to me nowadays."

"It's a curse," the woman said. "The god must be angry with us."

"I'll bet there's a woman behind it," the man answered.

Before anything else could be said, Gill took the keys and ushered the rest of the party to the rooms—two large rooms with a door in between. Once they were settled, Gill called them together.

"You have to remember, this isn't Maclin," Gill said. "As long as Mace has ruled here, there's been a spell that causes everyone within Tashtalon's ring to sleep between two hours following sunset and two hours before sunrise."

"No wonder they're tired and disoriented!" Rowan said.

"What was that about a woman behind it?" Saris asked.

"Tashtalon's priests have told the story for centuries that all evil comes from women," Gill explained.

Saris and Rowan gasped. Bryce whistled.

"It's going to be difficult for them to accept a queen," Collin said.

"They don't have to accept me as queen," Gill said. "They just have to accept me as someone who knows what she's doing. I'll settle for them accepting that they're only part of a larger human community that they have to re-enter."

Collin sat on one of the small beds. "Eminric has known Somerlie for quite some time. Maybe he can advise us."

They made good time the next day, and as the sun neared the western horizon, they reached the city gate to find Eminric waiting for them with his greathorse.

"It's about time," he said. "We need to talk." He swung up into the greathorse's saddle and led the way to Alia's house. Once inside, they all took a hand at preparing a supper.

Rowan opened the cooler door and gasped. "What, no electricity?"

Eminric bent down and lit the stove. "Mace never took any thought to maintaining it."

"I would think that you would like a kitchen with no electricity, Rowan," Saris teased.

"There are some basics one must have," Rowan said glumly.

"It'll be done," Gill said. "But there are other things to tend to first."

After they sat at Alia's large dining table, Eminric talked about the situation in Arcacia.

"Boreas and Cyril have managed to keep anarchy from breaking out," Eminric said. "The city guard spreads their orders through the neighborhoods, as they've always done, but more often now than before."

Collin put an elbow on the table. "What are they saying?"

"The image of Mace over the city Boreas explained as a warning that the people were slipping away from Tashtalon's commands, and should heed Boreas more. When the sleep of Tashtalon was removed, Boreas told everyone it would return if they would be more obedient. Since a lot of them are sleep-deprived, it's been easier to convince them of this. At least it's prevented panic or rioting."

"I would think that people would be happy to be able to sleep on their own." Saris said.

"Some are," Eminric answered. "I've seen gatherings where people lie on the top of a flat-roofed house, watch the stars, and cheer at sunrise. Truth be told, not everyone is having trouble sleeping. But parents with young children, or the infirm, or the troubled—they're the ones who miss it the most. Still, the novelty is starting to wear off, and people are grumbling that they want the sleep of Tashtalon to return."

Collin took a sip of wine. "They've become habituated."

Eminric nodded. "Which brings us to Gill, here."

"Yes," Rowan said. "She already explained the problem."

"We're lucky that Gill is not Silmariae, with all due respect to her memory." He turned to Saris, then Rowan, before continuing. "She would have ridden in with full regalia and expected immediate deference. Gill, here, in her riding pants and jacket, looks just like everyone else. She knows Cyril and Boreas. Even more important—they know her."

"So what do we do?" Collin asked.

"Getting Somerlie's citizens to accept a woman in charge is a high hurdle to jump, but not impossible, especially if we make Gill more appealing than Tashtalon."

Rowan snorted. "That shouldn't be hard to do."

"Harder than you think," Eminric said. "Tashtalon may have taken loved ones, but he also took troublemakers out of the community, gave everyone a good night's sleep, and kept Somerlie from drought or flood—something the priests knew quite well. We'll have to at least match that in order for Gill to be accepted."

"We may even do better," Collin said, with a scheming look in his eye.

Eminric turned to Gill. "I'm willing to reinstate the sleep of Tashtalon over Somerlie. It won't be nearly as hard as putting Maclin to sleep for five centuries. You can take the credit for that."

Gill nodded.

"It won't be hard to keep the weather stable, either—Eldswold has always done that for the human settlements," Collin added.

Rowan looked from Eminric to Gill. "The Wye also help us identify troubled children and keep them from growing up to be bullies. Crime has always been rare in Maclin."

"That kind of social support system can take time to set up," Collin pointed out.

Eminric fingered a teacup. "Still, it's something Gill can offer to them." He leaned toward Gill. "The most important thing is not to threaten anyone's authority, or to disturb anyone's life, unless absolutely necessary. If people are assured they can get on with their lives as usual, they'll be less resistant to a change of administration. You might even want to leave Cyril in charge, at least for a while, as your deputy here."

"I insist, however, that Boreas go," Gill said.

"I agree; but unless you're planning to execute him, he'll have to do something, even if it's just sweeping streets," Eminric replied.

"No prisons here?" Saris asked.

"Houses of detention for the unruly," Gill said. "Tashtalon has always taken the harshest offenders, sometimes right out of detention."

Rowan crossed her arms in front of her. "We don't use our prisons all that much, either, when it comes to it."

Eminric moved his dinner plates around to rest his arms on the table. "What I think we ought to do is make a well-orchestrated plan...."

Rowan groaned and rolled her eyes.

"...a *plan*," Eminric repeated, staring at Rowan pointedly, before turning back to Gill, "for confronting Boreas and Cyril tomorrow. They hold open court together every day now."

Gill leaned forward. "As long as it's understood that *I* take the lead. I know Somerlie better than any of you."

"Of course, your majesty," Eminric said genially.

Bryce raised a hand for attention. "Before we go on, I have a question: are you going to stay here and rule?"

"No. I doubt that the people here will accept a woman in charge, at least right away. If everything goes well, I'm returning to Maclin."

"Then you'll need a representative here." He took out his transmitter. "I can keep in communication with you, and advise whoever you put in charge here about policies set in Asquith."

Eminric turned to Gill. "I think that's a good idea."

"Aren't you staying here?" she asked.

"For the present, at least, to use whatever magic is needed to join Asquith and Somerlie again. But I think it's better to have a human here as your representative."

Gill looked over to Bryce. "Are you sure you want to stay?"

"As Eminric says, once the two kingdoms *are* joined, I too can go back home. I've been an advisor to the court in Maclin for some time; this gives me a chance to go back to what I used to do in a new setting. And frankly, after Mace, I think I still need some time to unwind before I go back home." He smiled. "Besides, Nils is a shameless flatterer. The idea of moving people in the right direction appeals to that part of his nature. As long as I have him, I may as well use him."

Gill and Eminric exchanged a look. "No reason why not," Gill said.

* * *

The next morning, Gill rummaged through her clothes—which Irina had dutifully moved to Alia's house, and stored in one of Alia's closets. She selected a fine, loose-fitting dress—the sort of dress she would wear on formal occasions. She put on the Wye armor first; the dress covered everything well. She declined headgear, but took her best riding gloves.

Saris, who was more Alia's size, went through her things and also took a dress loose enough to wear armor under. Rowan scoffed at all the elegance and just selected the best riding outfit she had with her. As was her habit, her thick arms remained bare. Eminric donned his usual fighter's outfit. Collin and Leni sorted through the clothes of Alia's father and brother, which Alia had never thrown out. Leni took a green jacket and matching pants; Collin took a richly embroidered purple jacket, a yellow shirt, and black pants. Bryce wore Mace's elegant clothes.

Once equipped, they rode to the castle gate. There was an area for tying horses; they dismounted there. All through Somerlie, Gill, Rowan, and Saris had carried their swords in a special flap in the saddles, so they would not stand out. Now, the women removed the swords from the saddles and belted them on. As they reached the castle steps, one of the castle guards walked toward them, agitated.

He pointed at the swords. "Ah, you can't, women can't...it's forbidden."

Gill looked him in the eye. "A lot of things have changed, Sconn."

He paused, examined her closely, and drew back, startled. "Gill?"

"Yes. We're seeing the Lord Protector and the priest of Tashtalon. I'll take the responsibility."

His mouth stayed open and his finger kept pointing, but he let them pass. Leni turned and imitated the confused guard as the party went up the steps, until Gill called to him to follow.

Gill halted just outside the audience room. Cyril sat in the Lord Protector's—actually the king's—throne; Boreas stood next to him. They appeared to be consulting on something. Two guards stood nearby, looking as if they were not expecting anything out of the ordinary that day. The room was otherwise empty of people.

Satisfied, Gill walked directly into the room, the others in her train. Immediately, Saris and Rowan bowed to Tashtalon's—the queen's—throne, something Gill had not anticipated.

Boreas picked up on the gesture immediately. "Blasphemy!"

"What?" Saris protested.

Immediately, Gill drew Silmariae. She held the sword, hilt in her hands, point resting on the floor. "They're with me, Boreas. If you have something to say, say it to me."

Cyril leaned forward, startled. "Gill?"

"Yes."

Boreas pointed at Silmariae. "You had better get rid of that at once, or Tashtalon will revenge himself on you. He may already have marked you."

Gill looked Boreas in the eye. "Tashtalon is dead, Boreas. I killed him."

A dead silence fell across the room.

Gill stepped up to the marble block between the thrones, shoved Boreas aside, swung Silmariae, and split the cube in two with a crash. Then she stepped back and resumed her stance with the sword's point on the floor and turned back to the two men. "Any questions?"

The guards gasped and turned to run, but Eminric and Bryce caught them. Gill turned to them. "You won't be harmed if you don't draw your weapons. Just close the door and stand this side of it, where I can see you."

At Eminric's look, they obeyed and stood quietly, if nervously.

Cyril gaped at her. Boreas's expression went from anger to confusion and back again. Neither man showed any fear.

Cyril composed himself first. "Because of your friend?"

"Of course."

"Lies," Boreas said. "You can't kill a god."

"Actually, it was Tashtalon who told all the lies."

"The ring of Tashtalon," Boreas answered. "That was not a lie."

"No, that was the truth, though the ring isn't there anymore. All of us crossed it harmlessly."

"What were the other lies?" Cyril asked curiously.

Boreas turned sharply to him. "You can't believe her!"

"I want to hear what she has to say."

Without waiting for further invitation, Gill said, "The biggest lie was that Tashtalon was a god. Powerful, yes, because he had powerful magic. But we can use magic, too—Tashtalon merely kept it from us. The laws about women, for instance. They weren't instituted because women were any more evil than men are. They were started because only a woman could command the sort of magic that could kill Tashtalon—and he knew it."

Boreas gestured to Gill. "But you are evil. See all the suffering you have caused. The sleep of Tashtalon is gone."

"The sleep of Tashtalon is gone because Tashtalon is dead. But I can restore the sleep—as early as tomorrow, because, as I said, I can use magic, too."

"You lie."

"Wait until tomorrow night and you'll see whether I'm right or wrong."

"You're stalling," Boreas said.

"No, I'm allowing for the fact that we can't drop the sleep on everyone again unawares. We have to warn people it is coming. And it will take longer for the messengers to go to the outer areas, so they will have to wait that much longer."

Boreas slowly advanced on Gill. "I don't know what you're playing at, but it's plain to me that you have become steeped in women's evil and I will put a stop to it." Quickly, he drew a knife.

Just as quickly, Rowan lunged at Boreas, disarmed him, threw him to the ground, put a foot on his chest, drew her sword, and put the point to his neck.

The guards gasped. Gill knew it was because they had never seen a woman fight expertly before. Gill had not moved as Boreas threatened her; now she looked down into his face.

"I'm here to tell you that you're out of a job. Tashtalon is dead. Just as I speak to you, the fire has gone out in Tashtalon's house. Your assistants will be unable to relight it. Soon, the ceiling will start to fall apart. By afternoon, the walls will start to crumble, and by sundown, there will be nothing left of Tashtalon's house but a pile of dust."

Boreas tried to wrench away and upward. Gill had not known that Saris had brought the energy weapon until she heard its whine. Boreas lay flat, eyes open, stunned.

Rowan gestured to the two guards. "Make yourselves useful: carry him to the wall and prop him up."

"He's not dead," explained Gill. "He's just too weak to move at the moment. He'll recover."

The guards looked from Rowan to Cyril. "Do as she says," he said.

Once Boreas was out of the field of view, Gill turned toward Cyril. "Now that we're free of distraction, I'm going to speak plainly to you."

"Please do."

"Tashtalon is dead. There will be no more disappearances. Tashtalon took away our history and our heritage. We will get it back. These people with me," Gill gestured, "come from beyond the ring. The ring used to be an area called Somerlie; this city's rightful name is Arcacia. It was a part of a larger area ruled by a male and a female Lord Protector." She indicated the thrones. "Those are their thrones. The one you're sitting in was for the man; the one that we call Tashtalon's was for the woman—which is why they," she gestured to Rowan and Saris, "bowed to it when they came in."

Cyril turned to the throne next to his. "That actually makes sense."

Gill walked up to the throne and sat in it. The guards in the room gasped. Cyril's mouth gaped. She turned to him. "You see, I sat on the throne and I didn't die. For reasons I won't go into right now, when I went to the area to the north of the Ring, the people there made me their female Lord Protector. This is my rightful throne."

Slowly, Cyril rose from his chair.

"There's no need for that," Gill said. "Sit back down."

Hesitantly, he lowered himself into the chair, but he remained perched on the edge.

"I fully realize that a lot of the people will be as set against the idea of a woman ruling them as Boreas." She nodded to him. "It's very possible that in the next year, the male Lord Protector, who they call a king, will come and reclaim this area. But until then, if I declare myself Lord Protector, that will cause more problems than it will solve."

"You always were sensible, Gill."

She lifted a corner of her mouth. "By the way, they don't call me Gill there. They call me Silmariae."

"Silmariae."

"After an ancestor who used to be their female Lord Protector, whom they call a queen. But, as I said, as far as I'm concerned, it's a good idea for you to remain in charge. You may still remain largely in charge after the king comes—I don't think he'll live here, and someone must govern the city. But you'll be in charge with the understanding that eventually, this area will be joined with the north."

"That's all that will change?" he asked.

"For the moment. Life is different in the north, in many ways easier. The ability to cook without using fire. A cooler that doesn't need ice. Ways of dealing with troublemakers that don't involve Tashtalon coming to kidnap them."

"Kidnap? You mean they aren't eaten?" he asked.

She shook her head slightly. "Speaking of which, there are 70 in Tashtalon's fortress still alive. I brought lists of the survivors which we can post in the city. What Tashtalon did to them was unspeakable; they suffered greatly and many are not right in their minds. But we have put people there to help them, and I hope soon it will be possible for relatives here to go and visit them."

Cyril's face showed optimistic astonishment.

"Is Finlay still alive?" one of the guards asked Gill.

"Yes," said Collin.

The guards turned hopefully to him and rattled off a list of names, which Collin either confirmed or denied as being still alive.

Cyril waved at them. "That's enough for now." The guards quieted; Cyril turned back to Gill. "You said you had a list?"

"Enough copies to post."

Eminric reached into a shoulder bag and brought out a stack of papers. He gave them to Gill; she handed them to Cyril. He quickly scanned the names, and turned back to Gill.

She cleared her throat. "I'm going to have to leave people here who can help get things back to normal and keep me informed of developments."

"Oh?"

She motioned Eminric and Bryce forward, and turned back to Cyril. "You'll still be in charge. Your day to day work will be much the same as when I was here. In fact," she held out a hand to Bryce, who stepped within reach, "Bryce, here, can be your assistant, just as I was."

Cyril rubbed his chin, considering.

"We've known each other for a long time," she said. "I think this is something you'll want to do. But if you're uncomfortable with this arrangement, or want to remain loyal to Tashtalon, then I'll have to give them more authority."

"Meaning in that case, I'm a figurehead."

"Precisely."

He looked at Eminric and Bryce, then back to Gill. "It's very hard to shake the feeling that Tashtalon isn't going to suddenly appear again and put the city back into his grip. On the other hand, I've never known you to lie, and what you say makes sense. It explains everything a lot better than he has." He nodded to Boreas. "So I'll take the risk that Tashtalon, or some agent of his, isn't going to creep up here and kill me for defying him and go along with what you say." He smiled. "Since I've waded in to the waist, I might as well dive in and take the swim."

Gill smiled back. "Good."

He waved at Boreas. "I can't have him walking around, though. He could cause insurrection." He nodded to the guards. "Carry him to a room with a secure lock and bring me the key."

The guards obeyed. Both of them lifted Boreas up and carried him out of the room.

"Should someone go and make sure that they do as you say?" Rowan asked.

"I think they're more afraid of what I can do to them than what Boreas can," Gill answered.

"They never liked him anyway; few of us ever did," Cyril responded. He held out his hand to the broken marble block. "Quite a trick you did with that."

"It wasn't a trick; I can do it again."

"If anyone could find a way to overpower Tashtalon, I'm not surprised it could be you."

Eminric stepped forward. "Cyril brought up a point. He and those of the city guard loyal to him could be in danger from Boreas's assistants and agents of Tashtalon in the city."

Cyril turned to Eminric. "You mean other than the ones in the house of Tashtalon?"

Eminric nodded. "I happen to know who and where they are, however."

"They're the ones who told Tashtalon who to take," Gill explained.

"You mean it wasn't random?" Cyril blurted out, outraged.

Gill shook her head.

"I know Boreas used to ramble on about those 'marked for the god,' but I never believed our own people...," He turned to Gill. "The city guard will be happy to find them and put them in detention."

"I thought they might," Eminric brought out another paper from his shoulder bag and handed it to Gill. "Here's the list."

Gill gave it to Cyril. His eyes widened as he read the names. "I would never have guessed."

"I presume I can leave things in your hands?" Gill said.

He looked around the room. "Yes."

Bryce turned to Gill. "May I stay here, majesty?" He turned to Cyril. "Not that we don't think you're competent to handle this, but...."

Cyril nodded. "I can use the guidance." He waved a hand over Eminric's paper. "Apparently there's a lot that I didn't know and should have."

"That went well," Collin said as they walked out of the castle.

"As Lord Protectors go, Cyril has been one of the more rational ones," Eminric said.

"What do we do now?" Saris asked.

"We go back to Alia's, for now," Gill said. "And I want to see my family. After that we can go back to Asquith, and I can show you your mother's tomb on the way there."

"I'd like that," Saris answered.

Gill paused and turned to Eminric. "There's a small item of personal business that Eminric and I need to attend to, also."

Chapter 20

Rowan insisted on coming with Gill when she went to see her parents. On the way there, they stopped at Lydia's house—a small cottage, much like Gill's grandmother's.

Lydia answered their knock at her door, and stared at them with a puzzled expression.

"I'm Gill," she said gently.

Lydia nodded. "Oh."

"I've seen your son, Lydia. He's alive. He asked me to come and tell you."

Lydia cried out with joy and hugged Gill. She began to weep. She quieted quickly and stepped away from Gill.

"Where is he? When can I see him?"

Gill took Lydia's hand and looked into her face. "I want you to wait a couple of days. Then go and tell the Lord Protector that you want to see your son."

"He told me to go away," Lydia complained.

"He won't this time; I promise. A lot of people have been found alive; we saw the lists being posted as we were coming here. You will be one of many people asking the Lord Protector to make arrangements."

"How can I ever thank you?"

Gill patted her arm. "It's not necessary; I'm just keeping a promise."

Lydia seized her hand and kissed it; then she went back to the house.

"You've made at least one person here happy; that's a start," Rowan said.

They next stopped at the house of Gill's parents. Gill asked Rowan to remove the saddle sling holding her sword and strap it on her back. Gill did the same so that others would assume that they carried long packs instead of swords.

Mavis answered the door when Gill knocked. "Gill! I wasn't expecting you back so soon! Come in!"

Gill made quick introductions; Mavis ushered them to a sofa and sat in a chair. "What happened to your year off? You keep coming back."

"This time when I leave, I won't be back for a while," Gill replied. "I just stopped in to say hello before I went to Grandmother's."

Mavis indicated Rowan's and Gill's muscled arms. "I see that you've been working," she said approvingly.

Rowan exchanged a glance with Gill. "Harder than you might imagine," Gill answered with a smile.

Suddenly, the front door flew open. Rowan stood and reached back for the hilt of her sword as Loris and Clede stormed in.

Gill stood and put a hand on Rowan's shoulder. "My father and brother," she whispered. Rowan nodded and they both sank back into the sofa.

"You should have seen what we saw!" Loris announced, then stopped when he saw Rowan.

"My new friend, Rowan. Rowan, this is my father, Loris, and my brother, Clede." They exchanged polite nods.

Loris and Clede put their work bags down and sat in chairs near Mavis. "You know the house of Tashtalon? It isn't there anymore."

"What did they do, move it?" Mavis asked.

"No, it crumbled right to the ground like a piece of stale bread. Clede and I saw it, just as we left the shop."

Clede added, "The city guard is out, too. Posting notices all over the city. Starting tomorrow night, the sleep of Tashtalon will return."

"That would be nice," Mavis said. "I've hardly slept in the past week. I keep nodding off during the day."

"Clede and I sleep just fine," Loris interjected.

"There's more, too," Clede said eagerly. "They've posted lists of names of people Tashtalon took. They're alive."

Loris looked from Mavis to Gill. "And wouldn't you know—my father, that mass of slime, is on there, too. I would have thought he was dead by now."

Mavis stiffened in her chair. "My brother isn't on it, is he?"

"No," Gill interrupted. The others turned to her. "We read the lists too, on the way here."

"Good. I wouldn't want him back." Mavis relaxed.

Loris gestured to Mavis. "You know what else they told us? Tashtalon is dead, too. No more people will be taken."

Mavis looked puzzled. "Dead? How could he be dead?"

Loris lifted his shoulders. "I don't know. But he's gone. Even more than that, some woman came to the Lord Protector this morning and announced she was in charge. She's the one putting the sleep back, though I'm not sure how a woman can use magic. Name's Silvery, or something like that."

"Silmariae," Gill corrected.

Loris, Mavis, and Clede turned to her. "Huh?" Loris said.

Clede reached over and nudged Loris's arm. "I bet she talked to Cyril."

Gill smiled. "Yes, and I'm the Silmariae you heard about."

Her parents and brother exchanged looks of confusion. Loris turned to Gill and examined her carefully. "You've been working hard, I see."

"Very hard, Father," Gill agreed.

Loris nodded to Rowan. "You're an older lady and a hard worker, I see. You looking after Gill?"

Rowan raised an eyebrow. "Very much so."

"Keeping her out of trouble?" Loris continued to address Rowan.

"As much as possible," Rowan answered.

"Got healers over where you are?" Loris asked.

"An excellent one. We'll be seeing him soon, in fact."

Loris nodded and rubbed his hands together. "Good."

An awkward silence followed. To fill in the gap, Gill said, "I came to give my regards while I'm passing through the city again. I'll be on my way, now. I need to get back to work, you understand." She stood and, Rowan behind her, headed to the door.

Before they reached it, Loris rose from his chair and hurried over. "Don't work too hard now. I know I said you ought to go to the mines, but I don't want you to overdo it."

Gill opened the door and kissed him on the cheek. "Don't worry."

As Gill and Rowan strode to their horses, Loris called after them, "You watch yourselves now."

"We will," Gill promised. She noticed that Loris stood in the doorway, gazing after them as they started down the road. Just before turning a corner, Gill glanced back to see Loris step back into the house and close the door.

Rowan leaned over to Gill as they rode along. "At first, I wondered why you just didn't explain what you've become, but I see now that the news would have been too much for them to absorb at this point. They really thought you had gone mad."

"If they'd known we were carrying swords, they would have become hysterical, thinking that we'd surely be found out and killed. It's going to take time for them, and for the city, to get used to the idea of women with power. I've told them the truth; they'll realize what that means eventually." She grinned. "With my grandmother, however, we can be more direct."

Irina opened the door at their knock, looked at Gill, looked at Rowan, let out a squeal of delight, and hugged Gill. When she let go, she grabbed Rowan by the arm. "Come in, come in."

When they were settled, Gill outlined the major parts of what she had done: found a kingdom to the north, where she was put in charge, then went to Mace's fortress and killed him. Irina took in the details without asking questions.

"So, you were Rose," Irina said when Gill had finished.

"Rose?" Gill asked.

Irina smiled. "In that story you love so much."

"What story?" Rowan asked.

Gill sketched out the story for her.

"So now it is true," Irina said, smiling.

"Yes," Gill took a breath. "Grandmother...Rand is alive."

Irina nodded. "Your father and brother stopped by and told me on their way home from work."

"I wouldn't recommend seeing him. I've talked to him; he doesn't want to see us again. Ever."

Her grandmother sighed. "It's just as well. As far as I'm concerned, those ties have long been severed."

Wanting to leave that distasteful subject, Gill asked, "What do you want to do now, grandmother? You're welcome to come north and live with us, if you wish."

"It's tempting, but I think I'd rather stay here."

"You could live in luxury there."

"I know. But I've been here so long. And I'm curious as to what will become of this place, now that Tashtalon is gone."

"It'll be a better place," Gill said.

"I don't doubt it," Irina answered.

The next day, Eminric prepared the spell of sleep. That evening, when the city was slumbering, Eminric and Gill—wearing a charm— went out to find Alia's grave. Eminric thought he could find it, since Alia had been dead only a couple of months. He brought with him a cylindrical device that cast light over a large area. They walked up the mountain, past the now-crumbled and deserted house of Tashtalon, and to the edge of a cliff. Eminric put the device on a stand and tilted it to shine into the abyss. Looking down the sheer rock face to the boulders below, Gill saw a collection of bones and rotting flesh. On top lay Alia's body, still in her bloody and decaying nightgown.

She held the seedling she had brought close to her, and buried her face in Eminric's chest. He embraced her.

When she pulled back, he said, "I should have expected they would do something like this; but I hadn't thought even Boreas would be so callous."

"What can we do?" Gill asked.

"I can bury her, and the others with her."

"Others?"

He nodded solemnly. "My guess is that every woman Tashtalon has killed in the past five centuries is down there." He held out his hand; Gill looked down and saw what appeared to be a dust storm. When the dust cleared, a layer of fresh earth covered the boulders.

Eminric nodded to the seedling. "Throw it down."

She did so. She saw it plant itself, and begin to grow. Green grass and flowers sprouted up around it. She turned to Eminric and found him leaning back, eyes shut, with his wand in his hand. He let out a breath and opened his eyes. "There. That ought to be a suitable memorial, for all the women who tried."

She shuddered.

"What is it?" he asked.

"But for luck, or fate, I could have been down there." On impulse, she drew Silmariae and set it in front of her, tip resting on the ground, hilt in her hands. Silmariae's brilliance turned the night into day and shone radiantly upon the newly-planted garden below. Gill heard a sound as if someone had plucked a harpstring. Closing her eyes to allow her ears to find the source, she realized that Silmariae was thrumming. She felt the vibration through her fingers. The key, again around her neck, added a hum to the chorus.

She turned to Eminric. He stood next to her with eyes closed, head bowed, and hands folded in front of him in a posture of reverent meditation.

Feeling that she must add her voice to the scene, she looked out over the garden and spoke. "Sleep in peace, Alia. Sleep in peace, my friends. Your sacrifices have not been in vain. Your daughters and sisters, your sons and brothers, are free, and I pledge by my life and heart and mind that they will never be slaves again, I and my daughters and my daughter's daughter's after me."

Silmariae let out a dazzling flash as Gill's words echoed in the canyon.

Eminric stirred beside her. "Moving words."

"I'll instruct Bryce and Cyril to tend the area. I want people to come here and see." She gestured at the garden. "It's time to tell their story now."

Eminric nodded.

"After we visit Silmariae's tomb, we'll make that a memorial, too."

"I don't think just anyone should come inside," he said softly.

"No," she agreed, "but we can make the area around it a garden, too. A place where people can come and reflect...as they can come here."

He smiled. "You'll make a good queen."

She tossed her head as if awakening from a dream. "Three months ago, I would never have thought this would be possible...a world without Tashtalon. A world I could only imagine. Now I have the power to make it the peaceful and prosperous place I only dreamed of."

"I endorse your idealism," he said gently, "but I would warn you that such things do not come without hardship."

She turned to him. "Any worse than what I've just been through?"

He looked thoughtful for a moment, then said slowly, "I doubt it."

She met his eye. "Good. In that case, I can't wait to get started." She sheathed Silmariae; he took down the light source. Together, using his glow to illuminate their path, they turned and walked back to the city.

Made in the USA
Coppell, TX
16 December 2021

69094899R00108